In Harm's Way

In Harm's Way

PAUL A. BREEZE

St. Martin's Press
New York

"A Thomas Dunne Book"

Library of Congress Cataloging-in-Publication Data

Breeze, Paul
In harm's way / Paul Breeze.
p.   cm.
ISBN 0-312-13094-5
I. Title.
PR6052.R37I5   1995
823'.914—dc20   95-15453   CIP

First published in Great Britain by Robert Hale Limited under the title *The Roughburn Cluster*

First U.S. Edition: July 1995
10 9 8 7 6 5 4 3 2 1

In Harm's Way

One

The telephone trilled and Marchbank cursed. Why did it always ring when he was in the toilet with his trousers around his ankles?

'You'll have to wait,' he shouted irritably at the closed bathroom door but the machine continued its incessant call, oblivious to his incapacity.

Eventually the ringing stopped, but only for a second. Then it started again. Someone was determined to winkle him out.

'Marchbank!' He answered curtly, the phone gripped between shoulder and ear as he struggled to zip up his trousers.

'Tony? It's Steven. Sorry if I've disturbed you.'

'Steven?' He suppressed his irritation. 'Yes?'

'Can you come out to my house?'

'Now?'

He looked at his watch although he knew perfectly well what time it was. Nine o'clock. A visit to the Albion was at the top of his agenda now he had dealt with his biological imperative. The pint of bitter he had imagined himself nursing beckoned warmly.

'Can't it wait until morning?'

'There's something I must talk over with you.'

There was an edge to the other man's voice, an urgency.

'It'll take me about an hour,' he agreed, reluctantly, his annoyance tempered by disquiet.

'I'll be waiting.'

They rang off.

Hamble – Steven Hamble – was head of the medical research department where Tony Marchbank worked. He had been its leader for six years. And yet, Marchbank reflected, Hamble still lived in the poky box of a house that he had bought ten years previously on a new estate close to London's Heathrow Airport. Surely he could afford somewhere nearer the centre of town?

Knowing Hamble as he did, however, Marchbank also knew that he didn't care where he lived so long as there was a roof to keep him dry. But what the hell was so important that it demanded his attention at nine o'clock on a wet Monday night?

Marchbank had driven as far as Chiswick High Road before he remembered that he hadn't left a note telling his wife where he had gone. I doubt if she'll even notice, he thought crossly. The observation was sufficient to release him from the obligation of going back. He didn't want to waste more time. The sooner this trip was behind him, the better.

The estate where Hamble lived was a navigational nightmare, a maze of interlinked roads in which all the houses looked alike. Usually Marchbank got himself completely lost but this night he drove to the front door without a single wrong turn. Lights were blazing from uncurtained windows as he parked. He rang the doorbell and waited.

Nothing happened.

He rang again. Still no answer.

'Steven!' He rapped on the glass of the door with his knuckles. There was no response.

A flimsy wooden gate on his right led to the side of the house. The gate was off its latch. Marchbank pushed it open and found a path leading to the side entrance. The side door was ajar but he walked past it and on into the garden first, thinking Hamble must be there. He was wrong. There was no sign of him. Even in the dark it would be impossible to hide in a garden the size of a pool table.

Back at the open door he called out Hamble's name again. There was still no reply. He went in.

The side door led directly into the kitchen. There were a few dishes on the draining board, dirty from Hamble's supper. Marchbank felt the kettle. It was hot; recently boiled. Maybe he's gone to get some milk, he speculated. But there was milk in the fridge when he opened it to look.

Marchbank felt awkward. He didn't want to w
into the house, uninvited, but he didn't want to
kitchen either. Eventually he went back outside and
car.

After twenty minutes he'd had enough. 'Blood
Steven,' he muttered angrily. 'Come on.'

Another twenty minutes found him back inside the ho
getting warm. This time he strayed beyond the kitchen into t.
living room. There were papers everywhere, on the table, or.
the floor, on the chairs. Most were in orderly piles but some
had spilled over untidily. Good God, this is worse than my
office, Marchbank thought.

But by now irritation was becoming concern. He went
upstairs. The lights were on here too but of Hamble there was
no sign. Downstairs once more he looked through the
documents laid out on the table, trying to find some indication
of the reason for his urgent summons. They were all research
notes from a study of leukaemia Hamble was engaged in.
Nothing was obviously out of the ordinary; nothing demanded
immediate discussion.

It was past eleven when Marchbank finally gave up waiting.
He closed the side door to the house and drove back into
London feeling extremely uneasy. Hamble had obviously left
hurriedly, soon after calling him. Why? He remembered the
tone of Hamble's voice on the phone. Thinking about it again
he could almost imagine he had heard the sound of fear. Was
his memory tricking him? Or was something terribly wrong?

His wife had returned home and gone to bed by the time
Marchbank arrived back. She had clearly been unmoved by his
absence. In contrast, he was feeling increasingly worried about
Hamble's. He poured himself a large gin and then rang
Hamble's number. There was no reply. He tried again ten
minutes later. This time, to his relief, it was engaged. It was still
engaged an hour later when he finally gave up trying and went
to bed.

Marchbank bustled crossly into the departmental office as soon
as he arrived at work next morning.

'Is he in?' he demanded, indicating the closed door to
Hamble's room.

answered Mrs French, the bespectacled and
matron who guarded Hamble's back.

ank looked at his watch. 'He's not usually this late is
oserved, brusquely. 'Let me know when he gets here
ن?'

d he repaired to his own laboratory where Christine
beth, his research assistant, was already on her second cup
coffee.

The internal phone rang an hour later. It was Hamble's
secretary. 'Can you come through?'

Her voice sounded as flat as a squashed frog. But if
Marchbank was expecting a simple resolution to the mystery of
Hamble's disappearance the previous evening he was in for an
unpleasant shock.

When he entered the office again he found two policemen
there. One was plain-clothed, the other in uniform. His eyes
had barely taken them in when a whimper drew his attention
to the grey-haired woman beyond. She was ashen faced and
struggling to hold back tears.

'What ... ?'

But he had hardly begun before the plain-clothed policeman
interrupted. 'Dr Marchbank, is it?'

'Yes.'

'I'm afraid I have bad news about Dr Hamble. There's been
an incident involving his car. I have to tell you that he's dead.'

Marchbank was struck dumb. Dead? Steven? He felt as if all
the breath had been sucked out of him.

'Why don't you sit down, Doctor?' the second policeman
suggested.

'When did this happen?' Marchbank asked finally.

'Last night at around eleven o'clock.'

'Eleven?' he repeated numbly. He felt cold. He had been at
Hamble's house at eleven the previous night, waiting for him.
He tried to make sense of what he was being told.

'How did it happen? Was anyone else killed?'

'There were no other vehicles involved. Dr Hamble's car left
the main road at some speed between Henley and Wallingford
and crashed into a disused barn.'

How could it have?

'But that's ridiculous. Steven called me at nine o'clock last night and asked me to go to his house. What would he be doing in the middle of Berkshire when he was supposed to be meeting me? There must be some mistake.' Marchbank suddenly felt relieved.

'There is no mistake, I'm afraid. It was Dr Hamble. The body was identified by his father a couple of hours ago.'

Marchbank's face fell. 'I don't understand. What was he doing there?'

'That I don't know sir. But I do know that his car appeared to contain several cans of petrol when it hit the barn. There was a fireball. I won't upset you with the details but it took the pathologist until the early hours to find any identifying features. We can find no obvious reason why his car should have left the road. Unless, that is, he drove it off on purpose.'

It took a while for Marchbank to realize what he was implying.

'You mean he committed suicide? That's impossible!'

The policemen soon left but not before they had asked Marchbank to call at the local station in Holborn and make a statement. It was, of course, an order not a request. After they had gone, the laboratory closed in on him like a prison. He felt claustrophobic, trapped. He needed to get away. It was impulse that propelled him to drive out to Hamble's house again.

He parked in the same spot he had occupied the night before and switched off the engine. Staring at the house through the windscreen he experienced a sense of unreality. The bricks and mortar in front of him were the same materials that had been there yesterday and yet they had changed. Hamble's death had mutated them. Previously they had been imbued with his life. Now they were cold and desolate.

Steven Hamble was dead. It was hard to comprehend. They had known one another for what, ten years? Both had passed through the hands of Conrad DeWyntz in Cambridge. Both shaped on his anvil, Marchbank three years after Hamble. Then, when Hamble had been asked to set up the epidemiology unit in the wake of the Black Report it had seemed only natural that Marchbank should join him as his second in command. Their destinies had appeared to be inextricably linked by the chain forged at DeWyntz's hearth. They were linked no longer. The chain was irrevocably sundered.

Marchbank sat for five minutes staring at the building before him. Then he got slowly out of the car and walked up to the front door. He wanted to knock, to see Hamble's face appear through the glass. He wanted it all to be a terrible mistake, even though in his heart he knew it wasn't.

The wooden door that led to the side of the house was ajar again, though he had shut it the night before. The police must have left it open, he supposed. He pushed it open wide and walked along the path to the side door. That was locked now. He followed the path to the back of the house and peered through the French windows into the living room where, less than twenty-four hours before, he had stood trying to find a clue among Hamble's papers to the reason for his telephone summons.

Something was wrong. He realized in an instant. All the papers had gone! Not one sheaf, not one sheet remained.

It was only then that he remembered the telephone. When he had tried to reach Hamble after driving home the previous night, the phone had been engaged. And that was after midnight. If Hamble had died at eleven, who had been using his telephone?

Leaving the police station, after making his statement, Marchbank felt grimly depressed. He walked slowly along Southampton Row and into Great Russell Street then fought his way through a gaggle of rucksacked and unkempt youths outside the British Museum before turning right into Bloomsbury Street. Across Bedford Square, Gower Street opened, a canyon of smoke-blackened terraces harbouring a ghetto of small hotels.

Beside the doors of some of the buildings he passed were blue plaques denoting the former residences of minor historical celebrities. Marchbank walked this way nearly every day on his way to work and he knew the names on the plaques by heart, stations on his route. Now he recited each in turn, taking comfort in their familiarity: Dame Millicent Garrett Fawcett, 1847-1929, pioneer of women's suffrage; Lady Ottoline (there was a name to conjure with – he liked to roll it over his tongue) Lady Ottoline Morrell, literary hostess; James Robinson ...

Deep in his reverie, Marchbank had almost reached his turning to the right off Gower Street when he spotted a red jacket, a flash of legs and a flounce of dark hair rounding the corner. What the hell was Margaret doing here?

He started to run but his wife was walking too quickly and had soon disappeared into a crowd of students. Marchbank slowed again and let her go. He would find out later.

The building housing the epidemiological department dominated the short side street. Its public face was a smooth, square, featureless façade, a blank, stone-faced monument to academia. In a flight of fancy when he first set eyes on it, Marchbank imagined the structure symbolized the calm surface beneath which deep intellectual waters turned slowly but endlessly in their quest for scientific perfection. Today, he thought, it looks like a mausoleum. With a barely audible sigh he pushed through the rotating door and crossed the chequerboard floor of the lobby to the staircase.

His own office was on the third floor, as was the rest of the department. In fact his was two offices in one. Originally a single long room running parallel to the corridor, it had been divided and equipped to provide a research laboratory and, at one end, a small private office.

Marchbank stepped from the corridor into the larger outer room. It was empty but there was a cardigan over the back of a chair and the two computers were switched on. A statistical analysis was in progress on one; the other winked at him quiescently.

Marchbank felt more at home here than in his own house. He surveyed the clutter proprietorially. This was his academic womb where he was nurtured and comforted. He needed to draw on that security now.

Most of the space available in the room was taken up by three desks. The computers hummed on the two opposite the door while the third, against the wall to his right, was where his assistant camped. Above the desks, the walls were covered with Marchbank's maps, small and large, many disfigured with an acne of brightly-coloured plastic-headed pins.

At floor level chaos ruled. A deluge of photocopies, folders and pages of scribbled notes flowed from untidy piles beneath the desks and lapped at the entrance, on his left, to the cupboard-like office hived off the end of the room that served as his inner chamber. He picked his way across to it and, once inside, stared for a moment out of the only attractive feature of this cramped sanctum, its window. The room behind him had to make do with harsh strip lighting for illumination, even in the middle of the day.

Marchbank was hanging up his jacket when a figure appeared through the doorway from the corridor with a mug of tea in her hand. It was Christine Lambeth.

Lambeth was clearly surprised to find him there.

'I didn't expect you back today.'

She sounded perturbed and looked shaken. Hamble's death, he presumed.

Lambeth was a young, athletic woman with a thin face, made even thinner by a frame of shoulder-length fair hair. Her lips were narrow and pale and she had light brown eyes; today her eyes were rimmed in red. Lambeth was wearing a knee length crushed velvet skirt the colour of antique pine, thick opaque aubergine tights and a sleeveless yellow Indian print blouse. On her feet were flat green velvet shoes with straps across the instep. Her bare arms were sprinkled with freckles and there was a coiled silver ornament on the upper part of the right one.

'Are you OK?' Marchbank asked her.

'I think so.'

But she appeared to be troubled. 'How could he do it?' she demanded suddenly.

He shrugged. 'Do we ever really know another human being?'

Lambeth shook her head, as much in disbelief as in agreement with him.

Contemplating the mystery of the human condition reminded Marchbank that he had seen his wife earlier.

'What did Margaret want?'

'Margaret? What do you mean?' Surprise opened up Lambeth's face again and she avoided his gaze.

'I saw her disappearing towards Euston Road on my way in.'

'She hasn't been into the office.'

Marchbank looked at her quizzically, then shrugged. 'I suppose I could have been mistaken.'

'Do you want some tea?' she asked, changing the subject.

'Please.'

Lambeth put her mug on a desk and headed for the door. As she brushed passed him, Marchbank detected the faintest scent of sandalwood. Its unexpected intimacy comforted him.

She returned a couple of minutes later with his tea.

'What's going to happen now?' she asked.

'Happen?'

'To the department I mean. Who will take over?'

'I hadn't thought about it.'

'It should be you.'

'I suppose so.'

They sat in silence, side by side, pondering the contents of their mugs.

By the time Marchbank got home that evening the strain of the day had almost overwhelmed him. All he could think about was collapsing into a chair with a mighty gin and tonic. To drink and to forget, that was his wish.

Home! Two storeys of yellow brick in the upwardly mobile hinterland between Goldhawk Road and Chiswick High Road, flirting with Hammersmith and Chiswick without quite being either.

The Marchbanks liked to call the place where they lived a house but to do so was cheating, strictly. It was true they owned all of the building above street level but there was a basement flat below them that was not theirs. In fact what was below the ground at the front became ground level at the rear by a process they had never been able to fathom. They didn't appear to live on a hill. Whatever the logic, the result was that while they could lay claim to three square metres of concrete and a wall in front of the building, the downstairs flat got the back garden. Perhaps it was just as well. They never had time for gardening anyway.

Marchbank opened the front door and stepped inside. A pair of shoes lay capsized in the middle of the hall, there was a red jacket slung over the banisters and a bag virtually blocked the way up the stairs. Margaret was home. Her husband added to the confusion at the bottom of the stairs and tracked her down to the kitchen where she was munching a piece of cheese while making herself a cup of coffee.

'Hello darling.'

She offered him her cheek which he pecked at unconvincingly.

Margaret Marchbank was thirty-three years of age but her skin was as perfect as an infant's and her hair shone darkly. To Tony Marchbank that perfection had once held hidden depths. In it he had discerned a hint of continental shape and colouring, a hint that had suggested mystery and passion to him when he first set eyes upon her.

Marchbank's wife was ambitious. She worked for one of the major insurance companies and had risen to heights which, while still a long way from the top, had previously been scaled only by men. She was determined her ascent would continue.

For work she dressed with the style and severity befitting one constantly defending the right to her position against the brittle masculine egos that surrounded her. But now, away from the battle, she wore a shapeless, buff coloured sack, belted around her waist and with integral arms and legs. It completely covered her from chin to ankles. She wore it often when she was not at work. It was a garment her husband had come to hate.

The Marchbanks had met when Margaret was taking her first tentative steps on the corporate ladder. Then, Tony Marchbank was already established in his research career with its gently rising slopes and theirs appeared a good match. But suddenly, or so it seemed to him, she had become a high flying executive and he had been left behind. He hadn't appreciated the driving ambition that burnt within her.

These days they only communicated at the most superficial level. Either they were both tired or one of them was out or there was some other reason not to discuss anything too deeply. Instead they skirted one another warily, like animals in the night. He had given up trying to tell her about his work. She never appeared interested. But then if he was honest the insurance industry bored him to death so he was as much at fault as she. Where would it end?

Today, for a change, he had something to say, something to which she would listen.

'Steven's dead,' he told her bluntly, without preamble.

'Steven? Steven Hamble?'

'Yes.'

'How?' she demanded in a shocked voice, although he noted coldly that the surprise didn't extend to her eyes.

'In his car. He killed himself, the police say. Loaded the back seat up with half a dozen cans of petrol and then drove it into a brick wall.'

'Tony! How horrible. Why?'

'God knows.'

'You poor thing.'

That appeared to be the extent of the comfort she had to offer but he needed to talk about Hamble's death whether she liked it or not. He plunged on. 'He rang yesterday evening and asked me to go over. I must have been at his house, waiting for him, when it happened. Why, for God's sake? Why?'

She watched him warily but said nothing.

'When I got there the back door was open. He had gone.' He struggled to understand but it made no sense. 'He'd already set off for his assignation with the inferno.'

He found he was shouting and realized he was angry; angry at Hamble for not waiting and not telling him what was troubling him. Angry that he hadn't confided in him. 'While I was sitting in his house, wondering where the hell he was, he was driving himself into oblivion by way of a brick wall.'

For a moment his wife really did look shocked.

'Why would he do a thing like that? Was he ill?'

'Not that I know of.'

But it gave him cause for thought.

'Well, at least that explains where you were last night,' she said, cutting the conversation dead.

The kettle boiled and he let the matter drop with a sigh, going instead to the cupboard for the gin. The bottle was almost empty.

'Where's all this gone?' he asked crossly, waving it at her. 'It was half-full last night.'

'Good God, Tony, I don't know. Somebody must have drunk it.'

'Who?'

'You probably.'

He puffed in exasperation.

'Were you in Gower Street this afternoon?' he asked her

abruptly.

'Gower Street? When?' she challenged him.

'Three – half past. I could have sworn I saw you.'

'What would I be doing in Gower Street at that time of day? I've got a job, you know. I don't have time to go gallivanting all over London.'

'It looked like your red jacket,' he added, mystified.

'Perhaps there's someone else in London with a red jacket,' she suggested sarcastically.

He poured the remains of the gin into a glass and filled it up with tonic, tossed in an ice cube, then took the drink into the open plan sitting room next to the kitchen and switched on the television.

Later that same evening, in an office overlooking the Thames from the south bank, opposite the City of London, a man was drumming the fingers of his left hand on the edge of his Scandinavian oak desk. With his right he held a telephone to his ear. The voice on the other end of the phone was guttural. The speaker was pronouncing each word carefully and precisely. It was a sign of his disturbed state of mind.

'You misled me. No harm would come to him, you said. Now, he is dead.'

'An unfortunate accident.'

'You expect me to believe that? What do you take me for? You have betrayed me. I would not have told you if I had known. I will give you no more help. Come, take your papers away.'

'You have finished?'

The speaker sighed wearily. He knew the betrayal was as much his as his interlocutor's. 'I have finished. But no more. Do you understand?'

'I can understand why you're upset. I would feel the same. But we mustn't lose sight of the grander objective. You'll feel better in a few days. I'll send somebody round.' He put down his phone.

'Problem, Guy?' the other man in the room asked.

'He's having to accept a slap in the face from reality,' the first man replied. 'These academics are all the same. But he'll come round eventually. It's his own fault. He should have kept his nose clean in the old country.'

Two

Oliver Earnshaw was fat, his face was childlike, and he was the new head of the special epidemiology unit. He had been appointed with unseemly haste, brought in from outside without any consultation with the other members of the staff.

Earnshaw's arrival meant Marchbank had been passed over. He supposed he should be outraged but in a way it was a relief. He wasn't ready to step into Hamble's shoes. But Earnshaw? The choice was incredible!

It was two weeks after Steven Hamble's death and they were all gathered in Hamble's – now Earnshaw's – office to meet their new leader. There was Marchbank, Lambeth, Colin Derwent their resident computer expert and Claire Blount who had only recently joined the group. Mrs French hovered in the background, uncertain whether she belonged inside or out.

Marchbank surveyed their new director. His round, schoolboy's face was topped with fine flaxen hair that was slicked across the forehead. In marked contrast to the infant façade, Earnshaw's dress was a pinnacle of adult absurdity. He had a predilection for ostentatious Italian clothing but he omitted to take his bulk into consideration. As a result he looked like nothing so much as a circus clown. Marchbank found it hard to suppress a smile.

Earnshaw was no stranger to Marchbank, nor to any of his colleagues. He had inhabited the fringes of the epidemiology world for several years now, the proponent of various outrageous theories that had made about as much impact on their discipline as a snowball on the face of the sun. What was puzzling Marchbank was where Earnshaw had acquired the academic credibility to support his new appointment. And if, as Marchbank suspected, he hadn't, then why was he here?

There were insufficient chairs to seat all the department members in the office and they shuffled around uncomfortably while they waited for the new director to begin his little speech. The director himself made to sit behind his desk, then thought better of it and stood too.

'Ahem. Thank you all for sparing the time for us to get acquainted.'

He paused, as if uncertain what he wanted to say now that he had their attention. 'I appreciate that I am taking over the helm under rather difficult, er, tragic circumstances but I can assure you that I intend to do everything in my power to make the transition as smooth as possible. I don't wish to make any major changes to the way things operate here.'

The sharpening of attention must have alerted him that he was straying into delicate territory for he deftly switched tack.

'Um, the minister is keen to ensure that our work continues without interruption ... '

'Pompous fool,' Lambeth hissed behind her teeth.

'He understands its importance, I am pleased to say. Now, I'm sure we are all going to get along famously and I have every hope that we will soon become once again the tightly knit little group that flourished under Steven Hamble's tutelage. That's all I really have to say but if anyone has ...?' His voice tailed off as he looked around expectantly but nobody ventured to speak. 'Well. If there are no questions, perhaps we should get back to work?'

They were only too pleased to be gone.

'A word, Tony,' Earnshaw said with uninvited informality as the others left.

Marchbank took a seat and waited until the new director had closed the door.

'I understand that you were the senior member of staff here under Hamble.'

Marchbank nodded.

'I hope you don't feel resentful towards me for taking over a seat which perhaps you considered to be rightfully yours. If it's any comfort, my appointment here was as much a surprise to me as it is to you.'

Marchbank offered no comment so Earnshaw continued; 'This unit appears to be one of the minister's pet projects. As I understand it, he wants someone here he knows, someone who'll keep him in close contact with what's going on. It would seem I was his choice. I'm telling you this because I think it's important that we rub one-another up the right way. Not to beat about the bush, where you lead, others will, um, follow.'

'As you suggested yourself, Oliver, I see no reason why we shouldn't get along famously,' Marchbank assured him with a wry smile.

'Good.' Earnshaw was oblivious to the irony in his voice. 'Now. There's another matter of importance I would like to discuss with you. The minister has asked me to take special care to see that the project Hamble was working on is completed as soon as possible. As you will appreciate I am going to have my work cut out getting my feet under the table here ...' Marchbank couldn't help smiling again though Earnshaw was completely unaware of the ludicrous image his words conjured up, 'and I would like you to take care of it for me.'

'The power station study?'

'Yes.'

'I thought that was virtually finished?'

'You will have a better idea than me but my understanding was that a certain amount of compiling remains to be completed.'

'Your understanding?' Marchbank was puzzled.

Earnshaw appeared irritated. 'I was briefed before I arrived.'

That explanation left Marchbank even more mystified than before but he let it pass.

'If that's what the minister wants, I imagine I will have to find the time.'

'Good man,' Earnshaw continued briskly. 'A number of the papers you will need are at Hamble's house. Perhaps you wouldn't mind collecting them yourself. Here is the key.' And he carefully placed a Yale key on the desk between them.

Looking at the key, Marchbank was about to object that the papers had gone. Then he thought better of it. No point in letting Earnshaw know more than was necessary, he decided. Instead he picked up the key and slipped it into his pocket.

The coroner had recorded a verdict of death by misadventure, a *carte blanche* for just about anything as far as Marchbank was concerned. Hamble's father had identified the body, or rather a number of personal items found in the context of the body. How the police had managed so quickly to determine whose remains were in the burnt out wreck still puzzled him.

Marchbank himself had given evidence. He had expressed his misgivings. They were noted. And that was that. Steven Hamble was consigned to the out tray. No explanation for what he did, just a fading memory.

But still a poignant one, Marchbank found as he drew up to the house. He paused before inserting the key Earnshaw had given him in the lock. In his mind this was still Steven Hamble's home. His memories of it brimmed over with Steven. He felt an irrational fear that as soon as he opened the door and went inside he would start erasing those memories, like files on a computer disk, and replacing them with new ones that didn't contain any reference to his old friend.

Don't be ridiculous, he told himself. Steven goes deeper than that.

There was a small pile of mail and free newspapers behind the front door, preventing it opening fully. Marchbank pushed them out of the way with his foot as he stepped across the threshold.

A door on his left from the hall led into the main living room. It was shut. He opened it quickly, trying to push Hamble's only too vivid memory out of the way too before it overwhelmed him. It was difficult. Everywhere he looked, memories crowded.

But once through the door the memories quickly evaporated. Instead of the empty room he had expected, there in front of him were the papers. Papers on the table, papers on the chairs, some in neat piles and others tumbling over. Papers on everything, just as they had been the night Hamble died.

Was he dreaming? The papers were real enough. He touched them to make sure. Then he must have dreamt that they had gone. But he hadn't been dreaming. The day after Hamble's death this room had been empty. And since then someone had carefully replaced the papers exactly as they had been before. It seemed a completely pointless exercise.

Marchbank began to gather the papers together. He made

four piles and tied them up with twine from a ball he found in the kitchen. Then he picked them up, two at a time, and carried them out to the car. He had no intention of lingering in Hamble's house and as soon as he had put the last two bundles in the car he went back to shut the door. But as he was doing so he noticed the pile of post again. Somebody should go through it, he thought.

There was nothing that required urgent attention, just two or three mail shots, a magazine and a telephone bill.

A telephone bill? His curiosity was aroused and he slit it open.

Someone had closed Hamble's account with the phone company. This was the final bill, complete with an itemised listing of Hamble's calls. And there, at the end, was the call that had been made from the house on the night Hamble died. A long call – over an hour – to a number outside London. Marchbank read the digits out to himself. He recognised the code. Cambridge. But not the number.

He had been right then. Somebody had been in the house that night. Someone who had used Hamble's phone, someone who couldn't be Hamble because Hamble was already dead.

Confirmation of the mysterious phone call coupled with the carefully replaced papers fanned the fires of Marchbank's suspicions once more. Who could have made the call? And why?

Perhaps it was a policeman who had used the phone. But that didn't make any sense. The call was made barely an hour after Hamble had died, if the police evidence was to be believed. And if their account at the inquest was also correct it would have been several hours more before they identified him as the victim of the crash.

Marchbank slipped the bill into his pocket. No doubt British Telecom would send another when they discovered nobody had paid the first.

Back in the office Marchbank contemplated the mountain of papers. What was in them? What did they contain, or what did somebody think they contained? What had prompted their secret examination? And by whom? If he wanted to find out he would have to scale that paper mountain.

He couldn't manage alone. He dumped two of the parcels of paper onto Lambeth's desk. She would have to help. Then he put one of the remaining parcels on his own desk and cut the string.

Hamble had been trying to discover if there was a link between childhood leukaemia and nuclear power. That was the purpose of his study and the burden of his papers.

But what is it that causes leukaemia in children? How could the disease be linked to a nuclear installation? For although there were clues, and plenty of theories, the precise genesis of the disease remained elusive.

Nevertheless, the only strong link that research had forged was with radiation. It was clear, for example, that if a pregnant woman was given an X-ray there was an increased risk of her child developing the disease.

There was one other connection. The disease favoured the middle classes. The better off were more susceptible than the poor.

Then, in 1983, a television programme claimed it had found an excess of childhood leukaemia cases in the village of Seascale and its surroundings in the north-west corner of England. Thirty-six cases were found between 1968 and 1982. The village just happened to be next door to a nuclear complex called Windscale.

The people running the plant were outraged at the suggestion that there could possibly be any link other than coincidence between the disease and its operations. But it was too late. The cat was out of the bag. Now the problem became how to identify the cat. The government set up the Black Inquiry with that purpose in mind.

Black recommended a comprehensive study covering the whole area. Meanwhile the Windscale nuclear installation decided it didn't like its name any more and became Sellafield instead. One or two observers took the jaundiced view that this might be an attempt to ditch the bad publicity associated with the older appellation.

Nevertheless, the furore continued. Soon there came suggestions that other nuclear installations should be examined and then other types of industrial plant. The shock waves were still reverberating.

One of the echoes was the epidemiology unit. It had been set up by the government on the back of Black's report to coordinate research into clusters like Seascale. Hamble had been chosen to lead it and he had been provided with a generous government grant. Part of that money funded the project he was involved with when he died.

Hamble had been looking at a group of five nuclear power stations, an equal number of industrial plants and twenty controls, places with no obvious source of environmental contamination chosen at random by computer. The idea behind the study was to see whether there was any evidence for a larger number of cases of leukaemia around the industrial or nuclear plants than in the control regions.

The objective was clearly defined. Achieving it was not. Marchbank knew only too well how much time Hamble had spent chasing round the country, trying to hunt down the statistics he needed in order to complete his work; he and Lambeth had frequently been roped in to help. Cancer registrations, death certificates, death entries, pathology records; all formed part of the source material Hamble had needed to consult.

Finding the records and identifying the victims was only the beginning. Then there was the question of when the disease was actually initiated on its course of insidious corrosion. Many scientists suspected that this was before the child victim was born. So, it was necessary to discover where the parents of all the children who had contracted the disease had been living at the time of birth. That meant more time-consuming legwork before Hamble could even begin to think of analysing the figures. And what about families that had moved out of the areas he was studying? Could they be located and had any of their children suffered?

In recent years the chance of surviving leukaemia had increased. Ironically this meant even more work because survivors were still important cases for the study but they didn't turn up in mortality records. Other sources of data had to be consulted to track them down.

But eventually, between them, they had amassed most of the figures Hamble needed. The next stage was to analyse them.

Hamble had used two different methods of analysis. One,

the more conventional, had confirmed the existence of the cluster at Windscale. It had shown no irregularities elsewhere. The second gave everywhere, including Windscale, a clean bill of health. This was not yet a perfect science.

Marchbank couldn't argue with Hamble's choice of analytical techniques but he himself would have added a third – sticking pins into maps. It hardly counted as scientific analysis, perhaps, and several of his contemporaries frowned on the practice, but Marchbank found maps reassuring in a way no table of numbers could ever be.

It was Lambeth who eventually spotted the anomaly. They had already been through all the papers from Hamble's house but could find nothing exceptional, just the normal confusion of notes and data that formed the basis of any study of this kind. Now they were looking at the material from his office.

Hamble had left a great heap of additional material: papers, computer printouts, notes and a box of computer disks. Until Earnshaw arrived these had cluttered the corners of his office. Now they lived in several cardboard boxes which were adding to the congestion in Marchbank and Lambeth's laboratory.

At the moment the two of them were going through Hamble's computer disks. Or at least Lambeth was. Marchbank was distracted, watching her, as she sat at the screen next to him. Lambeth had a fine covering of down on her neck and face. It provided Marchbank with a source of endless fascination which he was indulging. She was concentrating on her screen and remained oblivious to his gaze.

As he watched a frown appeared on her face and she looked up.

'I think there's something wrong with this Tony.'

'Wrong?'

But she had got up and was shuffling through a pile of Hamble's papers. She found the sheet she wanted.

'Look,' she said, handing it to him. 'Here are Steven's figures for the incidence of leukaemia in the twenty controls. And here,' – she indicated the computer screen – 'are the figures he got from the OPCS. The two sets of data don't match.'

Marchbank looked over her shoulder. All the figures on the page looked the same as those on the screen, all except one. A place near the bottom of the list, a town called Roughburn.

According to the OPCS (the Office of Population Censuses and Surveys) data the incidence of leukaemia in Roughburn had been unexceptional for thirty-seven of the forty years covered by the study. But during three years, 1955, 1956 and 1957, it had risen. Over that period five children had died of the disease. The number of cases was not startling but it was unusual. More unusual, however, was the fact that these deaths were not accurately reflected in Hamble's figures in the papers that Marchbank had collected from his house. In those, the number of deaths appeared completely normal, even during those three years.

A mistake? Or was it intentional?

Marchbank suddenly felt a wave of apprehension. The bottom of his stomach sank towards his knees, and a face swam in front of his eyes. It was a face from the past, a face he preferred to forget, the face of Elliot Cromby. Cromby had been a colleague during Marchbank's postgraduate days, a brilliant student who had been expected to go far. That expectation was never fulfilled because when he was halfway through his doctorate, Cromby had been uncovered as a fraud – uncovered by Marchbank. The man was perhaps the only person Marchbank could truly name as his enemy.

Cromby's deception had been to engineer the results of his statistical analyses to support the theory he was propounding. Quite by chance Marchbank had discovered what he was doing. And now, also by chance, he appeared to be faced with a parallel situation.

Why had Hamble doctored one of his controls? Was the real incidence of leukaemia too high to support his thesis? It seemed inconceivable. Hamble had been married to his work. He could never have accepted the intellectual treachery that such a deception involved. And yet, he had killed himself for no apparent reason. Here, now, was reason enough. Any man guilty of fraud must be prey to insufferable fears, not least that he be discovered.

Perhaps Lambeth realized what was going through Marchbank's mind.

'Tony. It's not possible,' she reassured him. 'Whatever Steven may have been, he wasn't a cheat.'

'Then why change the figures?'

'Perhaps he didn't. Look.'

She held the sheet of paper up to the light. There dark blobs appeared.

Somebody had carefully doctored the figures, whiting out the originals and replacing them. It had been expertly carried out but nothing could hide the telltale marks. Hamble could have changed the figures himself of course. But then so could somebody else.

The man called Guy was feeling rather pleased with himself. It wasn't often that things went according to plan in his line of work. In his hand he held a photocopy of a scientific paper published that week in a monthly epidemiological journal, a paper entitled, *Further Studies in the Industrial Genesis of Leukaemia* by S. Hamble, C. Lambeth and T. Marchbank.

'Wrapped up rather neatly, if you don't mind me saying so. As inconclusive a piece of work as you are likely to see.'

'The standard of scholarship in the country isn't what it used to be, eh?' his companion replied. 'I put it down to the fluorine in our drinking water myself. So that's it then?'

'No loose ends that I can see. We must pray that the gods who guide us see fit to prevent this wearisome place from popping up on the celestial roulette wheel again.'

'Isn't there some way we can make the place disappear, once and for all?'

'A nice thought, but impossible, I'm afraid. If you've got any ideas though ...?'

Three

The graveyard was on the opposite side of the road from the church, behind a low stone wall. It was neat and well tended, a comfortable place to contemplate eternity. Marchbank opened the sturdy iron-bound wooden gate, stepped inside, then closed it again carefully behind him.

Turning back from the gate he surveyed the scene before him, wondering where to start. The graveyard sloped upwards from the entrance, following the contours of the river valley. A wide, gravelled path led straight ahead from the gate, bisecting the graveyard, while two narrower ones to his left and right skirted its perimeter.

The oldest graves, grey stone shapes smoothed and sculpted by the weather, were in the most prominent positions alongside the central path. Later burials had followed the edges of the perimeter paths until these too were completely occupied. Now the dead had to settle for places farther from the paths and higher up the hill. How ironic that in death people still fought for the most advantageous spot.

In the distance, against the far wall of the graveyard, Marchbank's gaze alighted on a group of burials beneath a large spreading tree. A small hedge isolated them from the other graves. He started to walk slowly along the broad path that rose gently up the hillside towards them.

Now that he was within the confines of the graveyard Marchbank felt a great sense of peace. It was mid October and here in the north of the country autumn had already taken a firm hold. He passed under a maple and found himself ankle-deep in asymmetrical yellow stars.

Stopping from time to time, Marchbank looked at the gravestones on either side of him but they were not what he sought. Then, on his left, his eye was caught by an incongruous white object thrusting up between two graves. It was a toadstool, a primitive, phallic growth bursting out of the ground, converting death and decay into new life.

It wasn't just life and death. The town's history was written on these gravestones for those who knew how to read the script. The tide of life, the ebb and flow of families, here the wealthy, there the poor. Even the tastes of the former inhabitants could be discerned from the style of their graves. Some tombs told of rich lives lived to the full, others of tragedy.

It was for tragedy that Marchbank was searching. He found it at the highest point of the graveyard where his instinct had drawn him. The graves lay in front of the boundary wall, beneath the tree he had seen from below, an ancient horse chestnut, and hemmed in behind a low yew hedge.

A special spot, this. The secluded enclave at the top of the graveyard had been reserved for the greatest sorrow. He gazed down at the tiny graves by his feet. Here lay the remains of the town's dead children. He could feel the pall of grief like a mantle laid over him as he stood, slowly reading the names on the stones.

Two of the graves he had been expecting to find were here. Both girls, though that was chance. One of them had been four when she died, the other three. It didn't say on their headstones that they had died of leukaemia.

Today they might possibly have survived. But not then, not in the early years of the 1950s. He looked at the dates on their grave. Both children had died in 1956, within three months of one another.

There were not many children's graves beneath the chestnut; perhaps twenty he estimated. Maybe others were buried with the adults. Few that they were, these were the real purpose of his visit. He took a notebook from his pocket and wrote in it the names and dates from all the other children's gravestones beside the two leukaemia victims. Even as he did so he was struck by one unusual fact. Most years either no children had been buried here, or perhaps one. In one instance there were two, brothers who died on the same day and were buried in a single grave. But in a two-year period spanning 1955 and 1956 five children had died and been buried in this one graveyard.

* * *

Marchbank couldn't have chosen a worse day to scour Rough-burn's graveyards if he had tried. His visit coincided with the biggest civic jamboree of the year, occasioned by the opening of the town's new health centre by the Right Honourable George Winfield, Secretary of State for Industry.

It was an oddly small-town affair to be graced by a minister, Marchbank thought as he left the graveyard, closing the gate behind him once more. Perhaps there was something he didn't know. Could there be a by-election looming in the area? Or maybe Winfield was the Member of Parliament for this part of the world? No, that seemed unlikely. The Secretary of State was far too urbane for the members of this isolated community in the Tyne valley to take to him. They would make uneasy bedfellows.

Whatever its motive, Winfield's presence was an unwelcome intrusion. Marchbank had arrived in Roughburn that morning to find the centre of the town cordoned off and he had been forced to park nearly two miles outside. Now he had to retrace his steps. He hurried in the direction of his car, impatient to be free of the crowd into whose face he struggled, townsfolk in pursuit of the Honourable Winfield. He kept his head down, avoiding the innocent stares from the inquisitive northern faces. He felt himself a stranger here, alone and isolated.

In his car again he sat for a moment to recover his composure. Then, performing a U-turn, he headed off in the direction of Carlisle.

Marchbank had decided to stay in a local hotel he knew that evening and make the journey back south tomorrow. The place he had in mind was on the edge of the Lake District, about forty miles distant. He'd ring his wife when he got there and let her know. She wouldn't mind. In fact she'd probably be pleased to have him out of the way.

Margaret Marchbank. Sometimes he wondered if she had married him in order to get her hands on the alliteration. Whatever the reason, it couldn't have been the right one. These days they just went through the motions. Or rather they never got close to the motions. The last time there had been any motions must have been three months ... four? God, he couldn't even remember.

Unfortunately his subconscious didn't forget. He liked to think that he was in control of his animal drives but recently he had caught himself in the most bizarre fantasies. Like imagining what Christine Lambeth would look like in …

He forced himself to think about something else.

The hotel occupied an idyllic spot on the shores of Ullswater, away from the main road at the end of a narrow track. A pile of grey stone that had once been a simple if rather large lakeside house, it had grown organically to meet the demands of its new role. An extension here, a new wing there, gables peeping out from unexpected corners of the roof. The result should have been disastrous but it wasn't. It reminded Marchbank of an eccentric old man.

He signed the register and the young woman at the reception showed him up to his room. He was pleased to find himself with a view over the water. After she had left him he unpacked his overnight bag. The task didn't take long and when he had finished there was still an hour or two of daylight remaining so he decided to take advantage of the opportunity for a walk. With coat and scarf he went downstairs.

The sun, low in the afternoon sky, stretched the shadows of the trees across the lakeside path. The soft golden light dappled the carpet of leaves beneath them creating a rich autumnal patchwork. There was an eerie silence about him but it wasn't until Marchbank had been walking for several minutes that he realized why. The wind; there was none. He looked out at the lake. Its surface was like a mirror. He didn't believe he had ever seen such stillness before. It came into his mind that the extraordinary calm was a portent, as if the earth was holding its breath in anticipation of some precipitous event. Even the birds were silent. Perhaps they too were waiting.

He stooped and picked up a pebble, weighing it in his hand, then tossed it into the glassy water. In an instant the perfect stillness was desecrated. He watched the ripples from the stone as they spread outwards, gliding effortlessly on and on over the water into the distance. Those that rolled towards him struck the shore and then bounced back, enacting a chaotic dance as they chased the ones that had already set out across the lake. He stood, immobile, while the ripples became smaller

and smaller, finally disappearing into imperceptibility in the dusk and the vastness of Ullswater. The lake had absorbed the disturbance and was still once more. Roughburn is like that pebble, he thought turning away, a small disturbance in an otherwise untroubled calm.

Roughburn. What could be the meaning of the tiny cluster in the town's past, if it really was a cluster? Five dead children, five distant memories. What could have caused their deaths? After all, there was no nuclear power station anywhere near the town. Indeed there was little industry of any kind. So why was the cluster there? And why did somebody prefer its existence to remain hidden?

Time passed, unnoticed, while Marchbank walked and pondered and the last remains of the day seeped away over the hills to the west. With a shock he realized it was almost dark. He looked at his watch, then turned on his heel and retraced his path to the hotel. He didn't want to miss dinner.

Marchbank gave his face a cursory inspection in the mirror as he slapped on some aftershave. There were the beginnings of lines around his mouth, traces of strain at the corners of his eyes, but otherwise he looked less than his thirty-nine years. His eyes were blue-grey and deep, his hair dark and cut neatly.

He was ageing well, or so he told himself. He clenched the muscles across his bare stomach and prodded at the flesh. His finger didn't sink in noticeably he observed, pleased. He could still get into trousers he had bought ten years ago, though it wasn't often that he wanted to.

Downstairs in the lounge, ten minutes later, Marchbank sat on an elegant sofa beside the fire sipping a glass of champagne and looking over the top of his dinner menu at the other people who were gathered in the hotel that evening. A group of elderly Americans were arguing nearby but his attention was caught by two women talking quietly in the farthest corner of the room. Wasn't there a certain resonance in their features? He turned to his menu, deciding they were mother and daughter.

The shooting season was taking its annual toll of the local wildlife and game was on offer in several dishes. After studying the choice he settled for pheasant. When he lowered the menu

he found that he was under observation himself. A smartly dressed woman was perched on the edge of the sofa on the other side of the fire staring at him. He smiled back feeling self-conscious and picked up the menu again, pretending to reconsider his choice.

'I hope you don't mind me asking; are you alone?'

A melodic voice wrested him from his discomfiture. He looked up. The woman opposite was addressing him.

'Um. Yes, I am.'

'Me too.' She smiled again. 'Would you mind awfully if I joined you for dinner? I do so hate dining alone.'

How could he refuse?

Her name was Evelyn Hope and she was in television, he soon learned. 'Acting?' he wondered out loud.

'Goodness no, nothing so glamorous.' She got up and crossed to sit beside him. 'May I?' she asked, as she sat.

He looked at her blonde bob and perfect little black dress and smiled inwardly. He had been picked up.

Her 'nothing so glamorous', turned out to be television publicity.

'And what do you do Tony?'

He soon discovered that she had a way of asking questions and then waiting for a reply with her glossy lips slightly parted and blue eyes opened wide that made him forget what he was supposed to be saying.

'I'm an epidemiologist,' he finally remembered.

'Tell me more,' she demanded, smiling into his eyes.

He obliged. 'I study the incidence of diseases. For example I might want to find out if more people in Carlisle catch colds during the winter than do people in Newcastle; or the other way round. And if there is a difference I try and find out why.'

'But that sounds fascinating,' she told him as if he had suggested otherwise.

'Yes, I think so too.'

When the waiter came to take their orders Evelyn Hope arranged, with an impressive economy of explanation, that they should be seated together. While she did so Marchbank took the opportunity to look at her more closely. She had a small, pointed face and wore expertly applied make-up. A minimum of jewellery, small diamond studs in her ears and a

fine silver bracelet, accentuated her natural features. There were no rings on her fingers, he noted. He guessed she was in her late thirties or early forties.

Dinner passed easily. At one point she asked him what he was doing so far north and he told her about Roughburn. He was surprised to learn that she knew the town well.

'How?'

'I was brought up close by.' The shadow of a memory passed briefly across her face. 'Do you know I had completely forgotten, but a childhood friend of mine died when I was young? Quite unexpectedly – it was a great shock. It must have happened around the time you were describing.'

'How did your friend die?'

But she didn't know. 'All I can remember is my mother telling me that God had taken her.'

Later, when they had finished eating, they took their coffee back into the lounge and Marchbank asked for a glass of brandy.

'Have you been to the hotel before?' Evelyn Hope asked him.

'Yes, once. And you?'

'Often. It's a favourite haunt when I have to come to the north. Which room have they put you in?'

'On the first floor, at the corner, looking out across the lake.'

She clapped her hands together, a child's gesture. 'Oh, I love that room. I stayed in it in the spring. The lake in the morning with the sun rising over the trees was wonderful. I'm at the other end of the corridor this time.' She blessed him with her smile again.

There was a pause in their conversation, a brief hiatus during which a cascade of ideas tumbled through Marchbank's mind. It struck him that if he said the right thing now they could both wake up to that view in the morning. But what were the right words and did he want to say them?

Before he had time to form his thoughts she confounded him by draining her cup and standing up.

'Thank you for a wonderful evening. I think I shall go up to bed now.' She held out her hand.

Foolishly, he almost kissed it but stopped himself and, standing, shook it instead. Again he felt a tingle as she held onto him for just a moment longer than necessary. She turned to go and he remained standing until she had disappeared through the door.

Later Marchbank lay in bed in the dark, half expecting to hear a tentative knock at the door. No knock came. It was his imagination playing tricks on him again and she had wanted simply what she said, a companion for the evening. But try as he might he couldn't dispel from his mind the conviction that an opportunity had passed.

But it was a relief too. He had never been unfaithful to Margaret and in spite of the way things were he didn't want to start now. And yet, if Evelyn Hope had been forthright, what would he have done?

The lake was shrouded in an autumn mist next morning when he awoke. So much for Evelyn Hope's view. There was no sign of her at breakfast either and he thought she must have risen early and left.

He stepped outside for a last breath of lakeside air before going upstairs to pack his things. As he was walking along the drive a car's horn startled him and when he turned round he found a bright red Ferrari at his heels. Behind the wheel was his companion of the previous evening. He stepped aside and she waved animatedly and beamed at him before roaring off. Not for the first time in his life he wondered if he had made a grave mistake.

Four

'Tell me about Roughburn,' Lambeth demanded when Marchbank got back.

So he described for her the sparse northern outpost with its red sandstone buildings that looked as if they had been steeped in blood. He recalled too the people and their guileless stares. And he recalled his own, uncomfortable, reaction to them.

'The place is a backwater,' he concluded.

'Did you find anything?'

Marchbank's pocket book was still in his jacket which was hanging in the inner office. He retrieved it and showed her the names he had recorded from the children's graves. There were about fifty in all from the three graveyards he had visited.

'I want to run a trace on these,' he told her. 'Find out how they died.'

She took the book from him. 'What are you looking for?'

'Anything. More leukaemia cases, perhaps, that didn't make it on to the OPCS database.'

Fifty names. It didn't seem many, but it took the pair of them the best part of a week to gather the information. And what they acquired offered them little inspiration. There were no more leukaemia deaths.

Marchbank ran his eye down the list Lambeth handed him; the names to which she had put causes of death. 'Some more cancer cases I see,' he remarked idly.

'Those two boys you found in the same grave. They burned to death together in bed.' She shuddered.

But he wasn't listening. 'Have you got a copy of my original list?' he asked abruptly.

She found the list and gave it to him. Quickly, he checked off the names from her sheet. Then he fetched his own notes and checked those names off too. When he had finished there was an excited look on his face.

'What is it?' she asked.

'I'm not sure. There were five children buried in one of the graveyards during 1955 and '56. I already knew that two of them died of leukaemia. Another, a boy, was killed in an accident. That leaves two more. Both of them died from cancer.'

'So what?' asked Lambeth. 'Two cases don't mean a thing.'

'Just a minute. I haven't finished. There's another three here from the other two graveyards who died during those two years. All cancer. And in 1954 there were ...' – he scanned the list quickly – 'two more. That's nine children in three years just from these three graveyards. It's quite a coincidence wouldn't you say?'

'Come on. You're a statistician. Don't tell me about coincidences. What are you suggesting?'

He thought for a moment. 'I'd like to see all the cases of childhood cancer in Roughburn.'

'And what about Earnshaw?'

'I think I would prefer him to know as little about this as possible for now. Have you still got a friend working at the OPCS?'

'I wondered when we'd get round to her.'

The starting-point for many an epidemiologic study is the Office of Population Censuses and Surveys, or OPCS in London. The public database it maintains provides the basic population statistics that form the background canvas against which epidemiologists can gauge the significance of the other figures they collect.

But the OPCS goes much further than this. Locked away securely within its computers it also keeps details of individual deaths and their causes, privileged information not available for general perusal.

The OPCS takes great pains to maintain the confidentiality of its information. Herein lay Marchbank's problem. If he wanted to tap into that database he needed specific authorization. But authorization could not be obtained easily; certainly not without Earnshaw being aware of what was going on. And if Earnshaw knew, who else would come to hear?

Marchbank was pinning his hopes on Lambeth's contact, a friend from her women's group, for an inside track to the data. It didn't look hopeful.

'Is she going to get the information for us?' he demanded anxiously after Lambeth had contacted the woman. He was impatient to get on.

'No.'

He looked downcast. 'Can't you persuade her?'

'You're asking her to put her job on the line.'

'Tell her it's important.'

'Tony! You don't know that.'

'I don't mind paying the cost of the search myself if that will help.'

'I'll give it one more try.'

After much persuasion Lambeth's friend eventually agreed to do what she could. They heard nothing for the rest of the week. Then, on Friday, she turned up, unexpectedly, at their office.

It was Marchbank who saw her first, though he didn't know who she was. For an instant he thought the figure at the door was a boy because of her cropped hair and the way she was dressed. Her face was taut – a mask – and she stood motionless, framed by the doorway, staring at him.

Lambeth caught the direction of Marchbank's gaze and looked round herself. Instantly, she was alarmed.

'Sam! What is it?' she cried, jumping up from her chair.

The words jolted the other woman out of her trance, or so it seemed to Marchbank.

'You and your sodding figures!' she shouted, launching herself into the room.

She was distraught, almost manic, teetering between anger and tears.

'Oh, shit, Sam! What's happened?'

'I'm out on my arse because of them.'

For a moment her eyes flared and her whole body tensed; it looked as if anger had won. Then she collapsed in a cataract of tears. Lambeth caught her and held her tightly. Her look in Marchbank's direction was none too kindly.

It was five minutes before they got any more out of Sam. When they did, they learned that the OPCS system supervisor had found out she was conducting a search of the database without authorization. It was a dismissing offence.

'How did he know?' Lambeth asked.

'This sodding place of yours, Roughburn; it's flagged on the computer. As soon as I tried to access the cancer statistics, the machine alerted the supervisor.'

Marchbank, who had thought it politic to remain in the background, couldn't help butting in.

'Flagged? What does that signify?'

The woman looked at him fiercely, as if she was about to release another tirade but the look quickly evaporated.

'The only other place I ever came across that was flagged was Aldermaston.'

'It's a security thing?'

'What do you think?'

'Why Roughburn?'

'I don't sodding know. You're the one who wanted the figures.'

Then, quite unexpectedly, she started to cackle humourlessly. 'I got my own back on the bastards though. I'm buggered if I'm going to let them hang me for a crime I didn't commit.' And from her bag she produced a wad of computer paper which she half tossed, half threw at Lambeth.

They both looked at her in surprise. 'You mean you've got the data?' Lambeth asked, amazed. 'How?'

But her friend had broken down again.

It was guilt that prevented Marchbank grabbing the papers immediately and poring over them. Up or down, there was no getting away from it. His insistence had cost the woman her job. Nothing he could say or do would erase that fact. The thought kept him shy of the printout for the whole weekend.

Marchbank rushed to the office early on Monday morning but Lambeth had got there even earlier. She was already bent over the figures when he arrived and she looked agitated. He took off his coat quickly and joined her.

'What have we got?' he asked.

She had started to compile a table listing the number of cases of cancer for each year from 1950 to 1970. Looking over her shoulder he could see immediately that the results were staggering.

In 1950 there had been a total of two reported childhood cancers in Roughburn. The next year and the year after, none. 1953 yielded one. In 1954 three cases had been reported. All three children had died. Then in 1955 there had been ten. During the next year, 1956, this number had risen to twelve. After that the numbers tailed off slowly. In 1957 seven childhood cancer deaths had come to light followed in succeeding years by five, three, five and one. From then until 1970 the numbers had oscillated around one.

They also had figures for a much larger area surrounding and including Roughburn. The Roughburn cluster had affected these numbers too but if Roughburn was excluded the underlying average incidence was under ten childhood cancers each year in a population of 200,000. On that basis Roughburn, with its population of 30,000, should have had one or at most two cases a year.

Lambeth was stunned. 'What the hell?' she muttered to herself.

Marchbank whistled and rapidly totted-up the numbers. 'Fifty-three cases between 1950 and 1970, and forty-five of those were between 1954 and 1960. Allowing for one natural case a year, there's an excess of thirty-seven during those seven years.'

He performed more swift mental calculations.

'Five are our original leukaemia cases, so altogether we've got forty new ones. Several cases of kidney cancer, a couple of brain tumours. Thyroid cancer...' He shook his head. 'It's unbelievable. These figures have been buried there for years, a latent image waiting to be developed.'

'An image of what?'

'I don't know Chris.'

A question was staring them in the face. It was Lambeth who finally voiced it. 'Did Steven know about this?'

They looked at one another.

'He may have known something.'

'Then why did he kill himself? It makes even less sense now. If he knew about these deaths he would have wanted to find out what caused them.'

'Maybe he didn't kill himself.'

'What then? You think he could have been killed?'

'It's crossed my mind.'

'Why? To keep these deaths hidden?'

It was a frightening idea, an idea full of menace. What was it about these numbers that made them worth killing for? What was the image to which they held the clue? And if they were worth killing for once, why not again?

'They can't kill the whole department,' Lambeth whispered. But she didn't sound convinced.

'Who would want to kill him?'

'Who would want to keep this secret?'

'What are we going to do?'

That was the nub. If Hamble really had been killed they had two choices. They could either walk away from Roughburn; pass the problem on to someone else – Earnshaw perhaps – with the certainty that it would once again become buried. Or they could try and find out for themselves what was behind it, with all the risks that involved. For though neither of them said it, one thing was clear. If their suspicions were correct, this was a matter of State. The machinery involved was too large for it to be anything else.

'I'm frightened,' said Lambeth.

'Me too.'

'Speed is the essence,' he told her later that day. 'We've got to find out what caused the deaths and get it out into the open as quickly as possible.'

It was a form of reassurance, something to hold on to. Or so they convinced themselves. But when they appraised the task objectively it seemed impossible to conceive of completing it quickly. Or quietly. There was so much to do.

'We'll have to track down every one of these cases. We need their birth records to find out exactly where each child was born. See if we can trace the families. Talk to them. Find out if there are any common denominators. Hospital reports. Doctors' records – we need to see those too if we can. Find out precisely what type of cancer each child contracted. Cross-check the diagnosis. We might pick up one or two additional cases at the same time that didn't make it on to the OPCS register.'

It sounded daunting. Yet not everything was against them.

In order to look at a patient's hospital records, even a dead patient's, required the permission of the hospital ethics committee. Obtaining its consent is usually a time-consuming business. In the case of Roughburn, Hamble had already done all the hard work for them. Consent had been granted. Using Hamble's name, Marchbank would be able to gain access to the records without any problem. Or so he hoped.

It was just after five when Lambeth rose from her chair and started to put on her coat. 'I'm off now Tony.'

'Got a date?' he asked jokingly.

'Uhuh,' she mumbled.

He smiled at her. 'Anybody I know?'

But she carefully avoided answering as she picked up her bag and left.

In another office across London Margaret Marchbank was also looking forward to an evening out. The anticipation caused her to curl her toes inside her shoes. Her day's work was still far from over, however. Seated across the desk from her was one of the banes of her working life.

Harry Buckman considered himself to be a straight-from-the-shoulder sort of man. He had been brought up in a town some way to the north of London and in this cradle of his childhood and early manhood, men had been men and women were for support and recreation. Having to accept a woman as his superior was providing him with something of a challenge.

Faced with the prospect, his first instinct had been to laugh it off as a joke and his second to try and win her over with his charm. Unfortunately for him Margaret Marchbank had come across all the devices that men like Buckman employed to cope with what they perceived as one of life's great iniquities and she was not impressed with either of them. Thus it was that Buckman was forced to resort to his third line of defence: sullen acceptance coupled with a hostile guerrilla campaign. But by now Margaret was an experienced guerrilla fighter too and the likes of Buckman offered her little danger.

They were discussing the marketing of a new product that was to be launched on an unsuspecting insurance world the following week. Buckman was earmarked to take a travelling show to the north of the country in an effort to woo the financial advisers in that part of the world and persuade them of the benefits of the new combined life insurance and investment package they had put together. Marchbank meanwhile would coordinate the main publicity thrust in the capital.

As usual, Buckman was protesting. 'I do feel, Margaret, that my place is here in the City where I can field the big punters.'

'You can feel all you like, Harry, but on Sunday evening you will be in Harrogate or I shall want to know why.'

'Will you be able to cope without me?'

'Harry! I coped perfectly adequately before you walked into my life six months ago. I shall cope even more adequately when you finally walk out of it. The real question is whether you will be able to manage on your own so far from the fold.'

'Oh, don't worry about me. It's second nature.'

Yes, she thought, imagining him in his double breasted suit and loud tie, strutting around behind his paunch like a cockerel overseeing its hens. Yes, he would be perfectly at home.

'Come on then. Let's get the details fixed. I don't want to be here with you all night.'

The obvious riposte started to take shape on his lips but he caught the look in her eye and swallowed it. He's finally learning, she thought as they got down to business.

An hour later he was gone and she heaved a sigh of relief. What in God's name have I done to deserve these pricks, she asked herself?

Alone, Margaret Marchbank brushed her hair and examined her make-up. Most of her lipstick had disappeared and she replaced it. Then she checked her face once more for signs of stress or encroaching age. Still, there were none. She sighed again. Every day she expected the strain of the juggling act she was performing in her personal life to make an appearance but so far it had not materialized.

Why did life have to be so complicated? It was amazing how easy it had been to slip into a routine of deceit. Was it only three years ago that she and Tony had got married? At the time she had imagined she would be blissfully happy for the rest of her life. Then work had begun to take its toll. Not in the obvious way; she enjoyed what she did and wasn't becoming washed out. No, the effect had been more subtle, more insidious. She had gradually become a different person, more aggressive, more critical, more – though she hated to admit it, – more like a man.

She thought differently now. That must be what it was. And looking at the world from her new perspective she saw a different Tony, a Tony who no longer fitted into her life. Of course it was nothing to do with him, she kept telling herself. He was still the same man, muddling on in his way; it was she who had changed. But it made no difference. What before she had found endearing, now she found irritating. They had lost the ability to communicate.

She ought to tell him, to get it out into the open. It would be the honest thing to do, but she couldn't bring herself to, yet. To do so would mean admitting more to herself than she was ready to accept. Or was it admitting it to others that caused her to balk? She didn't know. And somewhere deep inside she kept alive the hope that it was just a phase she was passing through; that everything would eventually turn itself back up the way it had been.

So, instead, she kept it all bottled up inside her. And now, while Tony thought she was working late again, she was going to keep a rendezvous with someone else. If Tony ever learned about it he would be devastated. She smiled at her face in her mirror. She looked forward to these evenings. They were the only opportunity she got to be herself.

Five

A sudden change in the weather brought fog on the day Tony Marchbank left for his second visit to Roughburn. He delayed his departure as long as he dared but even so the fog still lay in thick patches across the Midlands. He was relieved when, in the early afternoon, a weary sun fought its way through the gloom and the conditions improved. But all too soon it was gone again, replaced by darkness. It was the tail-end of the year and the days were in a rush to be over.

The late start and terrible weather meant it was nearly eight o'clock before he passed the sign telling him that he was entering the town and entreating him to drive carefully. It was just as well he had already made arrangements to stay in a local pub. That night he slept soundly.

The next morning he was greeted by snow. There had been a light fall overnight and Roughburn was already having to come to terms with the onset of winter.

'It'll be heavier on the fells,' the landlord told him while he was eating his breakfast. Marchbank felt even colder.

Outside the wind, bitter and cutting, funnelled through the narrow stone chasms that were the streets. Marchbank fought his way through it to the local infirmary, wishing he had packed some more suitable clothing. But inside the hospital conditions were tropical and he was grateful for the warmth as he waited anxiously for the administrator.

Eileen Hughes was in her late fifties. She had a magnificent head of grey hair and was dressed in what Marchbank deemed sensible, rustic clothing. He was reminded, obliquely, of a gamekeeper he had once met and nurtured visions of her stalking the moors, a twelve-bore shotgun slung carelessly under one arm.

'We were all sorry to hear about Dr Hamble of course,' Hughes told him briskly. 'Now. I haven't been able to find you a spare office I'm afraid but we have made room for an extra desk in the records department. It's a bit spartan. I hope you won't mind.'

Roughburn Infirmary was a small but efficiently run hospital and the records department was no exception. All the patient records and reports were kept on a computer. This computer had been installed during the early part of the 1980s.

At the time the computer had arrived an effort had been made to log existing files as well as new ones on to it. Initial enthusiasm had carried the work back as far as the middle of the 1970s before its momentum had begun to fail. That, coupled with political pruning of the health service's funding, had resulted in work on the old records being abandoned at 1973. All the earlier records remained in the form of bulging manilla folders spewing a miscellany of reports and notes.

Soon after the work on the old files stopped the files themselves were relegated to the basement. It was there that Marchbank found them, just as they had been dumped, in no particular order, keeping an old central-heating boiler company. They, like it, were slowly disappearing under a thick carpet of dust.

Marchbank viewed them with a sinking heart. The dark green metal shelving looked as if it had been constructed with a giant's Meccano set. The racks of shelves had been shoved so close together that it was almost impossible to squeeze between them. Almost, but not quite. Gritting his teeth, Marchbank exhaled and edged his way in.

Marchbank wanted to locate the files of all the children who had contracted cancer and been treated in the infirmary. His preliminary search of the card index holding the hospital's pathology records had told him that forty-two of the fifty-three children who had contracted the disease between 1950 and 1970 had died here. Two other cases, children who had survived their illnesses had also been treated in the hospital.

The search of the pathology records served a second purpose too – to discover if there were any cases that had not made it on to the OPCS cancer register. There was always a possibility that one or two had been misdiagnosed or slipped through the net for some other reason. If so, Marchbank was determined to find them. The pathology index had yielded four possibilities. He added them to his list.

It took him a day to locate the files of the children from his original list. These he took out and put on one side. Since any pretext that the filing system was maintained in alphabetical order had long since been abandoned he had no qualms about introducing a little extra chaos.

He also found the files for the four additional cases from the pathology records. Two of them were not cancer after all and he returned them to the shelves. The other two he added to the pile.

Before he left the hospital he carted the forty-six manilla folders up out of the basement and into the records office. Then he went back to the pub where he was staying and had a long, hot bath, washing away the dust that had insinuated itself into every crease and crevice of his body. He spent most of the remainder of the evening sitting near the fire in the saloon bar downstairs, getting quietly plastered. Afterwards he slept so deeply that next morning he couldn't recall a single scene from his dream about green metal shelves towering over him like skyscrapers in a nightmare city while he ran between them searching for something he knew he would never find before his time ran out.

Marchbank was impatient to get to work on the records. He was up early the next morning and in the hospital by eight. Soon he was immersed in a sea of grief and suffering.

The files made pathetic reading. Through the blank style it was too easy to picture the doctors with inadequate facilities and little knowledge trying to deal with impending tragedy while knowing that in the end they were bound to fail. After the first three or four he attempted to curb his imagination and stick to what was written on the pages in front of him.

Marchbank didn't know exactly what he was looking for so he worked through each set of notes methodically, jotting down from each a list of details that he had already drawn up. He also kept a lookout for any unusual features, anything that might give him some sort of a lead to what had caused these deaths.

Three factors interested him initially: the exact diagnosis of the cancer, the age of the child when the illness had been contracted and the address of the family at the time. He also made a note of the consultant who had treated each one. If one of these doctors could be traced, his knowledge might prove invaluable.

It was three o'clock that afternoon when he put the last of the folders aside and got up from the uncomfortable wooden chair. He was done with them, for the moment at least. Before leaving the hospital he took the folders back to the basement and placed them all together on a space he created at the end of one of the lower shelves. He wanted to be able to find them again easily if he needed to.

It was too late to drive back to London today. He would have to stay another night. He thought about the information he had collected, information that was burning a hole in his briefcase. Should he spend the evening working on it? He dismissed the idea. He was far too tired to make any sense of it tonight.

But later, when he was lying in bed, his mind unexpectedly made a connection. He was certain that many of the children who had died of cancer had been born in 1952 or 1953.

There was a definite clustering of the birth dates of the children. A quick look at his notes the next morning confirmed his suspicions. What did it mean? Marchbank had the whole of a long, tedious journey back to London to ponder the significance of this discovery. Perhaps they were victims of a nuclear accident? It seemed an obvious possibility but for one objection: Roughburn had no nuclear installation. Something being transported through the town then? In those days virtually all nuclear activity was military, he realized. A cold draught raised the hairs on the back of his neck.

He tried to think of an alternative. Something less sinister. How about a virus, say, that was active when the children were born? But why affect them alone? Why not older children too?

There was one, more compelling, possibility: X-rays. What if there had been a faulty X-ray machine in Roughburn during the period in question or a suspect screening policy. It could arise simply enough. X-ray all the pregnant women, and unknowingly give them an overdose. The theory offered a cast iron-link with birth. Natal records would quickly reveal if it was correct.

Marchbank's mind ran off along one tangent after another. For most of the three-hundred-mile journey he worried continually at these ideas, going backwards and forwards, trying to fit them into a pattern. By the time he got back to Shepherd's Bush his brain was numb.

Home was much as he left it, barren. Nevertheless Marchbank spent a passable, if rather edgy, weekend with his wife. On Saturday evening they went out for dinner with some friends to an Indian restaurant on the Goldhawk Road. Sunday passed inconsequentially. He weighed into the newspapers in the morning after rising late and went to the Albion for a drink at lunchtime. Margaret remained in the house working on some project or other. Later they ate and then he watched television.

Chris Lambeth had taken to cycling into work two or three times a week for exercise. On Monday morning she appeared at the office door breathing heavily and wheeling her bike. Her face was covered with a bright red face mask that protected her from the noxious London air. She had a rucksack on her back.

A bicycle left in the street, even one chained to the railings, was likely to be stripped clean by evening so Lambeth always carried her's up to the third floor and left it in the corridor outside their office. She disappeared after leaning the bike against the wall and reappeared ten minutes later, her cycling shorts and training shoes replaced with a skirt and velvet pumps. In her hand was a mug of coffee.

Lambeth had an armourer's love of metal. Bangles, bracelets, amulets, rings; she wore them all. Marchbank didn't usually take any notice but this morning he saw that she was sporting a broad silver bracelet set with a single smoky-grey stone. It looked familiar. After a moment he realized why.

She saw him staring.

'Do you like it? It was a present.'

'Cairngorm, isn't it? Margaret has one very similar.'

'Um.'

'Yes, I do. Like it, I mean.'

Lambeth's life beyond the laboratory door was a closed book as far as Marchbank was concerned. She went to a women's group regularly; that much he knew because she had interested Margaret in it for a while after they had met once at a departmental get-together. Margaret had been enthusiastic initially, then abruptly she had dropped it. He presumed Lambeth still attended. But other than that he had no notion who she saw or what her interests were.

During the time Marchbank had been away in Roughburn, Lambeth had been busy on the telephone calling hospitals in Carlisle, Newcastle and Manchester. Her diligence had accounted for a further five cases on their list. Of the fifty-three children that the OPCS had turned up only four remained outstanding. Including the additional two Marchbank found in Roughburn they had tracked down fifty-one child victims.

When Marchbank told Lambeth about the birth dates she quickly sorted out all the birthdays from fifty-one sets of notes and plotted a graph. The result was unequivocal. The earliest birth among the victims they had identified was in 1948 and the latest in 1967. There was a scattering of births between 1948 and 1951 and between 1954 and 1967, but the majority – over thirty of the fifty-one – were born either in the last six months of 1952 or the first six months of 1953.

'There's not much doubt,' said Lambeth. 'Whatever caused the cancers was active during that period.'

Marchbank was more cautious. 'We can't be certain until we know where they were born,' he warned her.

Gwen Halpern had been twenty and married for two years when Michael was born. He was a small child, underweight at birth, but normal and healthy in every respect apart from that. She had weaned him when he was six months old and he had developed into a strong boy, walking soon after his first birthday.

Everything had seemed fine until Michael was two years old. Then he began to show the initial signs that something was wrong. The first thing Gwen noticed was his loss of balance. Before long he couldn't stand up at all and reverted to crawling. His attempts at speech suffered as well. He had started to talk but never got further than a handful of clumsily articulated words. Gwen watched helplessly as her son regressed, becoming physically weaker by the day. Within six months he was dead. A growth on his brain, the doctor said.

There was nothing anybody could do.

The loss of their son had been too much for Gwen and her husband George to cope with. George started drinking and became more and more moody, swinging between fits of silence and anger. Eventually he had become violent, hitting out at the person closest to him – Gwen. And before long Michael's death became her fault. Gwen was emotionally stronger than George but she needed someone to share her grief. With him in a bottle most of the time she felt isolated and when he started hitting her she reached the end of her tether. She left him.

It was the wrong thing to do as far as her friends and family were concerned. She found herself even more isolated than before. She went back home for three or four weeks but her mother didn't want her in the house and her father shunned her. In despair she attempted a reconciliation with George but it was hopeless. Within a few days it was as if she had never been away. Finally she packed a bag and walked out of all their lives for good.

Gwen had never worked to earn her living but she was resourceful. She became a trainee nurse in a hospital in Leicester and settled down to start a new life. She missed home at the start but the Midlands was a breath of fresh air after the claustrophobia of the conservative northern community she had left behind.

The divorce from George took years to complete because she refused to pretend she had been having an affair with another man in order to provide grounds, but eventually she was able to remarry. Bernard Halpern, her new husband, wanted children but Gwen was terrified, fearing it was something in her that had killed Michael.

In spite of her misgivings Bernard prevailed and she conceived Susan. Gwen spent the next three years waiting for the worst to happen. It never did. Their second child prospered too and eventually her fears were laid to rest. Now the two children were grown and had left home. Even so, it was still painful to remember.

She'd discussed it with her husband before agreeing to see Marchbank. Her instinct was to say no to him but she knew she couldn't. Not if it could prevent the same thing happening again to someone else's child.

They were seated in her living room. Bernard had wanted to stay too but she had sent him off to work. It would be easier to talk on her own.

'Thank you for agreeing to help me, Mrs Halpern.'

'I don't know that I can be of much help. It was so long ago.'

'Anything that you can remember....'

'I don't know where to start.'

'Where were you living when Michael was born?' he prompted.

'Oh, that's easy. Fifteen Maitland Road. George's mother lived at the end of the street and my mother was two streets away. It was that sort of town.' She gave an embarrassed laugh.

Marchbank made notes while she talked.

'Were you ill while you were carrying Michael?'

'Not that I can remember. I may have had a touch of flu over the winter. That was all.'

'Now, think carefully, this is important: can you remember whether you had an X-ray during your pregnancy?'

'I don't think I did. No, wait a minute. Yes, I did have one. It was about two months before he was born. The doctor was unhappy about the way he was lying in the womb and sent me to the infirmary. But it was all right.'

'Who was your doctor?'

'You've got me there. H ... Dr H....' She tried to recall his name. 'It began with an H, I think.'

'Never mind. Tell me what you can remember about Michael's birth.'

'There's not much to tell. I went into labour at about four o'clock in the morning. My husband – Michael's father – took me to the hospital in his dad's car. He was born about lunchtime. A tiny little thing.' She hesitated, the memory real and painful again after years of lying dormant.

'How much did he weigh?'

'I don't remember rightly. Four, four-and-a-half pounds?'

'A small baby? Did you smoke?'

'Goodness me no! George did though.'

'Any complications?'

'No, we went home after a week. Everything seemed fine until ... you know.' She stopped again.

Marchbank gave her time to compose herself.

'Did Michael play with other children?'

'Well he must have done sometimes, but it wouldn't have been often. He was barely of an age. And then he was too ill.'

'Anywhere that you took him regularly where he would have come into contact with other children?'

'Only the surgery.'

'Can you think of anything out of the ordinary that happened to him, anything at all?'

Try as she might, she could recall nothing.

Marchbank had one last question. 'There were other children, quite a few, who died around the same time as Michael. Did you know any of them?'

Gwen Halpern struggled to remember. 'No ... no, I don't think so. It wasn't long after that I left, see. Sorry.'

Each story was different. In many cases the parents found the strength in one another to weather the loss. Perhaps they already had children so they weren't plagued with the sort of misgivings suffered by Gwen Halpern. Others remained childless. It occurred to Marchbank that they dared not take the chance of going through the same suffering again, though they wouldn't put it into words. And for some, like Mrs Halpern and her former husband, the strain became too much and the fabric of their relationship was rent asunder.

Quite a few of the families moved away from Roughburn soon after their children had died. For them, perhaps, it was the only way to escape the memories conjured by the place, memories that were too poignant to bear. One mother took the ultimate escape – suicide.

And yet each story was similar too. All the people Marchbank visited carried a mark, a stigma. It seemed to make no difference whether they had come to terms with their loss or still bore it, there was something that linked them. It was like a special sadness or resignation, but more than that, perceptible just below the surface of their lives. He had tried to dismiss it as a product of his imagination but the more families he met, the more he became convinced it was real.

He and Lambeth couldn't visit all the parents. Two of the mothers were dead and several more couldn't be traced. Of those they did obtain addresses for, a number refused to cooperate. They didn't have time to go and see all of the remainder and to some they sent questionnaires. But where it was practical they tried to make personal visits.

It was a month before they had collected all the data from the families of the dead children but one thing had become apparent very quickly: X-rays couldn't be held responsible for the deaths. A high proportion of the mothers, perhaps as many as fifty per cent, had been given X-rays while they were pregnant but the other fifty per cent had not. Even if they discarded half the cases they were still left with a significantly sized cluster. There was no way round it. The X-ray explanation didn't fit the facts.

With all the statistics in their hands they started to tabulate and collate, to analyze and to plot in the hope of uncovering a bigger pattern to the deaths. If it was a nuclear accident that had caused them, they needed to know when it had happened. If it was something else, the data had to tell them what.

One of the first things they checked were the places where the children had been born. In spite of Marchbank's earlier caveat only two of the children had not been born in Roughburn. The others had spent the whole of their short lives in the town.

Marchbank was working through the addresses they had collected from the families. 'I never expected to become a postcode expert,' he joked, as he stuck another pin into a large scale map of Roughburn he had fixed on to the office wall.

Marchbank was not the first epidemiologist to discover this new area of expertise. Postcodes are a handy way of collating the incidence of a disease prior to statistical analysis, more particularly so since national registries use them to identify cases in their databases. There are over one and a half million postcodes in the United Kingdom, each home to around forty people. Unfortunately these useful little areas hadn't been defined in 1955 so Marchbank was having to take each address, find it on the map and then decide into which of the modern postcodes it fell.

After he had stuck in the last pin, Marchbank stood back and examined his handiwork. The heavily populated urban regions had the most pins while the outlying districts showed fewer, exactly as he would have expected if the cases were scattered randomly throughout the population.

'What do you think Chris?'

Lambeth looked up from her keyboard. 'Not a lot.'

In other words it told them nothing new. He sighed.

One of Marchbank's colleagues in the unit, Colin Derwent, had developed a computer program that could analyze scattered incidents of a disease and determine whether they had been caused by a single point of infection or contamination. Derwent was a computer fanatic. He spent all his waking hours in front of a terminal. The most noticeable effect of this was in his eyes; he blinked constantly. There was speculation within the department that when his blinking became rapid enough to synchronize with the beat of his computer's silicon heart, he and the machine would fuse into a single entity. Marchbank rang him.

'Colin? It's Tony. Can you run some figures through your computer for me? I need to know if they support a single source hypothesis. ... Thanks. I'll bring them through this afternoon.'

Statistical analysis is a tedious business. Marchbank often marvelled that he, or anyone else, found the patience to carry it through. To provide the raw data for Derwent's program, Marchbank had to key into the computer the grid references of the centres of each of the hundreds of postcodes that made up Roughburn and its surroundings. For each one he also had to enter the number of cancer cases it contained. It took him all the afternoon and most of the next morning.

By comparison, the program was swift. It took a mere forty minutes before indicating that as far as it was concerned the cancer cases did not originate from a single point. So much for that idea.

While Marchbank was busy with the addresses, Lambeth was completing the task of sifting through all the notes and questionnaires they had accumulated and putting the information about each case on to her computer. She broke the data down under a series of different headings such as who the doctor was that treated the patient or whether the child had been in contact with any of the other children and if so, where.

When she had finished she was able to furnish Marchbank

with the news that the children had been registered with eleven different general practitioners, that only twenty-four of them had blue eyes, that their average age when they had died had been three years, ten months and seventeen days and that they had 102 living full siblings and twenty relations who would have been their half brothers or sisters.

For all that, they were no nearer pinning down the cause. They needed help. A fresh mind. There was only one person Marchbank knew he could trust: Conrad DeWyntz.

Six

The journey from Kings Cross to Cambridge took just over an hour. Marchbank used to make it more often when he first left the university and moved to London but most of the people he had known during his post-graduate days had gone elsewhere now. In fact the only remaining reason for his once or twice yearly pilgrimages was Conrad DeWyntz.

When Marchbank was an undergraduate, DeWyntz had been his director of studies. That was not necessarily the basis for a permanent friendship but the older man had developed a certain fondness for his student. The relationship had been reinforced when Marchbank showed an aptitude for epidemiology, DeWyntz's own discipline, and the former's decision to take a doctorate in the subject had cemented it.

It was two years now since the old man had retired from his chair but he still kept his rooms in college and was rumoured to haunt the department too, popping up unexpectedly, it was said, in faculty meetings or suddenly appearing in laboratories. Marchbank suspected most of the stories were apocryphal. It was true however that DeWyntz remained active in his field; his opinion was still sought regularly and his views highly regarded.

Theirs was a curious relationship, Marchbank reflected as the train left Bishop's Stortford and headed slowly towards Cambridge and the Fens beyond. He supposed he could truthfully call DeWyntz his mentor, an academic father to whom he turned with scientific problems he couldn't master himself. Personal problems too, sometimes. But what did DeWyntz draw from it? Contact with Marchbank's generation and through that with new trends in their shared subject? Perhaps; but there was more to it than the dry stuff of academia. He felt a genuine warmth from the old man and hoped he returned it.

DeWyntz's college was close to the centre of town in one of the warren of streets that surrounded the market square. Like all the old colleges it preserved a sense of otherworldliness within its bounds, whatever the bustle outside. But, as Marchbank was about to discover, even these hallowed confines were not immune to progress. DeWyntz's rooms had moved and when he reached the staircase to which he had been directed he found that the original college building was now merely a shell. The whole place had been gutted and the topsy turvy rooms replaced with regular modern ones.

'Tony m'boy. Come in. Sit down.' Conrad DeWyntz greeted him at the door. A slight harshness in his consonants was all that remained to indicate his eastern European origins.

DeWyntz had managed to convert his new rooms into a replica of the old ones. The same books, the same furniture, even, Marchbank could have sworn, the same piles of journals on the floor that had accompanied his tutorials fifteen years ago.

'Conrad. You look well.' Marchbank shook his hand and looked into his face. Pale blue eyes shone back at him. 'Retirement seems to suit you.'

It was true. DeWyntz appeared to get slightly smaller each time they met but he radiated good health. He was about five feet six in height, shorter than Marchbank and slightly rounded. His hair was completely white but it still grew vigorously. He wore tweeds, as befitted his advancing years, and in his left hand was the ubiquitous pipe, a hooked affair that spent more time being lit than actually alight.

'How's Ester?' Marchbank asked.

'Getting older, like me. Her hearing's not so good any more.'

Ester was DeWyntz's wife. It was a curious fact that though Marchbank had known DeWyntz for all these years he had never been introduced to his wife and never visited their home. They only ever met in his college rooms. Marchbank had long since given up trying to fathom why the old man kept his life so tightly compartmentalized.

'And Margaret?'

'She's thriving.'

It didn't come out right. The old man caught the hint of sarcasm in his voice.

'All is not as it should be?'

'Insurance is a boom industry. She's become a busy woman, Conrad. We don't see as much of one another as we should.'

'That's not healthy. She doesn't have another man?' He was nothing if not direct.

'No, of course not. Nothing like that. It's just, well, I suppose we are growing apart.'

'So soon. That is very sad. But maybe it is just a temporary thing?'

'Perhaps.'

They were sitting by this time, when DeWyntz erupted from his seat with a start. 'You will have some coffee?'

The question was rhetorical. Without waiting for an answer he shot off into the corner where a kettle and a chipped enamel coffee pot stood on a tray with an already opened bottle of milk. From a cupboard he produced a bag of fresh coffee and ladled three healthy spoonfuls into the pot and when the water had boiled he filled it almost to the brim. Now, Marchbank knew, it would stand for precisely five minutes before DeWyntz would strike it smartly with a table knife he kept by just for the job. This was supposed to make the grounds sink to the bottom of the pot. Upon completing the ritual DeWyntz poured them each a mug. The knife trick never worked and the coffee was always full of gritty grounds but Marchbank was so used to it by now he didn't even notice. Today, however, the slightly bitter taste of the drink reminded him of Hamble. Steven had never been able to get used to it.

'I still find it hard to believe Steven is gone,' Marchbank confessed to the old man, voicing his thoughts. 'Sometimes I hear his voice. In the street. Even in the lab. Do you think he was capable of killing himself?'

'You doubt it?'

'He had no reason to.'

'Are you certain? In my experience the human mind is full of hidden corners.'

'He was working on something Conrad. By himself. He wouldn't simply abandon it. He would have told someone – me – first. I know he would.'

DeWyntz looked at Marchbank curiously for a moment then began to tend to his pipe. Soon a pile of matches started to grow in the ash tray. 'Tell me.'

'It concerns a place in the north. Roughburn. It was one of Steven's controls in his power-station project. When I went through his papers I found out that he – somebody – had altered the leukaemia figures for this Roughburn. It made me inquisitive. So I made some enquiries.

'Steven called me the night he died. Wanted to tell me something. I think this was it.'

DeWyntz had abandoned his efforts with his pipe and was listening intently to Marchbank. He looked troubled. 'What?'

'I'll show you.' Marchbank opened his briefcase which was beside his chair and got out a folder with the Roughburn figures. He passed it to the old man.

DeWyntz had become very still. He pulled out the pages of notes and read them slowly. 'Where did you get this?' he asked when he had finished.

'The OPCS. Roughburn Infirmary.'

'What do you think it means?'

'I'm not sure yet.'

The old man returned to his pipe. For a moment it caught and billows of aromatic smoke drifted past Marchbank. When he was satisfied he sat back in his chair.

'You have an idea? Tell me.'

'There aren't many options. I've ruled out X-rays. A vector is possible, I suppose, but it's a bit of a long shot. No, the only thing that makes sense is radiation. But I need more to go on.'

'Has it occurred to you that some of these are not common childhood cancers?' DeWyntz asked. 'Have you checked all the diagnoses?'

'As far as possible. Sixty per cent I should think.'

'You should check them all m'boy. Diagnosis was more of an art than a science in those days. What about post mortem reports?'

'We haven't had time to look at them yet.'

DeWyntz prodded at his pipe. 'Have you asked Earnshaw's opinion?'

'Earnshaw?' Marchbank looked at DeWyntz in surprise. 'No. I've told nobody but you. Besides, he would probably launch into one of his bug theories.'

Ten years previously Earnshaw had proudly unveiled to the world his theory that a number of types of cancer were caused by a small and as yet unidentified insect. The proposal had raised a few eyebrows within the academic community but by and large it had been taken in good spirit and quietly brushed underneath the nearest carpet. Earnshaw had eventually taken the hint but he could never quite abandon his theory completely. Given an opportunity he was only too happy to brush it down and try again.

'What do you think Conrad? Would Steven leave this unresolved?'

DeWyntz was slow to answer. When he did his reply shocked Marchbank.

'Tony, m'boy. I think you should drop this line of enquiry before you get in above your head. You are walking into quicksand. It will swallow you up.'

'But Conrad,' he protested. 'What about Steven?'

'Steven is dead and you are alive. Let's keep it that way.'

DeWyntz refused to discuss the matter any further. Marchbank was disturbed by his mentor's attitude. It was a side of DeWyntz he had never come across before.

On the train that evening, returning to London, Marchbank finally stopped trying to understand DeWyntz's response. It still made no sense. Then, something else the old man had said came back to him. Could Margaret really be having an affair? No, it was impossible. He would be bound to know. But for a brief moment he wasn't quite sure.

'What the bloody hell do you mean? Somebody's been ferreting about at the hospital in Roughburn! Who?' Guy was livid.

'It looks as if it was one of Hamble's colleagues. A fellow called Marchbank.'

'Looks as if ...?'

'It was this Marchbank.'

'And what was he doing there?'

'Looking at hospital records, apparently. Old ones.'

'Old ones? Jesus Christ! Why hasn't someone torched them?'

'What?'

'Never mind. Get somebody up there. Find out exactly what

he's been doing. And make it yesterday.'

Slamming the phone down roughly into its cradle, Guy jumped up from his slab of Scandinavian wood and crossed to the window. The glass was angled and slightly darkened. Anybody inquisitive enough to train a pair of binoculars on to it would see a fine reflection of the sky above his head. Nevertheless, Guy felt vulnerable. He was from the old school and had no liking for this new openness, however cosmetic. Perched up here on his designer mountain he felt as naked as a nudist on Brighton beach. And as cold.

He picked up his phone again.

'That OPCS business,' he barked when a voice answered. 'Are you certain it was Hamble back from the grave?'

'Yes.' But the voice sounded hesitant.

'Well let's be two hundred per cent certain, shall we? Put out a tickler or two.'

Chris Lambeth switched off the computer and tidied her desk. It was early, but with Marchbank away in Cambridge until tomorrow she was her own mistress for once. Lambeth had a date for dinner that evening and she intended to take advantage of his absence to indulge in the luxury of going home to change first. Usually it was such a dreadful rush to get to the flat and then back into town that she didn't bother and ended up dining out in the same creased and tired clothes she had worn all day.

Lambeth had been working with Marchbank for about two years. She had joined him at the unit after completing research for her PhD. People with her skills were rare and Marchbank had persuaded her to start work even before she had finished writing up her thesis.

In retrospect that had been a bad move. The thesis was still waiting. Some day soon, she kept telling herself, she would take one or two month's unpaid leave and complete it. But there was always another project that had first call on her time. Perhaps she shouldn't worry. After all she had already got her name on several prestigious scientific publications as a result of their work.

She pushed the office door shut while she changed into her cycling clothes. Normally she had to use the toilet along the corridor but with Marchbank away there was no need. The clothes she had taken off she packed into her rucksack, which she slipped onto her back.

A quick look around made sure the computers and printers were switched off and the window in Marchbank's office was shut – the caretaker would check when he came round later. He was a fussy old creature who left notes if absolutely everything wasn't done to his liking. She opened the door again, turned out the light, picked up her cycle from the corridor outside and left.

The time was 4.30 and the traffic, though bad, was light compared with the weight she would have encountered an hour later. Not that it mattered very much when she was on her bicycle although if it got really jammed up, the cars squeezed so close to one another that it could be difficult to thread a path between them. Fortunately she didn't have to cope with that problem this evening.

It took Lambeth about an hour to get to her home; a first floor flat, part of a semi-detached house in Finchley where she had been living since she arrived in London. When she and her bike were safely inside she tossed her rucksack on to a chair and looked at her watch. 5.30. Time for a quick bath. She ran the water while she made the bed, left from the morning, and stripped off.

Lying submerged up to her shoulders in the water, Lambeth started to think about the evening to come and then her thoughts drifted to Marchbank. What did Tony know about her life outside the office? Nothing, she hoped. She had made every effort to keep its details concealed from him.

It was surprising how easy it was to deceive people, she had found. In most cases a confident tone and a direct look did the trick. Tony was a doddle, but then he was so unsuspecting. Naive? Perhaps.

She smiled ruefully to herself. It was, in part, her own choice, she supposed, but she had found it necessary to play a double game with her fellows for longer now than she liked to remember. Pushing the thought aside, she sat up in the water, picked up the bar of soap, and started to lather her body vigorously.

* * *

The restaurant was in Hampstead and awkward to reach using public transport but it was discreet. Margaret was already there, and had ordered a bottle of white wine, when Lambeth arrived. Sancerre, Margaret always chose Sancerre.

'Chris.' Margaret Marchbank rose part way out of her seat when Lambeth joined her at the table and they exchanged kisses cheek, by cheek. A white-frocked waiter approached and then hovered, waiting to take her coat. Coat and waiter gone, Lambeth brushed Margaret's cheek again, gently, then sat herself down.

'Hi, Marg.' It was a mutually agreed diminutive, chosen after Lambeth complained that Margaret's name was too long. She hated to be called Maggie.

'Wine?'

'Need you ask?'

'Quiet day?' Margaret enquired as she filled the glass.

'Yes, I suppose it was. A little too quiet I think. Strangely enough I miss your husband when he's not there.'

Margaret grimaced but she didn't say anything.

'What about you? How's the insurance business?'

'Oh, the usual antics from the tailor's dummies that masquerade as colleagues. There has been one ray of sunshine this week though. The company's allowed Harry Buckman to slip the leash.'

'Given him the push? Why?'

'He disgraced himself at a product launch in Edinburgh last month with a lady from the press. I'm convinced that man's brain is in his prick.'

Lambeth laughed. 'What did he do?'

'What do you think? I suppose he imagined he was winning a notable victory, drinking her under the table and then into his bed. She is reputed to be a hard nut to crack, I gather. It wasn't the bedding that caused the upset, it's no more than is expected of our boys, trouble was, she's got a better head than him, and she kept it. Pumped him between the sheets. The MD wasn't particularly impressed when he saw the firm's dirty linen being aired on the gossip page of one of the weekly rags. It didn't take long to find out who had left it in the launderette.'

'Oh dear, poor Harry. She must be a dedicated woman. Sleeping with Buckman seems to me to be taking devotion to duty a little too far.'

'I doubt if she had to pay much for her story. From what I've heard he was so far gone that night he would have been about as much use as an overripe banana.'

A waiter glided up to the table as she finished the story. '*Mesdames*. Would you like to zee the menus now?' he asked, in an inflated French accent.

Marchbank and Lambeth both tried hard to suppress their giggles.

A little while later, after their first course had been cleared away, Marchbank refilled their glasses and then leaned towards her companion.

'Have you ever been to bed with a man, Chris?'

'Isn't that a dreadfully coy expression? Do you mean, have I been to *bed* – or have I *been* to bed?'

'You know very well what I mean.'

'The answer is no. I almost did though, once. When I was twenty. Someone – another Harry – at college. He plied me with drink too. The only thing I can remember about him was an enormous boil on the back of his neck.'

They paused while the waiter served their next course. When he had left their table, Marchbank continued, 'Was that when you found out you preferred women?'

'No. I'd known for a long time. That's what was so stupid about the college incident. Perhaps I was testing myself. Trying to find out if I could do what all my friends were doing. I don't know. Sometimes I think it would be wonderful just to be normal.'

'Chris. There's no such thing as normal.'

'You know what I mean. Nobody treats you in quite the same way once they find out you are a lesbian.'

'When did you find out?'

'It was when I was fourteen that I first began to suspect I was different to most of my friends. They had started getting stupid over pop stars and the boys in the class above ours. I couldn't understand it. The boys were a bunch of stringy looking kids as far as I was concerned. But my friend Sheila; I used to get worked up thinking about her.

'One night I went to stay at her house. We had to sleep in the same bed. It was the summer – hot – and she wore nothing but her knickers. White cotton ones, I remember. Her skin was so white too. I wanted to stroke her but I didn't dare. I just lay there in the bed, rigid, waiting for her to roll over against me. Every time her body touched mine it felt like a bolt of electricity. I tingled all over. I don't think I slept until it was light.' She laughed. 'It's a good job we weren't both boys. She would have been able to tell my feelings at a glance. There are some advantages to being a woman.' She toyed with her glass. 'I suppose that was when I knew.'

'Did you ever tell her?'

'No.'

'What did you do?'

'Nothing. I kept quiet. It felt very lonely sometimes.'

Marchbank took her hand and held it, squeezing tightly.

They dispensed with a dessert and over coffee Marchbank became quiet.

'Chris, I've been thinking,' she started after several moments' silence.

'Mmm?'

'I want to tell Tony.'

Lambeth's face dropped. 'Marg. Why? Don't be crazy. You can't tell him.?'

'But I can't go on deceiving him like this. It's not fair.'

'Not fair on who, him or you? He'll be devastated if you tell him. Besides, what about me? How am I going to work with him, knowing he knows?'

'What if he finds out by himself?'

'He'd never guess in a million years. Tony's mind just doesn't work that way. Even if he discovered we were meeting he'd think nothing of it.'

'You seem to know a lot about my husband all of a sudden.'

'Yes, well I probably see more of him than you do.'

Marchbank looked angry, then her features relaxed. 'Sorry. It's becoming such a strain. Sometimes my brain feels like a balloon getting tighter and tighter. If I told him – you know – I think I could relax again.'

'Marg, don't be silly. This isn't going to last for ever. One of these days you'll want a man's attention again. Besides, if you tell the world, you tell it about me too and I don't want that, thank you. I'm quite happy with the way things are.'

'Don't you ever feel the strain of having to keep it a secret from almost everybody you know?'

'I don't think of it in that way. It's my private business; like how often I go to the toilet. As far as I'm concerned there's no reason why anybody should know unless I choose to tell them.'

'I wish I had your resilience.'

'Don't worry. You'll learn. I had to.'

Marchbank sighed. 'I suppose you're right.' She signalled to a waiter. 'I fancy a brandy. How about you?'

'Why not.'

Seven

The first person Marchbank met when he reached the third floor on the morning after his trip to Cambridge was the last person he wanted to see – Earnshaw. Marchbank came through the door at the top of the stairway to find the director squeezing his bulk out of the lift.

'Good trip to Cambridge?' Earnshaw asked when he was free of the vehicle's confines.

Marchbank nodded.

'How was Conrad?' He referred to everyone by their first name if they were distinguished. It made him feel more important.

'Very well, thank you.'

'Good. Well pop along to my office will you, when you've disrobed. There's a good fellow.'

Marchbank pulled a face behind Earnshaw's back. A chat with the director was the last thing he needed.

Earnshaw's office was the complete antithesis of Marchbank's. It was as well ordered as a furniture shop display. The room boasted two windows and his desk was beneath one of them. A small bookshelf to the left of it carried a handful of regulation tomes, neatly arranged by size, and the parquet floor was completely devoid of clutter.

A man with an office like this doesn't deserve to be taken seriously, Marchbank thought.

'What can I do for you Oliver?' he asked. He was seated at the other side of Earnshaw's desk. By now Earnshaw's feet were firmly planted under it.

'Roughburn.' It sounded like an accusation.

Marchbank looked at him sharply. 'It was one of Steven's controls,' he replied. 'What about it?'

'Seems someone has been trying to get hold of information about the place from the OPCS without the right dockets. Bit of a ballyhoo, actually, a couple of weeks ago.'

'Why are you asking me?'

'Hamble's name came up. Unfortunately he's no longer with us. Thought you might know something.'

Marchbank's mind was racing. It was well over a month since Lambeth's friend Sam had been dismissed. Why had the matter surfaced now? And who had put Earnshaw on to it?

'Don't think I can help, Oliver. Sorry. What's it all about?'

'Probably nothing.' But his face told a different story.

Marchbank was almost out of the door when Earnshaw called him back. 'Got much on at the moment?'

'Quite a lot.'

'Well try and clear a bit of space. The minister's got an industrial project coming up that I may need your help on. See what you can do, eh?'

Lambeth still hadn't arrived when Marchbank got back from his little chat with Earnshaw and he had their offices to himself. He stood in front of the window staring blankly at the building opposite. It was a dull March morning, almost twilight in his room. The sky and the buildings before him mirrored his feelings, a symphony in grey. And it wasn't only Earnshaw's interrogation that was bothering him. He had Margaret on his mind too.

The house had been deserted when he got back from Cambridge the previous evening. His wife had arrived home a couple of hours later, at about 10.30, smelling of cigars. He'd noticed she had taken to smoking one on occasion, though not yet at home, thank God.

Some business contacts had to be entertained, she'd told him when he had enquired where she had been. She'd mentioned it to him earlier in the week; obviously he hadn't been listening. Normally he wouldn't have paid any attention now either. It made little difference to him whether she was home or not. But after DeWyntz had planted the suspicion of infidelity in his mind he found himself listening alertly, awakened to a new interpretation.

Was she telling him the truth? He realized he didn't know. But looking at her, he made another discovery. Whether she had been doing as she claimed or not, she had enjoyed herself. He could see it in her face. And Marchbank couldn't remember the last time he'd actually enjoyed himself. He became aware with a start that he was jealous.

It was absurd. For months now he hadn't cared in the least what she did. As far as he was concerned they were little more than fellow lodgers. So long as she made no unnecessary demands on him he was content to continue the charade, sharing with her the hollow shell that their marriage had become. He had even thought, hypothetically of course, about the possibility of being unfaithful himself.

Then, out of the blue, the idea that she might be seeing another man was planted in his brain and he was outraged. He'd almost confronted her with it there and then. Such was *the* power of this suddenly discovered jealousy. Fortunately, at the last moment he had realized how ridiculous he would sound. After all he had absolutely no reason to suspect her of being unfaithful. It was the idea that she *could be*. He'd never even considered it before.

He wondered if he needed to talk to someone about her. Who? Perhaps he could mention it to Chris. He dismissed the thought. The whole idea was absurd. The best thing to do was to try and forget it.

The sound of Lambeth's bicycle banging against the thin partition wall that separated their office from the corridor interrupted his meditations. She came in as he was emerging from his inner office and caught him still wearing a downcast expression.

'Hey, I didn't think I looked that bad in the morning.'

He forced a smile. 'Sorry. I was miles away.'

Even now it was on the tip of his tongue to pursue his uncertainty about Margaret with her but he held himself in check.

'Have a good day yesterday?' she asked as she slipped her rucksack off her shoulder.

'Not really. DeWyntz didn't want to discuss it. Warned me off, in fact.'

She looked up. 'Not like him?'

'No. I've been wondering if he knows something. Perhaps Steven confided in him before he died. By the way,' he added as Lambeth disappeared to get changed. 'Earnshaw's been asking about Roughburn.'

She checked and turned around.

'Don't worry. He doesn't know anything,' he reassured her, seeing the alarm on her face. But her reaction reminded him that they mustn't allow themselves a false sense of security.

Marchbank and Lambeth had reached an impasse. They had analyzed the Roughburn data to death and got nowhere. Now they needed inspiration. DeWyntz had offered none. If it was going to come from anyone it would have to be one of them. They shut themselves away one afternoon for a brain-storming session.

'What do we know?' Marchbank asked to start the ball rolling.

'We know it isn't X-rays.'

'But it is radiation?'

'Yes.'

'What radiation?'

She shrugged. 'I think we can assume nobody dropped a bomb on the place.'

Marchbank stared at her. 'Chris. That's brilliant. I should have realized before.'

'Come on, this is no time for sarcasm,' she told him crossly.

'I'm being serious; not about the bomb, I mean. It was something Conrad said about the cancers being unusual in children. He questioned the diagnoses. He's right. They are unusual. But they're not unknown. There's been a similar incidence before in another part of the world.'

'Where?'

'Think back to your student days.'

Suddenly Lambeth's face fell. 'But Tony that's impossible!'

'Nevertheless it's true. Japan after the end of the war. Hiroshima and Nagasaki!'

It was quite true. They had no need to check. Every epidemiologist is brought up on the studies of those two Japanese cities after the Second World War. Both knew that the types of cancer they were seeing in Roughburn had appeared in the Japanese population. But knowing didn't get them much further down the road. They still had no idea where the radiation could have come from.

'If in doubt, draw up a list,' Lambeth suggested.

It wasn't a very long list, three items to be exact.

Marchbank read it out. 'Something in the environment, contamination from an industrial plant that we don't know about, or some sort of nuclear spillage. Let's take them one by one. The environment first. Any ideas?'

As far as radiation was concerned, the environmental options were severely limited. The only real contender was radon. This radioactive gas is known to leak slowly from granite. But, as they already knew, Roughburn was not built on granite.

'Besides, radon on its own won't do. We need a cocktail of nucleides to get the mixture of cancers we've got,' Lambeth pointed out. 'And something that is present all the time couldn't possibly account for the short time-scale of the cluster at Roughburn.'

The time factor appeared to be a severe obstacle to any environmental source.

'Unless?' Marchbank began.

'Unless what?'

'Suppose there was a mine, a coal mine say, a small one that supplied local needs. And suppose the seam was contaminated; suppose it was radioactive. Not throughout; just a small part, so that the contaminated material was all mined and distributed over a short period of time. It needn't be coal, but couldn't something like that account for the pattern of deaths we've found?'

'It's possible.' She sounded unconvinced. 'How would it become contaminated? With what? And why only Roughburn?'

'Look!' he replied irritably, 'let's find out if there are actually any mines there first and worry about the hows and whys afterwards.'

One straw for the pile, Lambeth said to herself.

Marchbank moved quickly on to the next item. 'Industrial plants?'

'You've been to the town,' Lambeth pointed out. 'What do you think?'

'It seems unlikely to me. And,' he suggested jokingly, 'it would need a plutonium factory to cause the number of cases we've found.'

'Perhaps it was.' She wasn't smiling.

'What?'

'A plutonium reprocessing plant.'

'In Roughburn? Don't be ridiculous. Where?'

'It needn't be in the town. Nearby. It's a remote enough place. Don't forget what happened at Windscale in '57 when the reactor got out of control. Hundreds of square miles were covered with radioactive iodine.'

'We're not talking about hundreds of square miles. Besides, you can't keep a place like that secret. The local people would be bound to know of its existence.'

'Maybe they do. Have you asked them?'

'Come on Chris. This is absurd. If there was a nuclear installation near Roughburn we would know about it.'

'Are you sure?'

'Yes, I am.'

She shrugged. 'OK, it's just an idea.'

They sat, silently, while Marchbank played with his pencil.

'All right. We'll make some enquiries. But I know what the answer will be. Now, what about the third possibility? A nuclear spillage.'

This option offered the most scope. Commercial nuclear power hadn't got off the ground by 1953, but there had been research going on, and a very active nuclear weapons programme.

'Which means,' Lambeth said, 'that if there was an accident in Roughburn it would have been hushed up in the interests of national security.'

'It would have to be a major incident involving a hell of a lot of radioactivity to cause so many deaths. How could an incident of that magnitude be kept under wraps? Like your factory, too many people would know.'

'But you don't have to keep the accident secret. Simply forget to mention that there is any radioactive material involved.'

'I wonder?' It began to sound plausible.

'More to the point,' she asked, 'what would it be doing there in the first place?'

'Roughburn is on the main Carlisle to Newcastle railway line. Where's the atlas?'

Lambeth found it and he flicked through the pages until he reached the one showing the town.

'Look.' He traced it with his finger. 'Roughburn ... through Carlisle and then over to the west coast. Well I'll be damned. It follows the coast all the way down through Seascale. And what's right next door to Seascale?'

'Sellafield!'

'Right! I wonder when operations started there?'

Marchbank began to get excited. 'If there was an accident at Roughburn it shouldn't be difficult to track down. There must be records somewhere. It would have been in the newspapers, the local ones, at least. Probably the nationals too.'

Marchbank was indeed clutching at straws. Nevertheless the first piece of information he acquired fitted in with his hastily assembled theory. A telephone call to the head office of British Nuclear Fuels, the company which ran the plant that was now called Sellafield elicited the information that while the site's Calder Hall reactor hadn't begun operating until 1956, the place had become a weapons establishment just after the Second World War. His theory was at least tenable.

How were they to track down the putative accident? It took a while before Lambeth thought of the obvious answer – ask the railway company. She picked up the telephone.

Statistics about accidents on the railways are kept by the Railway Inspectorate, part of the government's Health and Safety Executive, she learned. Yes, she was instructed upon further enquiry, the figures for accidents were published and accessible to public inspection.

And there the trail dried up. Because there had been no incidents on the line at Roughburn between 1949, when there was a minor signal failure and 1958, when a local passenger train jumped the points just outside the station. Neither had there been one within twenty miles of the town. It looked as if they had reached another dead end.

'Bugger,' Marchbank said rather loudly when he heard.

But by now Lambeth had been infected with his enthusiasm for the idea and refused to give up easily.

'Just because it doesn't appear in the statistics doesn't mean it didn't happen. Don't forget we're probably dealing with a secret military operation. Just think how easy it would be to leave one accident out of the figures. A word in the right ear and it's gone. Erased – as if it never happened. Scientists are supposed to carry a healthy burden of scepticism, Tony. What's happened to yours?'

'But if there's no record of the accident how can we track it down?'

'We'll have to go through the newspapers.'

The newspaper section of the British Library is based in Colindale in north London, nearer to Lambeth's Finchley flat than either central London or Marchbank's home. She volunteered to visit it the next morning before coming in to work.

It proved to be a morning wasted. With no idea of when the accident might have happened except the vague notion that it would probably have to be in 1952 or 1953 she found herself faced with the impossible task of reading through all of the papers published over a two-year period. She tried to narrow it down by picking only one newspaper, *The Times*, and assuming that if it had happened it would have appeared somewhere within its pages. But even that proved too much. After four hours she had barely scratched the surface of the task. She gave up.

'It can't be done Tony,' she said when she got into the office early that afternoon. 'Not unless we know when it occurred.'

'There's only one solution then,' Marchbank declared; 'another visit to Roughburn. The answer to this, whatever it is, must be there: somewhere.'

'Well don't think I'm going to stay here on my own. I'm coming with you this time.'

The following evening, soon after Lambeth had returned home, she received an excited telephone call from Margaret.

'Chris, it's great news about Tony.'

'What?'

'Going away next week, for the whole week! We'll have it all to ourselves.'

'Marg. I've got some bad news for you. I'm going with him.'

There was a silence from the other end, followed by a wail. 'Oh, Chris, no! Can't you get out of it?'

'It's my work. I have to go with him.'

She hadn't told Margaret anything about Roughburn.

'Damn your work!'

'That's not fair.'

'I know. Sorry. I didn't mean it. Forgive me? But I was looking forward to....' Her voice trailed off.

'Where are you?'

'At the office.'

'Why don't you come round?'

'I can't. Tonight I really do have work to finish.' She lapsed into silence.

'Chris?'

'Yes?'

'I've got to do something. I can't go on like this for much longer.'

Eight

On Saturday morning Margaret Marchbank went to her hairdresser and instructed him to scalp her. He left an inch all over. Freshly shorn, she walked to South Moulton Street and bought herself a short, tight-fitting dress and a new pair of shoes.

'I want to go out tonight,' she told her husband when she got home later that afternoon. 'Somewhere exciting.'

Marchbank, who was still struggling to come to terms with her absence of hair, peered at his wife curiously. 'Exciting?' he repeated doubtfully. 'Such as?'

'I want to dance.'

'You hate dancing.'

'Come on Tony. Don't be such a bore.'

He agreed, uneasily.

'What do you think?' She had put on the new dress and shoes.

Marchbank whistled. It was so long since he had been granted a sight of her legs, he had forgotten what an asset they were. What the hell is going on, he asked himself?

They took a cab up to town and went for dinner first, to a small Italian restaurant not far from Victoria bus station. The dining-room was upstairs and the head waiter fussed over them like a father shepherding his children. He knew Margaret it seemed – from business lunches, her husband assumed.

It was gone eleven by the time they finished their meal. They left the restaurant and took another cab to a nightclub in Piccadilly, Margaret's choice too. Marchbank felt increasingly at a disadvantage. His wife knew her way around the city much better than he did.

The nightclub-night was just beginning when they arrived

and the place was only half full. They found a table and ordered drinks. Lights flashed in time to the pulse of brash metallic dance music. Smoke from a hundred cigarettes swirled around them. The music and syncopated light heightened the effects of the alcohol and before long Marchbank felt himself floating, half an inch above his chair.

They had been seated for perhaps twenty minutes, watching – it was impossible to hold a conversation – when Margaret took him by the elbow and steered him to the dance floor. She immediately picked up the rhythm of the music but he felt stiff and uncomfortable even though he had drunk amply.

Several men stood around the edge of the floor, jackals seeking prey. He saw the glint of lust in their eyes as they stared at her. Their attention encouraged his wife; she appeared to revel in it. Yet her eyes ignored them. Her look remaining fixed on her husband, trying to draw him under her spell.

He was drawn in. He found himself moving with her to the animal beat. He didn't know her. She was a mysterious woman who was luring him on towards he knew not what. So they danced and drank and danced again for two or three hours. And by degrees their dancing became closer, more erotic, more sexually charged, more laden with promise.

At two in the morning the club was packed, a single creature heaving in time to the music, when Margaret announced that she wanted to go home. They piled into yet another taxi, the static sexual charge still crackling between them. But even through his alcoholic haze, Marchbank sensed a hardness in her. She was cool, in control, while he was not. He had the irrepressible feeling they were following a script.

He shut the front door behind them after paying the taxi driver. She had kicked off her shoes at the bottom of the stairs and now sat half-way up the first flight.

'Come on up,' she beckoned.

Obediently he followed, the heat of passion burning in his loins. In their bedroom she slid sensuously across the bedspread looking invitingly at him.

'Do you want to make love?'

'Mmm.'

'Fetch me a drink first, will you?'

He went down, slavishly, and poured her a whisky with a dash of soda.

He was only gone for two minutes, he was sure, but when he returned she was fast asleep, fully clothed, stretched out across the bed where he had left her. There was a smile on her face.

Marchbank couldn't believe it. He was furious. His pent-up sexual energy demanded release. She had done it on purpose, he told himself, irrationally. He tried but was unable to rouse her. She was dead to the world. Resisting the urge to shake her like a rag doll, he left her where she lay and, downstairs again, poured himself a large drink.

He awoke, in his chair, a couple of hours later with a thick head. It was still dark. The glass was overturned beside him. A wet patch was all that remained of his gin and tonic. Groggily he dragged himself upstairs. Margaret had woken while he had been downstairs. She was undressed and in bed, fast asleep again and still smiling. He undressed himself and climbed in beside her, pondering ineffectively the purpose of the evening.

On Monday morning Marchbank picked up Lambeth from the Metropolitan Line station at Shepherd's Bush. After their Saturday night out, he and Margaret had spent Sunday in uneasy and uncommunicative silence. He was relieved to escape the house. It felt like the beginning of a holiday.

He had booked rooms for them in the pub in Roughburn where he had stayed during his last visit. The publican greeted him like an old friend when they arrived that evening.

'I've put you next to one another,' he told them, and winked conspiratorially at Marchbank.

There had been no further falls of snow in the Tyne Valley but the countryside was blank and barren. A bitter wind swept in from the east and down along the river, keeping a firm grip on the weather. It was still unmistakably winter. This time Marchbank had come prepared for the conditions but he shivered as he quickly dressed himself next morning.

Their first port of call after a leisurely breakfast was the town library. The librarian, a helpful young woman of about the same age as Lambeth, directed them to the back copies of the local weekly broadsheet. At least it had been a broadsheet in the 1950s. In the middle of the 1980s it had changed to the ubiquitous tabloid format that was now on sale in the town's newsagencies.

The papers were kept in enormous cardboard folders, each containing about six months' issues. Before long Marchbank and Lambeth were each poring over one of the mammoth, musty binders.

Lambeth had already sampled the delights of a newspaper library but it was a new experience for Marchbank. Like her before, he resolved to search each issue thoroughly for any story that might hold a clue to the cause of the children's deaths. His resolve rapidly withered before the magnitude of the task and he was soon only skimming the newspapers hoping to spot a story about an accident. There was none.

By lunchtime they had covered all the issues from the first five years of the 1950s and found no trace of a railway accident, or of a major accident of any other sort. They were getting nowhere.

Lambeth had discovered one thing however. 'The papers aren't all here,' she whispered to Marchbank.

'Are you sure?'

'Look.' She showed him where two issues were missing from the binder in front of her.

They pointed out the absence to the librarian.

'Och, I'm afraid there's no respect here for the collection,' she told them. 'If they see something they want, like as not they'll take it. You'll have to go on down to Hexham to find a complete set.'

Hexham was the town, a few miles down-river towards Newcastle, where the paper was published and printed.

Over a lunch of fish and chips and a mug of tea, they discussed what to do that afternoon. The plan they settled on was for Lambeth to return to the library while Marchbank took a stroll to the station to see if he could strike a more profitable vein there.

Back in the library, Lambeth gave up searching the newspapers and turned instead to the natural history collection. There, among books about the Cheviots, iron smelting and local flora and fauna were several local histories. They all mentioned mines.

It didn't take long to discover that the area had once been

alive with mining of one sort and another. Lead and silver had been won from the hills around Hexham. North towards Bellingham there had been a flourishing iron industry and everywhere there was evidence of coal mining, lime pits and quarries.

The books were also very specific about the mining's fate. None of it had survived beyond the first two decades of the twentieth century. Apart from one or two stone quarries, the hills were silent. The sound of tools on stone was little more than a distant echo.

The first of their carefully gathered straws had been blown away. With dampened enthusiasm Lambeth returned to the front desk and enquired about large scale ordnance survey maps of the region.

The railway station was on the outskirts of the town, not within strolling distance, so Marchbank picked up his car and drove there. The line was little used and the place had a quiet neglected air about it.

The station was a long stone building, Victorian in style, and constructed from the same red sandstone as the rest of the town. Marchbank parked his car and got out.

A pair of wooden doors were propped open in the middle of the frontage. Passing through them, Marchbank found himself in the ticket hall. A closed magazine stall faced him. To his left was a ticket window and on his right, behind another door, the waiting-room. A second open door to the left of the magazine stand led to the platform. The wind howled through it and out of the doorway behind him.

The whole place was deserted. At least, that was how it seemed at first. However a systematic search eventually revealed that someone was hiding in the rear of the ticket office, huddled over an electric bar fire with his back to the window.

'Hello!' Marchbank called through the ticket window, trying to attract the man's attention. It had no effect. He appeared to be deaf. How were customers supposed to get tickets?

Marchbank went out onto the platform and found a door marked private. He knocked, then receiving no response, opened it. Inside, a young man looked up with a start from a magazine he was reading. On seeing Marchbank he hurriedly folded the magazine and stuffed it into a bag beside him. He was not quick enough, however, to prevent Marchbank noting that it featured fit and barely clothed young women adopting unusual poses for the camera. That, plus the headphones of a personal stereo, explained why he hadn't heard Marchbank call or knock.

'Private in 'ere. Can't you read?' the young man told him angrily.

'I've been knocking on the window for five minutes,' Marchbank replied equally crossly.

'Next train's not for forty minutes,' he countered.

'I'm not here for a ticket.'

Marchbank realized he would get nowhere unless he could pacify the other man. 'Look, I'm sorry I barged in on you. I'm trying to find the station master.'

'Well 'e's not 'ere mate.' The man looked at him warily.

Marchbank took a deep breath. 'Perhaps you can help me then?'

The other waited, expectantly.

'I'm trying to find out about an accident on the line here in the 1950s.'

'Can't help you mate. I weren't born then.'

'Is there anybody here who would remember?'

'Why'd you want to know?'

Marchbank's instincts told him that he would be better off not mentioning the real reason but he couldn't think of a plausible alternative so he tried to avoid explaining altogether.

'It's for some research I'm doing.'

'You with the papers or something?'

He was about to say no when he realized he was probably being offered just the excuse he needed. He nodded.

The man seemed to soften. 'Well, I reckon you need Geordie. Geordie White.'

'Where can I find him?'

'He'll be along right enough. You can wait if you want. Outside.'

An hour later Marchbank was in the station waiting room, stamping his feet to keep warm. An hour and a half, and he was still there. He felt as if he would never recover from the cold. Cross once more, he went outside and hung around by the ticket window, hoping to catch the eye of the attendant inside.

Eventually the man saw him.

'On his way now, I shouldn't wonder. Usually here about tea time.' And he disappeared again.

In the end it was two hours before a big framed, bald headed old man pushed his way into the waiting room.

'You the feller what's asking questions?' he demanded.

'Yes.'

'With the papers, yon lad says?'

Marchbank nodded.

'What's it about?'

'I want to find out if there were any accidents here during the early 1950s. Say between 1951 and 1955.'

'Why?'

Marchbank looked at Geordie White more closely. He wasn't dressed in the uniform of the railway company. Indeed he looked old enough to have retired. 'Do you work here?'

'Used to.'

'Then?'

'Yes.'

He was going to have to take someone into his confidence or he would get nowhere. 'Can I buy you a drink?'

There was a pub called the Railway Tavern about fifty yards down the road from the station. They sat over pints of local beer and Marchbank explained who he was. Then he told White about the deaths. The other man listened intently, a growing look of consternation on his face.

'What's this got to do with accidents?' he asked presently.

'Something killed those children. It could have been radioactivity spilled during an accident.'

'Poisoned the bairns?'

'It's possible.'

White was silent, deep in thought. Marchbank waited.

'My sister, her lass – she died. Would've been two years past the coronation.'

'1955?'

'About then. She never got over it.' He paused. 'But an accident you say? There was no accident.'

'Are you certain?'

'I was a signalman. If there had been an accident I would have known.'

It was a crushing disappointment. Even though his theory had been based completely on guesswork, Marchbank had high hopes for it. Now it was dashed apart. He tried to salvage what he could.

'Could there have been any other sort of accident? Perhaps an aeroplane crash or ... well anything?'

But White could recall nothing.

He remembered his promise to Lambeth. 'You've lived here since the war, haven't you?'

'Aye.'

'Could there be a secret military establishment near the town?'

'How near?'

'It would have to be within ten miles.'

'No. Nearest place is the firing range. That's Otterburn way. Thirty miles at least.'

Marchbank thanked the old railwayman with another drink and left. He found Lambeth back at the hotel. Her study of the local maps had been fruitless too. They had been in Roughburn for less than twenty-four hours and all three of their theories had been eliminated.

Over supper that evening they tried to formulate a new plan.

'The answer is here. It's got to be.' Marchbank was adamant.

'Sure Tony. Where?'

In the end the only concrete idea they had was to get in the car and drive around, hoping for inspiration. So, after breakfast next morning, that is exactly what they did.

The man sat in his office overlooking the Thames as twilight softened the harsh city skyline. But his mind was not on the city. It was on Roughburn. Marchbank was there again. One of his pairs of eyes had informed him earlier in the day.

Marchbank clearly knew something. He was going to have to be stopped. The only question was how. He reached for the phone.

'What's Roscoe's schedule?'

'Gets back from Portsmouth this evening.'

'Pack him straight off up to Roughburn, will you?'

'After last time? You sure?'

'The man may be a lunatic but he is an opportunist *par excellence*. This business is getting out of hand. I want a result.'

'On your own head, then.'

'What are we looking for?' Lambeth had done up her seat belt, and was opening out the map they had just bought from a newsagent's.

'We'll know when we see it.'

'Brilliant!'

'If we head north we might find a place where we can look down on the town.'

'OK.'

But there was no vantage point from which they could overlook Roughburn. The country north of the town was rough and harsh, rising and plunging without warning and the road followed its contours. Though the main road north gained height as it left Roughburn, the town rapidly disappeared behind a wooded ridge of land. They tried to find a minor road that would lead them to the eyrie they sought but eventually they were forced to give up.

Returning to the valley they turned west and drove towards Carlisle, then east, retracing their steps and searching in the opposite direction. Nothing leapt out of the landscape at them. Finally they crossed the river and meandered through the roads in the hills to the south of the town. But all they found was sheep.

'What a damned waste of time,' Marchbank complained when they finally pulled up outside the pub again in the middle of the afternoon. 'I hope the bar's open.'

But it wasn't.

It opened an hour later and that was where Lambeth found him, huddled up close to the log fire, nursing a pint of beer.

'Drink?'

'Gin and tonic please. Large.'

He fetched it.

'Face it Tony,' she told him when he got back. 'Wherever the radioactivity came from, we're not going to find it.'

Marchbank stared into his drink. Was she right? What if it wasn't radiation after all. Could there be some unknown third cause? Maybe there was no explanation. Perhaps the town would remain a mysterious footnote, like the margin note scribbled by the mathematician Fermat claiming he had solved an unsolvable problem without revealing his proof. That proof remained a riddle to this day. But Roughburn wasn't a riddle. Roughburn was a secret. A secret he intended to uncover.

'We'll have to search the papers again, thoroughly. In Hexham.'

'Cheers.' Lambeth said caustically, draining her glass. 'Another?'

In spite of the setbacks a holiday camaraderie developed, almost unnoticed, between Lambeth and Marchbank. It was as though they had both unconsciously decided that if they couldn't solve the scientific conundrum they would at least enjoy their time away. Consequently, the next morning they decided to take a picturesque route to Hexham rather than the direct road.

The most promising way, they determined after studying their map, was a straight looking road that followed the course of the old Roman defence, Hadrian's Wall. Once on it they soon discovered that while an aerial view might confirm that the road was as straight as a Roman die, at ground level it bore a striking resemblance to a roller coaster. As they nose-dived over another brow, Lambeth squealed like a child and Marchbank laughed.

To their left the land rose, wild and rugged. It was littered with great grey stones like a giant's playground. Off in the distance, perhaps half a mile away, they could see the escarpment where the Roman wall had run.

'Shall we stop?' she suggested, when they passed another sign for a Roman fort.

'Why not?'

The fort itself, when they found it, was visible only as its foundations. Neat rectangular patterns – trenches of exposed brickwork cut into spongy green grass – outlined where soldiers had slept, eaten and abluted nearly two thousand years ago. It was so remote in time and place, this ancient way of life, it was hard to imagine. They pottered around, looking at this and that until the wind drove them back to the car.

A little later in the journey, as they neared Hexham, the road converged with the line of the wall. A shallow depression alongside the road was for the most part the only evidence that they were virtually close enough to touch the Roman remains. Then, unexpectedly, five or six yards of the wall itself emerged from the ground.

Marchbank experienced a sense of unreality. Patterns. Remains, just below the surface. It was as if the land itself was taunting him, laughing at him.

The newspaper in Hexham was reluctant to let them look at its private archive but after some discussion and checking of credentials they were finally granted access. This time they set out determined to examine every item that appeared during the years 1950 to 1955. They needed a marker, like the part of the Roman wall still above ground, to show them what lay beneath the surface.

The old newspapers painted a picture, built from innumerable mundane snippets, of life in the post war years. New hope dawning as memories of the terrible conflict began to fade. Too few young men. Never enough money. Rationing, phased out slowly. The period marked a turning point too, the gradual erosion of a rural way of life that had survived for centuries. The paper recorded the changes in a series of historical vignettes.

Weddings, birth and death notices, auctions, agricultural fairs: Marchbank and Lambeth read them all. Curiosities like a six legged pig born to a sow near Roughburn and leeks as thick as a man's wrist winning the local competition in Hexham. Even so they almost missed the vital clue.

The paper devoted a page each week to letters from its readers. One correspondent, a hill farmer, wrote during the spring of 1953. It was a letter born of desperation. His lambs were dying and he didn't know why. Nearly half had been born dead that year, or too weak to survive and many more had been grossly deformed and rejected by their mothers. After the letter the editor appended a comment referring readers to a story that had appeared in the previous week's issue.

Lambeth read the letter with vaguely stirring interest but her progress was arrested by the editor's adjunct. She couldn't remember the story to which he referred even though she must have read it herself barely ten minutes earlier. So much for being thorough!

She turned back and eventually found the report.

Lambing deaths on Roughburn fells

White Peak Farm, in the hills south of Roughburn, has lost over half its lambs this season. 203 were stillborn and another fifty-five were born so deformed the ewes would not suckle them.

'I've never seen anything like it before,' declared the farmer, Mr Harold Mickleson. 'I normally lose ten or fifteen but not two hundred and fifty. It's a financial disaster.'

The local veterinary practice has been unable to offer any explanation for the tragedy.

Lambeth filed the story away, mentally, but she soon had cause to recall it. In the issue after the one containing the letter, the paper ran a follow-up story. Five other farms in the hills around Roughburn had reported similar experiences.

The following week there was yet another story.

Lichen Blamed for Lambing Losses

A rare lichen is responsible for the death of hundreds of lambs in the hills around Roughburn this spring.

Hill farmers have reported losing up to fifty per cent of their lambs and local vets have been unable to explain why. Now a boffin from the ministry has come up with the answer.

Dr Crawford, called in to try and find out what was going on, said the ewes must have grazed on the poisonous lichen. 'It is a very rare form that only appears under exceptional circumstances,' he told the farmers. 'I'm sure it will disappear during the summer and everything will be back to normal by next spring.' The ministry plans to monitor the plant's progress, just in case.

'What do you make of this Tony?'

She showed him the four items. As he read, Marchbank's face slowly lit up. When he had finished he could barely contain his excitement.

'Damn it Chris. Well done. This is just what we've been looking for.'

Nine

Was radioactive contamination responsible for the deaths of hundreds of lambs on the hills around Roughburn during the spring of 1953? And was it responsible for the deaths of thirty and more children from the town too? Marchbank thought so.

'The fells must have been covered with radioactive fallout. Remember Chernobyl? This was much worse. It must have been humming.'

As they drove back to Roughburn his brain worked overtime, spilling out ideas chaotically.

'Where did it come from?' Lambeth demanded.

'There was a six-legged pig too,' he went on, ignoring her question. 'It all fits the pattern.'

'You haven't answered me.'

'Damn it, Chris, I don't know.' He turned towards her. 'I'd like to see the data for miscarriages during those two years.'

'Careful,' she warned as the car swerved erratically. 'Watch where you're driving.'

He laughed. 'Lichen? I wonder who thought that one up.'

The stories from the newspaper were the breakthrough he had been hoping for. They were confirmation that something really had happened sometime during 1952 or 1953. Corroborative evidence. It was an excuse for a celebration.

The publican recommended a place to them, a hotel in the ragged country about five miles to the north of the town. Washed and changed – Marchbank in a rather conservative suit he had packed unthinkingly in his rush to get away on Monday morning, Lambeth in a dress she had acquired from Oxfam several years earlier – they found their way there by taxi.

The hotel turned out to be an austere stone structure perched on the edge of a river where the paths of the water and a road crossed. Their taxi deposited them at a door recessed deep into a rough stone wall. Small window openings on either side of it, covered by thick curtains, allowed no light to escape and gave the place a cold, uninviting air. The sound of water cascading over an invisible fall somewhere beyond the building made them even more sensible to the chill. Once inside, however, they found a more comfortable welcome.

It was Thursday and Marchbank had intended to return to London the following day. Now he was determined to stay until Saturday.

'I want to check out the miscarriages,' he told Lambeth as they sipped their drinks.

'If we'd searched the papers thoroughly on Tuesday,' Lambeth answered as she selected a peanut from the dish on the bar and prepared to pop it into her mouth, 'it would have saved a lot of time.'

About twenty minutes after their orders had been taken a girl dressed in black and white led them to their seats in the corner of a square, wood panelled dining room. The lighting was discreet and there were candles burning on their table. A bottle of champagne stood waiting for them in a silver bucket.

'Where did that come from?' Lambeth demanded.

'I ordered it.'

'But we can't afford it,' she declared.

'My treat. Besides, it's too late now.'

It wasn't quite, because the cork had yet to be pulled. That situation was remedied a few moments later.

'Is this why we came by taxi?' she asked while the waiter poured her a glass.

Marchbank's grin confirmed her guess. Before long they were both behaving like conspiratorial school kids.

They were almost alone in the restaurant. Only one other table was occupied, this by a man on his own. As they talked and laughed, champagne and crystal and candlelight began to weave a spell around them. They became engulfed in a world of their own.

It was hard to say when Lambeth realized she was straying into dangerous waters. Perhaps the thought crept up on her slowly, sneaking into senses dulled by the champagne and *bonhomie*. Or maybe it came as a sudden awakening, an inspiration fuelled by her knowledge of the situation between Marchbank and his wife, the knowledge that their marriage was virtually at an end and that very soon, if not already, he would consider himself a free agent and be on the lookout for someone new with whom to sport. But however it dawned, she became aware of a curious glint in Marchbank's eye and an intimacy in their conversation that properly belonged to exchanges between lovers.

It had the effect of a bucket of cold water. Good God! Tony's got designs on me. And yet here, in the warmth and in the bosom of their intimacy she didn't mind, in an academic sort of way. The problem, she nevertheless grasped through the champagne, was that if she didn't do something about it the idea would become reality and while she quite liked Tony – actually had become fond of him – the prospect of his loins thrusting like the piston of an engine to her cylinder was about as appetizing as a face full of junket. No, less appetizing. She liked junket.

But how to extract herself without offending him? Of course she could come out and tell him, casually, of her persuasion. But somehow this didn't seem the time or the place. So what the hell was she going to do?

In fact she did Marchbank an injustice because the idea only dawned on him at about the same time as it occurred to her. And, to be fair, his thoughts were not immediately carnal. He found himself noting that here he was enjoying himself, in itself unusual. From there he progressed to the recognition that he was doing so in the company of a woman who he found attractive and likable, a contrast, at least in the last respect, with his feelings towards his wife. And then he wondered what he should do about it. At that stage his ideas did become more down to earth.

'Chris. I'm growing rather fond of you. I hope you don't mind me saying so.'

The table had been cleared and they were sipping port.

'Mind? Of course not. I'm enjoying myself too.'

'I was just thinking ... .'

He sounded unsure what he had been thinking. Be tactful, she told herself. She put her glass down.

'There's something I should tell you Tony,' she started

carefully. 'It's about Margaret. You probably don't know that I see her sometimes. We've become quite close friends since the women's group. She talks to me; talks about you and her. I know your marriage isn't going well. And – well – I think I know what you're thinking. I'm flattered. But I don't think the idea is very practical. It would lead to terrible complications.' Such as you couldn't imagine she added, to herself.

He looked shocked. At first she thought she had made an awful mistake, that he hadn't been thinking what she imagined after all. But it was the fact that she and Margaret had been meeting, unknown to him.

'Why did you keep it a secret?'

'It seemed simpler, with you two having problems. I didn't want to be caught in the middle.'

He touched her hand, fleetingly, on top of the table. 'Yes, I suppose you're right.' There was a pained look on his face, a look of betrayal. She had hurt him although she wasn't sure why.

'What's going to happen?' she asked. 'Between you and Margaret.'

'I don't know.' He shrugged. 'What does happen? I suppose we'll drift along until something stirs one of us to act and then that will be that.'

With talk of the doomed marriage a gloom descended on the evening and their joyous spirits evaporated. Or perhaps they had just had too much to drink. In next to no time they had ordered a taxi, paid their bill and left.

Back at the pub there was an envelope waiting for Lambeth. She opened it quickly. The message inside was simple. Ring Marg. She shoved it into her handbag.

'Not bad news, I hope?' Marchbank asked, seeing the look on her face.

'I don't think so. It's from a friend. She wants me to ring her.'

They had telephones in their rooms so she hurried upstairs and called from there. Five minutes later she was knocking on Marchbank's door.

'Tony,' she started as soon as it opened. 'I have to go back to London tomorrow. I'll get the train. Will you be all right, finishing up here on your own?'

'Is everything OK?' he asked, concerned.

'Yes. Nothing to worry about.'

But her face conveyed a different message. The sudden change of plans brought their little holiday to an abrupt end.

Outside, fifty yards up the street, a man sat in a parked car. He was a small man with dark hair and he was cold. Bitterly cold. He rubbed his hands together and shivered. He had spent most of the evening outside a restaurant in the wilds of Northumbria. Now he was in a foul mood. And when his frame of mind deteriorated, he became unpredictable.

It was going to be a long journey back to London by rail for Lambeth the next day. She had to catch an early train from Roughburn, one of the few that went to Carlisle, and await a main line connection from there to the capital. She and Marchbank met for breakfast. It was a subdued meal after the previous evening. Then he took her to the station.

'See you on Monday,' he shouted, waving, as her train moved off. And he was alone again. It was an unexpected sensation. Not being alone, he was used to that, but being aware of it. It was so long since he and Margaret had filled the role of companions, one to the other, that he had forgotten what it was like. With Lambeth over the past few days he had been reminded what companionship was.

'Miscarriages,' he said out loud, determined to distract himself.

The reason for Marchbank's interest in miscarriages was simple. Radiation had caused both deaths and stillbirths among the newborn lambs on the fells in the winter of 1952-3. There had been human deaths too. It seemed logical to suppose that there might be a surfeit of human miscarriages.

Where would he find the data? In the infirmary? He was on the point of driving there from the station when it occurred to him that to do so could prove a mistake. Earnshaw's enquiry showed someone was still monitoring any interest in Roughburn.

Was he really in any danger? It was difficult to believe so. But perhaps it was as well to remain cautious. Whoever had alerted Earnshaw about the OPCS database breach could also have instructed the hospital. If so, to show his face there would be like placing an advert in *The Times*.

Then how was he to get hold of the information? It was a while before the means occurred to him. The medical files he wanted to look at were in the basement of the infirmary. And as his previous excursion had proved, nobody ever went near them. The dust was an inch thick. If he could slip down there again he could find what he needed without anybody knowing.

The entrance to the basement was at one end of a corridor that stretched the full length of the building. He waited until lunchtime when he knew most of the hospital staff would be in the canteen. It was 12.15 when he strode purposefully through the infirmary doors. Five minutes later he was standing at the top of a flight of steps, the steel basement door shut behind him.

The warm, dusty smell greeted him like an old friend. He descended the steps, following the central-heating pipes that led to the abandoned boiler. There was a faint odour of tar or oil; like the bowels of a ship, he thought. Past the boiler, the green metal shelves of files were as he had left them.

The basement was really a half basement, not completely underground. A dull light filtered in from narrow lights high up its walls. There was light enough to find his way around but not enough to read by. He dare not use the ceiling lights so he had brought a torch.

He looked at the shelves of files, wondering where to start. They were in no particular order, he recalled. Start at one end and work along to the other, then. He rested his torch on the shelf beside him, pulled out the first file and opened it.

A cloud of dust greeted him. He spluttered and coughed. It seemed worse than last time. He brushed the dust away and examined the contents. Tuberculosis. A man. He put it back and took out the next.

After an hour he felt as if he had been in a desert for a year. His throat was parched from the dust and his eyes were gritty and irritating. He had found two miscarriages, both during 1952. At the rate he was going it would take him a week to finish. The task looked hopeless but he forced himself to go on.

3.30; he had been there for three hours and found three miscarriages. The light from his torch was beginning to fail and he felt as if he was asphyxiating. To cap it all he could hear a rat scratching around somewhere behind him. He couldn't go on. Even Hercules would have been taxed. He cursed his own stupidity at even attempting the task. If he had two brain cells to rub together he should have realized it would be impossible.

Perhaps he could come back again after their discoveries about Roughburn had been published. He picked up the three files, intending to lodge them with the forty or so files he had found during his first visit. But when he got to the shelf where he had left them he couldn't. The children's files had gone! He touched the bare shelf in disbelief.

Marchbank looked around, suddenly feeling very exposed. How stupid could he be, thinking nobody knew what he was up to? If they knew about the unauthorized OPCS search they wouldn't just alert the hospital. They would ask questions. And then they would know all about his previous visit; know all about the files he had found. Here was the proof if proof were needed. Were they watching him too? Did they know he was here now? If his eyes had not been caked with dust he would probably have cried.

It was the faint smell of petrol that first alerted him to danger. Then he heard the whispered crackle of burning paper. And then he smelled the acrid smell of smoke. Oh, God! Someone had set fire to the files.

Within ten seconds the crackle had become a roar and he could feel the heat burning his face. The files were tinder dry. In moments he was witness to an inferno.

Marchbank panicked. He ran. He couldn't go back, towards the stairs and the door: the fire blocked his path. Instead he tripped and scrambled his way between the shelves in the opposite direction, away from the exit and into the gloom.

The fire followed him, racing along the shelves with alarming speed. The smoke was already beginning to engulf him. He was trapped; cut off from the door. There was no escape. Whoever had set the fire knew that. It was pointless. Within seconds he would be unconscious, within minutes, dead.

Fortunately for Marchbank his mind no longer had control over his body, which blundered on regardless. And somehow, coughing and spluttering, he found himself at the end of the shelving. Ahead of him the basement yawned in the flickering glow of the conflagration.

Roughburn Infirmary was a symmetrical building; two long arms reached out either side of a central block. The basement stretched beneath its full length. Marchbank had entered through a door at the end of one of the arms. Symmetry implied there might be a door at the other end too. It was his only chance.

The smoke was already overtaking him as he staggered on. He cannoned into a chair and fell to the floor; picked himself up and continued. By now all light had gone. But for the moment he was outpacing the fire. He couldn't tell how near he was to the end. Then with a crash his head banged into brickwork and he collapsed to the floor again, dazed.

Dragging himself up he felt the rough brick of the wall in front of him and followed it to the right. If there was another exit it would be in that direction. He came to a corner. Now he was going back the way he had come, back towards the fire. There was no break in the wall, no second set of stairs.

Suddenly the wall fell away from him and he toppled into a recess. Steps! He clambered up them with hands and feet. At the top there was a door. He grabbed the handle and pushed. It wouldn't budge. He banged and banged and began to choke. He grabbed the handle again. Pull, you fool! The door opens inwards. It did. He lunged through and fell full length across the corridor.

Out in the body of the hospital, mayhem ruled. Fire bells were ringing and people were rushing in every direction, evacuating the building. Nobody seemed to notice one extra, coughing and rather grimy figure. Marchbank joined the tide and was swept out into the open air. He looked at the sky in amazement. Such light. So much air. He could breathe once more. He was alive. It was as much as he could do to prevent himself falling on his knees in thanks.

Somehow he found his way back to the pub and into his room. There he stripped off all his clothes and plunged into a bath of steaming water. He stayed there for an hour letting the pain drain from his body.

Now a curious change came over Marchbank. He knew he should feel terrified but he didn't. He felt elated. Ever since he had admitted to himself that Hamble might have been killed he had lived with a gnawing uncertainly and fear. He could be next. Now there was no more uncertainty. He knew he was a target. They had thrown their worst at him. And they had failed. He had survived. What was more, they had broken cover. He knew now for certain that he was right.

He was a match for them. He would win.

But fate hadn't finished dealing Marchbank's hand.

Ten

Marchbank knew Margaret had gone as soon as he opened his front door that Saturday evening when he arrived back from Roughburn. There was the silence of desertion about the house. Or was it just an absence of clutter in the hall?

It's your imagination, he told himself. He dropped his bag and briefcase and rushed from room to room, downstairs then up. But there was no doubt. His wife had left him.

It had been a possibility for far too long. If it hadn't been her, it would have been him. Yet now that it had happened it was a shock. He needed someone here. He had nearly died in the fire in the infirmary. The desperation of his escape haunted him.

He felt a surge of anger. He had been right then. She was seeing someone. Why else would she have left so precipitously? He felt the hot coals of jealousy burning in the pit of his stomach once more.

He tried to reason with himself. What did it matter to him that she was in bed with another man?

Yet against reason he felt betrayed. How dare she! What right had she to go off, abandoning him so selfishly for another? He knew then, briefly, the rage that caused men to kill in their desire to avenge their injured hearts. He imagined himself striking out brutally at her unknown lover in an effort to cauterize the pain. Striking at her too, blindly.

But soon the flames of his rage subsided. He felt lonely. And that was worse because there was no remedy, no-one else to blame. Loneliness had to be borne alone. Tears came to his eyes.

He was in their bedroom. He threw himself face down on to the bed they had shared and in the dark and silence of the empty house he let himself go, allowed self-pity to take over his body. For fifteen, twenty minutes he was a child. When it was over he felt cleansed, empty. Slowly he got up and switched on the lights.

Downstairs, he made himself a drink and when he felt calmer he began to take stock of the situation. It was then that he found the envelope. It had been propped against the pepper mill on the dining-table but had slid down so it lay flat on its face. He picked it up and turned it over. *Tony.* Just that one word, in Margaret's barely legible writing.

He tore it open quickly and pulled out the single sheet.

Tony
I know it's cowardly to run away like this but how long will it drag on, otherwise? I've made arrangements to stay with someone, a friend, while I sort myself out. I'll call you when I can.
Margaret.

PS. I've asked Jonathan to represent me. Hope you don't mind finding yourself another solicitor.

'Cold hearted, practical bitch,' he muttered. He read the note again. Friend? Who was that a euphemism for? He tried to imagine her with some sleazy insurance salesman but it didn't work. Whatever else she was, Margaret had disgustingly good taste.

Marchbank tried to be pragmatic. What actual difference did her absence make? If she had been here, few words would have passed between them. She would have gone off to bed early and he would have watched the TV. But it did make a difference, however hard he tried to persuade himself otherwise. He had been abandoned, left alone. The feeling of isolation could not be rationalized away.

He wondered if she would disappear completely. He might never see or hear from her again. He felt a sudden moment of panic. With no address or telephone number, how could he contact her? She could have been kidnapped or murdered and he would never know. But of course she would be at work on Monday. He could contact her there.

What had she taken? He began to look around. One or two ornaments had gone. A few books? He couldn't be sure. Upstairs he found that a few of her clothes had disappeared, but not all of them. Cosmetics, jewellery: some of both still remained too. She would have to come back eventually for the rest. He felt a warming sense of relief.

The next morning when he awoke there was an instant before he remembered that he was alone. When he did, he buried his face in his pillow.

He had a whole day to himself. How was he going to fill it? But when he forced himself out of bed, routine took over. He walked round to the local newsagent and collected a bundle of Sunday papers before eating breakfast and then spent the rest of the morning sprawled on the sofa reading them.

Newsprint gave way to introspection. He didn't want the space to think. Marchbank looked at his watch. It was past noon. He could escape down the road for a drink. But when he arrived at the Albion the practical ramifications of his new situation made themselves felt for the first time. People would have to be told.

He thought of his father, a lonely man himself since Marchbank's mother had died. He was very fond of Margaret. How would he take it? And all the relatives and friends who had to be informed. How would they react?

Not yet. He could put it off for a day or two, he told himself, at least until he had spoken to Margaret again. And he wondered what would be left of their life together when the dust had settled.

When he got home again he felt restless. He needed someone to talk to. He picked up the phone intending to call DeWyntz but with the receiver in his hand he changed his mind and dialled Lambeth's number instead. There was no reply. He felt let down.

He pressed the code and number for DeWyntz but the old man was not in his college rooms. Stupid to expect him to be on a Sunday. He didn't have his home number. Frustrated, he eventually tracked down an old friend from his university days and arranged to meet for a drink that evening.

* * *

On Monday morning a postcard bearing a picture of an orang-utan was waiting on the doormat for Marchbank when he got downstairs. It was from Margaret. She had posted it in London two days earlier; Saturday, the day he found she had gone. The message it bore was that she would be away from work for the next week while she sorted out her new domestic arrangements and would telephone him when she could. He couldn't help thinking the picture she had chosen was part of the message too.

He was himself late for work that morning and arrived to find a sharply worded note pinned to his door instructing him to go to Earnshaw's office without delay. Of Lambeth there was no sign. He found her in the director's office, in conference with a shiny looking civil servant from the Department of Trade and Industry. He knocked and went in. It was half past ten.

'What bloody time do you call this?' Earnshaw demanded angrily while Marchbank pulled up a chair.

Marchbank shrugged. 'Sorry Oliver.' He had no intention of parading the reasons for his late arrival in front of the director let alone the Civil Service.

'Well we're not going over everything again. You'll just have to pick it up as we go along.'

Marchbank looked at Lambeth as he sat down but she avoided his gaze.

The object of the meeting was to discuss a new study. He and Lambeth were to carry it out, or so it seemed, under Earnshaw's guidance. The plan, Marchbank managed to piece together, was to examine the statistics for industrial accidents throughout the United Kingdom to see if they could discern any pattern or logic in them. In theory this would eventually lead to remedial measures. The work was sponsored by the government which was under growing pressure to act on a rising toll of industrial deaths. Instigation of the study would be used to support the minister's claim that action was being taken.

The meeting dragged on most of the morning as they explored possible strategies, discussed how long it should take

– as long as possible appeared to be the ministry's preference –
and decided what effects they ought to be on the lookout for.
Marchbank's mind drifted. He found it increasingly difficult to
concentrate. So, he was caught by surprise when Earnshaw
stood up and showed the man from the ministry to the door.

Lambeth stood too. Marchbank jumped up and followed in
her wake. They were barely out of Earnshaw's earshot when he
started quizzing her about Margaret.

'Where is she?' he demanded without preamble.

He was keenly aware of her hesitation and discomfort.

'Don't ask, please, Tony. You know that I can't tell you.'

'Have you seen her?'

'Yes.' She looked at her feet.

He was having to drag every word out of her. It was unfair,
he knew, but he had to find out.

'At least tell me if she's moved in with another man.'

Again he detected hesitation.

'No. She hasn't left you for another man.'

'You're sure?'

'Oh, yes. I'm certain of that.'

He felt better, as though the fact that their marriage was in
ruins was of little consequence so long as she hadn't betrayed
him.

Lambeth, in contrast, felt depressed. What she had feared
most was beginning to happen. She was stuck between the
Marchbanks, a handy whipping boy for either of them.

As it turned out, her fears were not realized. After that
morning, Marchbank avoided the subject of Margaret as much
as possible. His estranged wife eventually called him on the
Friday, by which time she had found herself a small flat in
Putney. Conversation was difficult with all the psychological
debris of their relationship now out in the open but they made
a tentative arrangement that she would come and collect more
of her belongings one evening the following week. She left him
her new telephone number but no address.

It was the end, however, of the camaraderie that had
developed between Marchbank and Lambeth during their
northern trip. In its place Marchbank adopted a cold
professionalism. He seemed unaware of this change in manner
but Lambeth noted it and was distressed. Was this hardness an

armour to protect his wounds or a reaction to her suspected complicity? She did not know. But she put far from her mind all thought of how he would react if ever he found out the truth.

Meanwhile Marchbank threw himself into his work. A quick resolution of Roughburn was imperative after the fire. His sense of urgency and danger had returned.

Later during the same week as Margaret's departure, Marchbank was attempting to pinpoint when the radioactive incident in Roughburn had taken place.

'The spread of the birth dates might give a fix,' he suggested to Lambeth. 'Plot them on a bar graph, will you?'

Lambeth had prepared a table, weeks earlier, containing the birthdays of all the children who had contracted cancers. It was a simple matter to draw up a bar chart from the figures. What it showed was that the number of cases started rising in August and September of 1952 and climbed erratically to a peak spread across March and April of 1953. From there the numbers tailed off more slowly until the end of 1953.

'When is an embryo most susceptible to radiation injury?' Marchbank asked after looking at the graph.

'During the early stages of development. The first two or three months.'

'I agree. So the mothers who were in the first three months of their pregnancies when the radioactivity appeared will have suffered the worst effects.'

'Roughly, yes,' she concurred.

'And if the peak is in March and April of 1953 it would mean the actual irradiation took place sometime ...' – he paused to count backwards – 'during July or August of 1952.'

'Hang on. The first cases don't appear until August.'

'Yes, OK. But children born close to the time of the incident would be almost fully developed and less susceptible,' he pointed out.

'What about this long tail? There are cases right through 1953.'

'Perhaps it was a dry summer in 1952.'

'Or the incident happened later.'

'Let's say that the earliest plausible date is July 1952 and the latest October 1952. How's that sound?'

'Fair enough.'

But knowing when still didn't help them discover what had happened.

The small flat in Putney was part of a modern riverside development. It had been built for sale but a dramatic failure of the housing market had forced the developers to rent the properties as a temporary measure. Their financial face-saving was Margaret Marchbank's salvation and she paced and prowled her new domain like a lynx might a well-appointed cave.

With her recently acquired freedom, Margaret Marchbank felt herself a different person. She hadn't realized how low she had sunk over the past few months. The house, the deceit, Tony himself; they had all contrived to weigh her down. Yet, with one decisive act, all those shackles had been broken. She wished she had done it sooner.

The flight itself had been hastily conceived. It was not something she was proud of. An overwhelming urge to run had overtaken her while Tony Marchbank was away in Roughburn and a terror that if she didn't act immediately she would be trapped for ever. Her Thursday call to Lambeth had been prompted by this panic.

She had packed as little as she dared – even that had proved a major burden in Lambeth's tiny flat – and had been waiting on the doorstep when Lambeth got back from Roughburn on the Friday. Chris is a darling, she thought, remembering, but there simply wasn't enough room for both of us.

But even after she had left Tony and the house near Shepherd's Bush she still hadn't felt free. Not until she had found the flat in Putney and then faced up to her husband had she finally felt the weight lift from her; felt she was her own woman again. And yet, she acknowledged, she wouldn't have been able to do it without Chris. The thought made her feel slightly uneasy. It was as if her freedom was still not her own to do with as she chose.

She was interrupted by a buzz from the entry phone. Lambeth was downstairs.

'Marg, you look wonderful.' Lambeth handed over an enormous bunch of red roses as she stepped across the threshold.

'Chris.' The two women hugged one another.

'Come on then. Let's see what it's like.' This was Lambeth's first visit. Marchbank laid the flowers on a table and gave her a guided tour.

'Hey, this is great.' She bounced on the bed and then rolled across it. 'It's twice the size of mine.'

They returned to the living room which overlooked the river.

'I love the view,' Lambeth said as she watched the water slide by. Today it looked like cast iron; black, cold and forbidding. Margaret slid her arm through Lambeth's and they stood staring at it, silently.

It was less than two weeks since Margaret Marchbank had left home but already, with characteristic efficiency, she had almost completely furnished her new flat. She had also removed all of her personal belongings from Shepherd's Bush.

A separation cannot be finalized in such a short span, of course. There was still the sticky question of how to resolve ownership of the things she and Tony both had an interest in. And the house itself. She was anxious to get on and sort out their affairs but she sensed a certain reluctance in her husband. She couldn't understand his reticence. He had been just as unhappy as she.

'How is Tony?' Marg asked, stirring from her reverie.

'Better. Working hard. I've a suspicion he went out one night last week with someone. No idea who.'

Lambeth hadn't mentioned the evening out in Roughburn to Marg. She decided to keep that to herself.

Margaret picked up the roses and took them into the kitchen. There were too many to fit into a single vase so she divided them between two, putting one on the table in front of the window. The other she carried into the bedroom. Afterwards she cooked dinner. In spite of the length of their affair this was the first time she had ever done so. In fact it was a long time since she had done any serious cooking. That was one of the activities that had suffered a terminal decline during the latter part of her life with Tony.

The flat was open plan and Lambeth watched from the living room. As with everything she did, Marg approached cookery in a businesslike way. Jointing a chicken was one of the jobs Chris would spend hours agonizing over. Marg had the bird sectioned in about ten seconds.

As she observed her lover at work, Lambeth marvelled at the change that had come over her. She seemed so much stronger, both mentally and physically. Even her posture was different. And her face was becoming more luminous with each passing day.

They were getting on well. Now that Marg no longer felt herself in the shadow of infidelity she had relaxed and their relationship had blossomed. At times Lambeth felt they were both floating effortlessly, like gulls on a thermal. It was luxurious.

And yet, Lambeth was worried. Worried because things were going so well, she wondered? Not that, no; worried because Marg was becoming so strong and independent. In the beginning Marchbank had needed Lambeth; now she didn't. The balance in their relationship was changing subtly. At the back of her mind was the fear which had always lingered that it could only be temporary. One morning Marg would wake up needing a man again.

'Open this will you?'

Lambeth took the proffered bottle of wine. 'Corkscrew?'

Marchbank waved vaguely at some drawers to her left. Eventually she found the implement in one of them and removed the cork. Only then did she bother to look at the label.

'Hey, it's not Sancerre!'

'Just shut up and pour it!'

When the meal was cooked they sat opposite one another, with the river moving endlessly past beside them.

'Shall we go on holiday somewhere?' Lambeth asked, pausing over a forkful of chicken.

'That's a nice idea. Let's.'

'Somewhere hot?'

'Like?'

'Tenerife. We can get our tits brown there.'

'Chris! You have a coarse vein in that otherwise flawless make-up.'

'But don't you just love it?'

'The feeling that I'm slumming does add a certain piquancy to our relationship.' She gulped at her wine. 'When shall we go?'

'God, as soon as possible. I'm fed up with dull brown skies and grey skin.'

'Brown sky?'

'You know what I mean.'

After they had eaten Marchbank insisted they do the washing-up.

'Do you ever think of the future?' Lambeth asked abruptly as she picked up a dripping plate.

'Give me a chance. I've barely got over thinking about the past.'

'I do. It frightens me.'

'Why?'

'I don't know where I'm going; what I want from life.'

'Does that matter?'

'I bet you know where you'll be in ten years' time.'

'Yeah. I'll be on the company board. Every time I twiddle my toes, little piggies will dance.'

'See, what did I tell you?'

'It's a joke, Chris.'

'With more than an element of truth.'

'Dry the dishes and stop being such a misery.'

She did as she was told.

Time was running out. They couldn't delay any longer. The Roughburn data had to be published. Marchbank had felt edgy ever since his return from the north. Although nothing had happened since he got back two and a half weeks earlier he still looked over his shoulder more often than was comfortable and took special care when crossing the road. Living in an empty house didn't help either.

There was little more they could do with the data now. They knew, to within a month or so, when the incident had occurred. They knew what effect it had had. All that was missing was the incident itself.

'Will anyone accept it?' Lambeth asked.

'Why not? The evidence is sound.'

But it was incomplete, that he couldn't deny, and after some discussion they agreed that the best format might be a letter to one of the medical journals.

It was the most difficult fifteen hundred words Marchbank had ever had to draft. He worried that their inability to identify the source might come across as a fatal flaw. After all it was a bit like finding the victims of a car crash but no car, he thought. On the other hand, if there were victims there must have been a crash.

He heard nothing more for three weeks. The waiting began to seem interminable. Then one morning a letter arrived from the editorial offices of the journal. Marchbank tore it open anxiously. His heart sank when he saw the contents. His draft had come back with the collected comments from three unidentified referees. All three had turned it down. Too insubstantial, said the editor's note.

He sent it to another journal. This time it was back within a week; three more opinions expressing disapproval. Their comments were depressingly similar to the first set. He sent it off once more.

A third journal, and a third rejection. Nobody would publish. Marchbank began to feel hunted and exposed. He had to get the information into print.

He read through the depressing list of criticisms that had just landed on his desk from the last journal. To him they seemed like nitpicking excuses for not publishing. Things like 'the sample size is too small to localize the event temporally in the fashion attempted'. Good God, he couldn't control the sample size. How many dead children did they need? Or, 'These cancers are not commonly found in children. Have the authors checked the diagnoses?' Of course they had. That observation was a crucial part of their argument. Didn't these people read what was in front of them. That was exactly what DeWyntz had said when Marchbank had told him about Roughburn.

DeWyntz? Marchbank started at the idea. Surely not?

No! He couldn't be one of these referees. However strongly Conrad felt about Marchbank getting involved, he wouldn't let his emotions obscure his academic judgment. He would realize that the paper must be published.

It was Lambeth who suggested going to a newspaper.

Eleven

Lisa Love had gone blonde; a surprising decision, perhaps, for someone endowed with a striking head of jet black hair. Nevertheless the whim had taken her and the previous day her hairdresser had, against his better judgement, removed the stopper from a bottle of hydrogen peroxide and done as she requested.

Lisa looked into the bedroom mirror. Not exactly Marilyn Monroe, she decided, but not bad, even if honey coloured hair and black eyebrows made a peculiar combination. She ran her fingers through the bleached and curled locks, still not used to the fact that they were hers in spite of the evidence of her own eyes. The hair felt odd, coarser than usual to her touch.

She hadn't warned her boyfriend, Richard Broughton, of her intention. When she had arrived home the previous evening and walked into the room where he was working the effect had been dramatic and rather gratifying. His eyes had grown out of his head on stalks and he had stood up from the table where he was working in such a state of confusion that he had almost knocked the whole thing, computer and all, on to the floor. His reaction had pleased her; she liked to surprise him.

But as she dressed for work, Love wondered whether he liked the new colouring. It had never occurred to her that he might not but he had been evasive, she recalled, noncommittal. She hoped she wasn't going to regret her impulse. Maybe he needed time to get used to the idea. Broughton was still curled up and fast asleep in the crumpled bed behind her. Looking in the mirror as she applied her lipstick, she could just see him, a mat of dark hair barely visible above the bedclothes.

Love was rarely retiring in her dress. Today she was all in black; a black wool jacket, black leather shorts, satin black tights and a pair of black ankle boots. She checked her appearance one last time before hoisting a black leather rucksack on to her shoulder and heading for the door. Today nobody was going to miss her.

Nobody did. As she walked to Camden underground station she could feel the pairs of eyes charting her progress. This is what being blonde is all about, she reassured herself. She never experienced so much attention with her hair its natural colour.

On the train it was the same. Everywhere she looked in the carriage she detected eyes hastily averted or heads turning away. Everywhere, that was, except the seat directly opposite her where a man leered for the whole journey. He had deep-set eyes and thick, lecherous lips. She began to feel uncomfortable and kept her eyes clear of his.

Women looked at her as well as the men and she thought she sensed animosity in their faces. Love started to doubt that being a blonde was going to be the pleasant experience she had anticipated.

Damn them, she said to herself when she had got off the train. I can have whatever colour hair I like. By the time she got to her office, opposite Smithfield Market, her discomfort had turned to anger. Love got out of the lift on the third floor of the building which housed the newspaper where she worked. This was where the feature writers scratched out their living. She was one of them. Through a pair of swing doors, she was in a large open-plan office. A few heads lifted as she walked in and one or two remained raised for longer than usual. She smiled. Nobody would ever say anything here. She could turn up with a cormorant on her shoulder and it would go unremarked. But her entrance had been noted. Now she was back on familiar territory she relaxed again and her anger gradually dissipated.

At the other end of the room were two small cubicles, tiny offices hived off from the rest of the room. As Lisa walked towards her desk a head appeared from the doorway of one.

'Good God. Have you had a fright?'

It was Fran McIntyre, features editor of the *News*. She'd forgotten about Fran.

'Thank you for that vote of confidence.'

'Do you know, once I almost....' McIntyre looked around the office and sensed heads cocked and ears pricking. 'Never mind, I'll tell you another time. Come in here, I've got a job for you.'

She pushed the door of the cubicle shut behind Love and waved her into a chair.

'What do you think? Really.' Love asked, twisting her head.

'It's great. I was only joking,' McIntyre assured her. 'What did Richard say?'

'I'm not sure he likes it.'

'He'll come round.'

'I hope so.' But she valued McIntyre's judgement and felt reassured.

'What's this job?'

'You've got a degree haven't you?' McIntyre asked obtusely.

Love nodded.

'I want you to cover a medical scare story. Cancer in some town up North.'

'My degree's in English, Fran! Why can't Maurice do it? He's supposed to be our medical correspondent.'

'Maurice is in bed dear. Flu, or so he claims. Chapped thighs, more likely. Either way he can't do it. Go and see this what's-his-name?' She looked at the notepad on her desk. 'This Marchbank, and find out what it's all about. There's a good girl.'

Marchbank was on his own in the office, eating a sandwich, when the telephone rang. It was Love. She arranged to come and see him that afternoon.

'We've got a journalist from the *News* coming over in an hour,' he told Lambeth when she returned from lunch.

'Good.'

He was not so sure. This wasn't the proper way to go about getting scientific work published. It went against his instincts. Whenever he saw other scientists courting publicity he was openly critical. Still, he consoled himself, they had no choice.

But when Love arrived, Marchbank's doubts returned with interest. He found it hard to accept that this girl with her bright hair and trendy clothes could be a serious journalist. And he felt resentful that the paper should send someone who, he unfairly decided, wouldn't understand the first thing about his work.

He met her in the lobby and brought her upstairs in the lift.

'This is Chris Lambeth. She works with me,' he said rather coldly as he showed Love into their office. Lambeth cleared papers off a chair so that they could all sit down.

The journalist slipped her rucksack off her shoulder and took a pad and pen from it. She had already sensed the antipathy in Marchbank's manner and hoped he wasn't going to be awkward. That wasn't unusual. Experts often treated journalists as morons, she had found. It could be a pain in the backside getting them to explain themselves. She mentally gritted her teeth and hoped that if he was going to be difficult his female colleague might prove some sort of ally.

In fact, after some initial feeling out of the ground the interview went much better than any of them might have expected. This was partly because once Marchbank began talking about Roughburn his enthusiasm for the subject overcame his suspicions. And in no small measure it was because Love asked him the right questions. As a result he was soon talking freely and at length. For her part, Lambeth didn't actually say very much but she observed Love at work with some curiosity.

Marchbank had decided from the outset that there was no point in mentioning Hamble's involvement at this stage. It would only confuse matters. Get the facts about Roughburn into print first and tackle that later, he decided. So he gave Love a brief outline of what they had discovered.

'How long have you been working on this project?' Love asked when he had finished, raising her sails cautiously.

Marchbank looked at Lambeth. 'Six – seven weeks?'

She nodded.

'Is that typical for a study like this?'

'No.' He didn't amplify.

She tacked in a different direction. 'Are clusters like this common?'

'It depends how you look at it. A cluster is only a pattern of incidence. Outbreaks of many diseases, typhoid for example, will look like clusters if they start from a single individual and then spread to others by personal contact. They will be localized too, you see. Food poisoning can show the same pattern. But in those instances the cause is known and we don't usually talk in terms of clusters. The difference here is that we don't know what is responsible. So I suppose the answer to your question is no, not common. Apart from a handful of leukaemia clusters I don't know of any that resemble Roughburn.'

'How did you discover it in the first place?'

'That was pure chance.' He thought quickly. 'It's ironic actually. The town turned up in another piece of work as a control.'

Love scribbled furiously while he spoke and Marchbank paused for her to catch up but she motioned him to carry on.

'Nobody had thought it could possibly harbour a cluster itself.'

'Why are you so certain that there is a cluster in the town?' she asked him.

'The figures speak for themselves.'

Love looked up. 'But they're just statistics. What do the numbers actually mean?' Marchbank raised his eyebrows slightly but she sailed on stoically, ignoring the implicit criticism. 'Can't you explain them more clearly?'

Marchbank did his best. 'In simple terms they mean that the number of cases of cancer we've found in Roughburn is too large to be explained by natural incidence.'

'Or at least it is extremely unlikely to be the explanation,' Lambeth interjected.

'You mean it's possible?' Love asked, turning to her.

'Well, I suppose theoretically ... ' she began but Marchbank cut her off.

'No. It would be impossible for this number of cases to have occurred by chance. Something caused them.'

'What?'

Marchbank and Lambeth looked at one another again.

'All the evidence points to radioactivity in the environment.'

'But what does that mean? Where did the radioactivity come from?'

'We don't know.'

'Then how can you be so confident it is radiation? You must have evidence.'

'Our evidence comes from comparing the cases in Roughburn with other incidents where these types of cancer have occurred in a similar distribution and over a similar time scale.'

'Other places? Such as?'

Marchbank answered automatically. 'Hiroshima and Nagasaki.'

Love stopped writing.

'I'm not saying that someone has dropped an atom bomb on Roughburn,' he elaborated quickly. 'Just that similar types of cancer were found among children born in those Japanese towns after they were bombed.'

Love's pen resumed its activity.

'It doesn't make sense,' she complained when he had failed to offer a fuller explanation. 'I hope I'm not being stupid but if there was all this radioactivity in Roughburn, why did it only affect children? Wouldn't adults be affected too?'

'Probably. But at the dose levels that seem to be involved here it would be extremely difficult to establish. You see a malignancy, a tumour for example, generally takes ten years or more to develop. In the space of ten years a lot of people would have moved away from Roughburn and many more would have settled there. To make a sensible study of the adult population we would have to trace everyone who was resident in the town at the time.' He looked at Lambeth, who nodded in agreement.

'We had enough trouble with the children. We have no plans to pursue the grown-ups.'

They continued for half an hour more before Love closed her notebook and stood up.

'When will this appear in the paper?' Marchbank asked.

'In the next couple of days I should imagine.'

'Will you send me a copy to check over before you publish please?'

'I'm afraid I can't promise that. I'll be working to a tight deadline.' She slung her rucksack over her shoulder as she spoke. 'Don't bother coming down. I can find my own way out.' And she made a hurried exit before he pressed further about seeing her copy. He would just have to trust her.

It didn't even cross Marchbank's mind to trust Love. He expected her to get her facts mixed up. He just hoped she didn't make too much of a hash of the story. But when she had gone he felt lighter. Roughburn was out of his hands now. However bad a job she made of it, the story would be out in the open. The pressure was off him. He could begin to relax again.

Back at the *News*, Love tracked down McIntyre.

'He said what?' There was a look of disbelief on the features editor's face. Love repeated Marchbank's comments about Hiroshima but the surprised look remained.

'I can give you his exact words if you like,' Love told her, pulling out the notepad.

'Don't worry. I believe you. Well, what are you waiting for? Go and get writing.'

It was two days later, on Friday, that Love's article appeared in the *News*. Marchbank bought a copy on the way to the station and looked at it on the train. His face started to burn as soon as he saw the headline:

North Country Nagasaki

What caused radiation deaths in Roughburn?

His heart sank further as he read the story that went with it. By the time he had got to the office, he was furious. Lambeth was there already and she had to bear the brunt of his anger.

'Damn that woman! I should never have listened to you. I knew it was a mistake to talk to her. I could have guessed she would twist whatever I said to suit her own ends.' Crossly, he flung down the paper on to the desk where Lambeth was sitting.

Lambeth hadn't seen the story yet. She picked up the paper and read it through while Marchbank continued to rage. When she had finished she tossed it back on to the desk.

'Be fair, Tony. She's only used what we told her.'

But he wouldn't be pacified. He picked up the paper again himself. 'Listen.' And he read from the article; *Dr Marchbank claimed the cancer cases found among children in Roughburn were similar to those that scientists discovered in the Japanese cities of Hiroshima and Nagasaki after they had been destroyed by American atom bombs at the end of the Second World War.* I never said that. She's bloody well made it up. And Nagasaki blazed across the top. It's the worst sort of sensationalism. Talk about the gutter press.'

'You did compare Roughburn to Nagasaki and Hiroshima.'

'Well I don't remember. And if I did I certainly didn't suggest that it had anything to do with the atom bomb.'

'Neither does she.'

'Whose side are you on?'

'Nobody's.'

'Thanks.'

'I'm just asking you to be reasonable.'

There was a squeak from the corridor. They both looked up. It was Earnshaw.

'A word Tony. In my office.' He didn't look very pleased either.

It was clear even before he opened his mouth that Oliver Earnshaw was not in a reasonable mood. His face was beetroot-red, a colour cleverly picked up in the tie he was wearing.

'What the hell is this supposed to be?' he demanded, waving another copy of the *News* at Marchbank; his own.

'You've seen it then?' Marchbank answered flatly.

'Of course I've seen it. And I've had two other newspapers on the telephone asking for comments. I want an explanation.'

Marchbank had known that as soon as the article was published a showdown with Earnshaw was inevitable. He took a deep breath.

'I'm afraid I lied to you Oliver. I felt it was for the best at the time. I knew about Hamble's interest in Roughburn. And about the OPCS data. This is it.'

The director frowned and several of his features were temporarily obscured by folds of flesh.

'Well it's a bloody disgrace. I was under the impression that you were a capable scientist. A scientist of integrity. I see I was wrong. You've been taken in. It's all nonsense, of course, old boy. Just some harebrained wild goose chase Hamble got involved in.'

'Nonsense?' Marchbank's ears reverberated with Earnshaw's collation of animal metaphors. He was attempting to be patient but his reserves were limited. Now they were exhausted. 'Nonsense! This bloody nonsense of yours cost Steven his life and nearly cost me mine.'

Earnshaw looked shocked.

'Don't move,' Marchbank ordered, getting up from his chair. And he disappeared from the office. He was back moments later with his Roughburn papers which he shoved in front of Earnshaw. 'Read!'

The director did his best with Marchbank standing over him.

'How do you know these figures are accurate?' he asked, half-way through.

'They came from the OPCS database.'

'Pah! That's impossible.'

'And I've checked them against hospital records. They're accurate.'

He read on.

'All this – all this rubbish about radiation,' Earnshaw spluttered when he had finally finished. 'It's pure speculation.'

'Then give me a more plausible explanation.'

The director opened his mouth and then shut it again in a passable imitation of a trout.

Marchbank sat down and looked at the director squarely. 'I think it's time you told me what you know about this, Oliver.'

'Know? I don't know anything,' he blustered.

'You knew about Steven's interest.'

'Only from the OPCS,' he backtracked hurriedly. 'After that woman tried to steal the data they checked back. Hamble had made some enquiries about this Roughburn place too. Hadn't received authorization, of course. They thought perhaps he'd set it up with her before he died.'

It was plausible.

'What happened at Roughburn?'

'I don't know.'

'Oh, come off it!'

'It's a security matter. That's all I can tell you – all I know.'

Marchbank wondered if he was lying. He was inclined to think not. Earnshaw was not a man in whom to confide secrets.

The director began to recover his confidence. 'I think you might have told me what you were doing, old boy. We're supposed to be a team here. Now we're going to be a laughing stock. The minister will be furious. You have behaved with a singular lack of professionalism in this matter. I'm beginning to have serious doubts about your suitability as a member of our unit. From now on I would be obliged if you would refrain from discussing this with any other newspapers. Refer them to me please.'

But Marchbank wasn't interested. He got up and left with Earnshaw still in full flow.

The ministry where Love's story caused the deepest concern was not, however, the one Earnshaw was thinking of when he upbraided Marchbank. In the Department of Trade and Industry the Secretary of State, George Winfield, was seated at his desk going through the basket of memoranda and papers that had accumulated as a result of the previous day's inter-ministerial activity. His permanent secretary, Clive Young, sat across the room scanning the morning's newspapers.

'Did you see this, Minister?' Young asked, a copy of the *News* in his hand.

'What is it?'

'A story about one of the towns you visited earlier in the year. Roughburn.'

'Show me,' the minister ordered.

Winfield took the paper and began to read. As he did so the blood drained from his face leaving it a disturbing shade of grey.

'Good God, Clive!'

'What is it Minister?' Young looked alarmed.

But Winfield didn't reply. Instead he opened one of the drawers on the left hand side of his desk and took out a telephone. He dialled a number from memory and waited impatiently for a response.

'Guy? Winfield. Have you seen the *News* today?'

'No.'

'Then I suggest you look now. Page three.'

He waited, while the man on the other end of the line had a copy of the paper brought to him and then read Love's story. There was the rustle of a paper being folded.

'Ah.'

'What the hell is going on?' demanded Winfield. 'You led me to believe you had nipped this in the bud.'

'I was under that impression myself.'

'Well I suggest you put a stop to it now, before it goes any further.' Winfield rang off and replaced the telephone in the desk drawer. Afterwards he sat for several minutes staring at the wall on the far side of the office.

Twelve

The other newspapers leapt on to the story in the *News* immediately it appeared. Nearly a week passed before the fuss generated by the original article died down.

Marchbank respected Earnshaw's embargo but that just made matters worse. In the vacuum it left the papers simply embroidered new angles for themselves. Several of the Sunday papers hurriedly sent news hounds to scour Roughburn and then ran follow-up features that weekend. And by the beginning of the next week the dailies were running follow-ups of the follow-ups.

It was a sobering experience for Marchbank. He was utterly confounded by a two-headed, six-legged monster he found staring at him from one tabloid on the news stands on Monday morning, purporting to be the result of radiation-induced genetic damage. More likely the product of a graphic artist's imagination than of irradiation he suspected. But he finally accepted that Love had treated the facts about the Roughburn cluster, as expounded by himself and Lambeth, with reasonable circumspection.

There was one other positive result of the blanket coverage the story received. On the same Monday morning following the appearance of the story in the *News*, Marchbank's telephone rang just as he was about to leave for work.

'Hello,' a female voice said when he picked it up. 'It's Evelyn Hope. I don't expect you remember me.'

It took him two seconds. 'Ullswater. The red Ferrari.'

'You do remember!' She sounded pleased.

'How are you?' he asked, trying to puzzle out why she had called him after all this time.

'Very well thank you. And you?'

'Weighed down by surfeit of publicity, but bearing the strain.'

'Yes, I've seen the newspapers. You poor thing. I'm afraid we have no shame. Actually that's why I've called.'

He had forgotten she worked for a television company. She's going to try and get me to agree to an interview, he realized. But he was wrong.

'I don't know if you would be interested but I think I may be able to point you in the direction of some useful information concerning your Roughburn mystery.'

'Information?' He was thrown off balance by her offer.

'You may remember I was brought up just outside the town.'

It came back to him then. 'Of course. You told me – at dinner.'

'What I didn't tell you was that my father used to be a general practitioner there. He's retired now of course. He and Mummy have moved to the Isle of Wight.'

'Good Lord!'

'I was at home over the weekend. Daddy had been reading about you and he seemed to think he knew something that might be connected with your discovery. I'm afraid I've no idea if it will be of any help but I've persuaded him to talk to you about it – if you want to that is. He wasn't keen but he finally agreed.'

Marchbank had already weighed the implications. 'Yes please.' He tried to control the excitement in his voice. 'When can I see him?'

'He's not keen on travelling up to town but if you like I could drive you down there one day. Next weekend perhaps?'

'Don't you mind?'

'I'd be delighted.'

'Thank you. Then it's a deal.'

'Oh, good.'

Marchbank replaced the receiver thoughtfully. Evelyn Hope! He had forgotten all about that little adventure. The memory was an island of warmth in his cold sea of loneliness. He still hadn't got used to Margaret's absence. The hollowness of the house was a constant reminder. He picked up his briefcase and headed for the front door.

* * *

On Tuesday morning Marchbank received a letter from his local tax office.

Dear Dr Marchbank.
An inspector will be calling round on Wednesday next to discuss an anomaly concerning your tax situation. Please have all the necessary documentation available for his perusal.

He looked at the date. It was tomorrow. What the hell did they want? He had enough to worry about without the prospect of Her Majesty's Tax Inspectors digging into his finances. And what documentation? He didn't have any.

He had no choice but to stay at home the following morning and await the tax inspector's arrival. On the stroke of ten – Marchbank later imagined the movement being synchronized with Big Ben – there was a tap at the door. He opened it to a short balding man with a Hitler moustache, wearing a dark suit and carrying a large black briefcase. He invited his visitor in.

The man soon came to the point. 'Dr Marchbank. It has come within my purview that you have been engaged in certain extracurricular activities, the remuneration for which you have not been declaring on your tax returns.'

'What?'

'I believe you do some teaching.'

'Teaching? Oh, yes. I occasionally tutor students.'

'And do you declare the income you receive?'

'Declare it. Well ... .' He didn't.

'I thought so. I am afraid this oversight on your part is going to necessitate a complete audit of your financial position over the last five years. Now if you could just give me details of your bank accounts....'

It took the rest of the morning to satisfy his inquisitor. When the tax inspector finally left, his briefcase, which had been empty when he arrived Marchbank discovered, was crammed full of bank statements, stubs from used cheque books, salary slips and every other piece of paper he possessed of the remotest financial significance.

As he was showing him out, there was a question Marchbank couldn't stop himself asking. 'How did you find out about my teaching?'

The tax inspector appeared pleased to be asked. 'An anonymous informant,' he replied proudly.

'And you took it seriously?' Marchbank was staggered.

'Oh, yes Doctor. You'd be surprised how often they prove to be accurate.'

'Bloody Gestapo,' Marchbank muttered as he shut the door. But he was worried. What if they prosecuted? What was the worst penalty they could impose on him? He tried to tot up in his head how much he could possibly have earned from his teaching. Surely it couldn't be more than a couple of thousand pounds at the most. That meant that even with interest they couldn't demand more than five or six hundred pounds from him. They wouldn't prosecute for such a tiny sum, would they? Or was there something else he had forgotten about? He couldn't think of any other income he had failed to declare.

If that's all, there's nothing to worry about, he told himself. But the anxiety remained lodged at the back of his mind.

There was another disturbing aspect. Who was the anonymous informer? Earnshaw? He seemed the obvious candidate. But why? And how had he found out about the teaching?

By Thursday the phones had stopped ringing and there was no mention of Roughburn in any of the newspapers. Marchbank thought that the media interest had finally abated. He was mistaken. On Friday it took a different and more sinister turn.

As a result of the attention he had been receiving, Marchbank had got into the habit of buying copies of all the daily papers on the way to the station and going through them on the train. That Friday morning one of the broadsheets, a competitor to the *News* and a newspaper that maintained a close relationship with the government, published an article that, it claimed, utterly refuted Marchbank and Lambeth's analysis of the Roughburn figures.

The paper's argument had been very carefully pieced together. He felt certain he could detect a guiding hand; the imprimatur of some official scientist he wondered? Although no source was quoted he was certain the journalist responsible hadn't the skill to put it together himself. This was the work of someone with a thoroughgoing knowledge of his discipline.

The argument was presented in a way that made it appear extremely plausible. In spite of that it was completely bogus. Only another epidemiologist would be capable of constructing it, he suddenly realized.

An epidemiological study relies entirely on statistical arguments to prove or disprove its thesis. And, as commentators have often pointed out, statistics are vulnerable to misinterpretation. Careful manipulation of the same set of figures can be used to support diametrically opposed positions.

That doesn't mean that statistics are an inherently unsound way of supporting a proposition. If an analysis is carried out thoroughly and correctly the results it provides are irrefutable. But they must never be taken out of context. Conversely, the context in which the analysis is made must be absolutely clear if the meaning of the result is to be understood. Somebody who was well aware of this, and with scant regard for the Marquis of Queensberry rules, had set out to make Marchbank and Lambeth appear at least incompetent, if not fraudulent.

The strategy the author had used was to suggest a number of minor, and seemingly justified, alterations to the analysis: massaging a few figures here, shifting a premise there. On their own each was inconsequential. Taken together they made possible a completely different interpretation.

The first piece of manipulation involved questioning the number of childhood cancer cases Marchbank and Lambeth had identified in Roughburn. That number appeared to be based on a sound enough corps of data, but was it? After all, medical diagnosis of this type of disease was patchy at the time in question. The article quoted figures suggesting that roughly twenty or thirty per cent of the cases were probably wrongly diagnosed, based on data whose authenticity Marchbank could not verify. Taking the larger percentage, the number of childhood cancers was swiftly reduced by nearly one third. He and Lambeth had carefully checked the diagnoses and only retained those they were confident of but someone reading the article had no way of knowing that. They would be taken in.

Then there was the population base from which the cases had been drawn. In their Roughburn study he and Lambeth had assumed that all the cases had occurred within a population of around 30,000, the inhabitants of Roughburn and the surrounding area at the time. What, the article asked, if that figure was too low? After all, towns had been growing rapidly in size during the 1950s. The author suggested that an error of as much as fifty per cent was plausible and then recalculated the population as 45,000 using the maximum error he had postulated. The effect of this was to reduce the statistical significance of Marchbank and Lambeth's figures in similar proportion.

The article proposed one or two other reassessments in like vein before delivering its *coup de grâce*. Lambeth and Marchbank had considered all the cancer cases together and argued that the concentration and types they had found indicated that the illnesses must have been caused by radioactive contamination of the area. In the reworked analysis the writer split up the cancers into generic types and considered each type separately.

Taking as a guide the now significantly reduced statistical incidence for each, he proceeded to identify another place where a similar concentration could be found; not of them all together but of leukaemia here, brain tumours there, cancer of the kidney somewhere else. And in each of these other places the level of incidence, he pointed out, was not caused by radiation. In other words, on the basis of this new interpretation all the childhood cancers in Roughburn could be accounted for by chance. There was no need to postulate an unknown source of radioactivity.

The article was an attempt to discredit them. Of that fact Marchbank was in no doubt. Whether these other places with their high natural incidences existed, he had no idea. Even if they did, there could be an unnatural cause in each case. But whether they were well founded or not mattered little. The argument could easily be demolished. The real incidences in Roughburn were several times higher than those quoted in the article.

Marchbank knew that he and Lambeth had detailed figures on their computers that would support their analysis and refute this new one. It would take time, for it is much easier to be destructive than it is to be constructive. And in the interlude perhaps some misconceptions would grow in the public mind. But Marchbank was absolutely confident that given a week he could present a cast-iron rebuttal of all these criticisms. The instigator of the article must surely know that too.

So what was its purpose? Perhaps the author knew of Earnshaw's edict and was relying on that to prevent Marchbank responding. But with his personal integrity at stake he had no intention of letting the matter pass.

Something else wasn't right, but it took Marchbank much longer to realize what it was. There were figures in this latest newspaper article that had not appeared in Love's original article. Some he hadn't even mentioned to her. But they had been in his letter, the one the journals had refused to publish. Whoever was responsible for the article had seen that letter. How had they got hold of it?

Marchbank arrived at the office before Lambeth that morning. He had barely crossed the threshold when the telephone rang.

'Marchbank,' he said tersely, picking it up.

'Dr Marchbank. It's Lisa Love here. From the *News*.'

If he had received this call a week ago he would have found it hard to prevent himself cursing her all the way to hell down the telephone. Since then he had seen the worst the newspaper world could offer and his opinion of Love had mellowed. Anyway, he needed her now if he was going to have a platform to defend himself. Even so it required a special effort to be civil.

'Yes?'

'Have you seen the article ...' she began.

'The one demolishing our Roughburn work. Oh yes! I read it on the train. Its absolute hogwash!'

'I'm glad to hear you say that. It looked pretty damning. We have to put the record straight as soon as possible. When can I come and see you?'

'Look!' He found himself raising his voice and took a deep breath. 'It's going to take me a couple of days to pull all the figures together.'

'But you do want to put your case?'

'Yes, of course.'

'Shall I call you on Monday then?'

'All right,' he agreed gruffly.

She hung up.

When he had replaced the receiver he found he hadn't even taken off his coat.

He did so, and hung it behind the door, then slumped into the chair in his inner sanctum. He felt despondent. Wherever he turned he met pressure in one form or another. Margaret, the tax man, the Press. It would have been so much simpler if he had chosen to ignore Roughburn. So much simpler. Yet he knew his conscience would never have permitted him to take that course.

Marchbank got up and went into the outer office. May as well get started, he said to himself as he sat down in front of one of the computers and switched it on.

He didn't pay much attention while the machine went through its usual start-up routine so it was a surprise when he looked at the screen and was greeted with the unfamiliar message. HAPPY BIRTHDAY MICHELANGELO.

'What the ...' Then his stomach turned a somersault as its significance dawned on him. The machine had been infected by a computer virus.

What was he supposed to do now? He had read something about computer viruses in the newspaper a couple of weeks earlier but he couldn't remember what action it had suggested he should take. Was the virus causing damage inside the computer while the message remained on the screen? He had no idea but he switched the machine off anyway. Then he did something extremely stupid. He switched on their second computer.

It was a reflex action. Certainly he didn't consider the consequences beforehand. Afterwards when he tried to recall what had prompted him to do it, all he could think of was that he had somehow intended to use the second computer to cure the first. By the time he realised what he was doing it was too late. There on the screen of the other machine was the same message. HAPPY BIRTHDAY MICHELANGELO. For the next five minutes the walls of the room blushed and reverberated under his barrage of curses.

The sound of Lambeth's arrival stemmed the flow of abuse.

The smile on her face as she walked through the door disappeared the moment she saw him.

'What the hell Tony? You look dreadful.'

'It's the computers. A virus. Three years' work out of the window.'

'Oh shit. You're joking.' It was an imperfect epitaph but the best she could think of at short notice.

If Marchbank had tried to imagine the worst thing that could happen to him professionally, this would have been it. Unfortunately he hadn't; otherwise he might have taken suitable precautions. Now it was too late.

It was Colin Derwent, their colleague and the unit's computer wizard who rekindled some hope.

'It's not necessarily the end of the world you know,' he told them cheerily. 'The virus may have done nothing. Even if it has, there are ways of recovering the data.'

Marchbank perked up at that. 'How do we start?'

'You need an expert for a job like this. Did you know there's a computer security company just up the road; in Gower Street?'

'Where?' he demanded.

Derwent had read about the company in a computer magazine and he still had a copy in his office. He brought it through for them to see. As soon as Marchbank saw the article he grabbed the magazine and rushed out of the door, not even bothering to put on his jacket and leaving Derwent and Lambeth speechless in his wake. He ran all the way to the address given at the bottom of the page, arriving breathless on the doorstep of one of the many terraced houses in Gower Street that had been converted for use as offices.

There were three doorbells. He pressed the top one and a speaker beside him crackled.

'Security Institute.'

'I've got a virus,' he blurted out, then realized how stupid it must sound. 'I need someone to help me,' he added.

Whoever was inside seemed used to such outbursts because the door clicked open. He walked in.

He found himself in a narrow hallway with a tall ceiling. There was a door on each side of him. One appeared to belong to a literary agency. The other was blank and locked. At the far end, steps disappeared downwards and into a corridor that led off to the right. He followed the steps and rounded the corner. At the end of the short corridor he found a third door marked Security Institute. He knocked and entered.

Through the door Marchbank found a secretary and immediately tried to explain his problem but she stopped him and called one of the firm's experts. The man was dressed in a scruffy grey suit. His tie looked as if it had been tied by a chimpanzee. In spite of that he had a doctor's manner and listened patiently while Marchbank told him what had happened.

'Michelangelo's birthday?' he asked, a slightly perplexed look on his face, when Marchbank reached the part about the screen message. 'Most odd.' He appeared to be miles away, deep in thought.

'Can you do anything?' Marchbank demanded.

'That depends. Where are you?'

Marchbank told him.

'I'd better come along and see hadn't I?'

It occurred to Marchbank that consultants usually expected to be paid for their services.

'Is this going to be expensive?' he asked.

'Let's agree that the initial consultation's free. You've aroused my curiosity.'

He picked up a briefcase and followed Marchbank out into the street and back to the unit.

Derwent had wandered off when they got back but Lambeth remained glumly on guard. After a hasty introduction Marchbank hustled the expert in front of one of the computers and sat him down. Then the two scientists stood looking over his shoulder as he set to work.

First he took a floppy disk out of his briefcase and placed it into the slot on the front of the first machine.

'What's that for?' Marchbank asked.

'It's a virus-free disk to boot the computer.'

'How will it help?'

The security man sighed to himself. He was in for a hard time. Academics were always the worst.

'A virus is a program, just like any other, and it can only get into the computer from a disk. Yours must be on the disk inside the machine. By using this I can get the computer started without letting the virus loose. See.' He switched on the power and the computer came to life but this time the birthday greeting was absent.

'Now,' he started before Marchbank had time to ask, 'I'm going to put in this other disk which has a special piece of software on it that will try and find your virus.'

He replaced the first floppy disk with the second and ran the program it contained. The software chugged away silently for about thirty seconds and then the computer started bleeping frantically.

'Aha! There it is. Michelangelo, right enough. A nasty little reprobate. A quick squirt of the antidote and you'll be right as rain.' He keyed in the appropriate instructions.

'Is that it?' Marchbank felt relieved.

'That's got rid of the virus. Now we have to see what damage it's done. What software do you normally run?'

Lambeth told him.

It took the security expert only a few moments to check the status of the computer. His diagnosis was bleak. 'It's all gone. No programs, no data, nothing. This machine is completely empty.'

'How?' Marchbank asked desperately.

'The virus has overwritten everything that was on the disk. That's what I would expect from Michelangelo I'm afraid. But don't despair yet. We may still be able to recover something.'

But after another quarter of an hour the truth was staring them in the face. There was absolutely nothing left on the computer to retrieve.

It took him a little while longer to ascertain that exactly the same had happened to the second machine. Marchbank and Lambeth stared at him blankly when he told them.

'Don't you keep back-up copies of all your work?' he asked.

'I thought duplicating it on the two machines gave us enough protection,' Marchbank replied.

A look of exasperation flickered across the virus expert's face. 'I'm sorry then. There's nothing more I can do.'

But he wasn't quite finished. 'Do you know why anybody would want to tamper with the internal clocks on these computers?' the specialist asked as he started to pack away his equipment.

'No,' Marchbank replied. 'Why?'

'Because the Michelangelo virus is triggered on the artist's birthday. March the sixth.'

'But that was over three months ago.'

'Exactly.'

The implication wasn't lost on Marchbank. His expression was grim as he showed the security expert out.

'What now?' Lambeth asked when the virus expert had gone.

Marchbank shrugged.

'Do you believe someone did it on purpose?' she asked.

'Why should they? It's all out in the open now.'

'You saw the article this morning?'

'So?'

'How are we going to refute it? All the data's gone. The only possible way is to collect the statistics again from scratch.'

Lambeth looked aghast at the suggestion. 'You must be joking! Besides, Earnshaw would just love us to do that.'

'Then as far as our jury is concerned, we are either fools or liars.'

'You think that's the reason for the virus?'

He shrugged again. 'Have you got a better one?'

'Come on Tony. You're beginning to sound paranoid.'

He looked at her oddly.

Thirteen

Evelyn Hope collected Marchbank from Goldhawk Road at eight o'clock on Sunday morning.

'Hello,' she said, leaning over and opening the passenger-side door for him. 'Jump in.'

Marchbank was not a man inspired by motor cars; as far as he was concerned they were a means of conveyance and nothing more. Nevertheless he had to admit to himself that climbing into the passenger seat of the low slung red arrowhead that was Evelyn's Ferrari gave him a certain small thrill.

The seat was almost touching the ground. It was covered with soft beige leather and gripped him as if he was sitting in the palm of someone's hand. He strapped himself in. When she pulled away he felt immediately the authority of the powerful engine behind their heads, pushing him down into the hide. It was a distinctly sensual feeling. He began to understand the attraction of such vehicles.

It was a warm June morning with the barest breath of wind. A day to lift the spirit. The streets were almost empty as Evelyn dropped down from Shepherd's Bush to Hammersmith and then picked her way towards Kew Bridge. She was a confident, fluid driver and Marchbank began to relax and enjoy himself.

Over Kew Bridge they joined the main road towards Portsmouth. His companion briefly let the car sail up beyond one hundred miles an hour before easing back to the speed limit. Ferraris were too conspicuous to take any chances with the traffic police.

'It's a beautiful car,' he told her as she settled the sports car at a sedentary seventy miles an hour, and he wondered how much she must earn to afford it. The cheapest would cost several times the amount he was paid in a year.

'It is, isn't it. They have pedigrees you know, just like horses. This one belonged to a famous racing driver once. I'm lucky to own it I suppose. I couldn't afford to buy a car like this on my salary.' She paused but Marchbank sensed she hadn't finished. 'It belonged to my former husband. We're divorced now. He took the house and I had the car. The way house prices have gone, I think I got the better deal.'

Marchbank looked across at her. Evelyn's hair was in the same style as when he had first met her, a blonde bob, but in place of the black dress she had worn then she now had on what he guessed to be a silk blouse tucked into a pair of expensively cut brown trousers. She displayed the same natural elegance that he remembered from their encounter six months earlier. Yet he sensed a vulnerability within her too that hadn't been apparent to him then.

'What did he do, your husband?'

'He worked in the City. Very young and very hungry. A millionaire before he was twenty-five. A magician with money. He swept me off my feet with it. Unfortunately he thought you could deal with people in the same way as stocks and shares. He didn't need a wife. All he really wanted was an asset.'

The explanation tripped off her tongue easily and Marchbank thought it sounded like a well-rehearsed speech. Something to hide behind? Maybe the truth it glossed over was too uncomfortable a memory.

'He sounds like a good companion for my ex-wife.'

'Are you divorced too?'

'Not yet but I imagine I will be soon – when she's finished picking over the carcass of our marriage.' He couldn't keep the bitterness out of his voice.

'You sound as if you regret her absence.'

'Not really. Just the manner of her passing.'

After that they drove on silently for several miles. Sunday morning traffic was beginning to build up but the motorway was still relatively uncrowded. In the fields alongside the road wheat and barley were ripening, turning from green to gold.

'What's it feel like to be a celebrity?' Evelyn asked him, breaking the silence again.

'My week of fame?' He pulled a face. 'I could do without it. I sincerely regret ever talking to the *News* about Roughburn now.'

'I can sympathize. Our divorce made one or two of the tabloids. Nothing like you've had to put up with though. I saw that dreadful article on Friday.' There was a brief pause. 'It was rubbish wasn't it?'

'Yes.'

He was aware of her body relaxing. She had been worried, he realised.

'You'll set the record straight?'

'It may not be easy.'

And he told her about the computer virus.

'But that's awful,' she exclaimed, sounding distressed, when he had finished.

It took them two hours to reach Portsmouth. In the town Evelyn followed the signs towards the harbour and the Isle of Wight ferry. Then, unexpectedly, she turned off and dived down a side street and into an underground car park beneath a hotel.

'I know the attendant here,' she explained. 'I don't like to leave the car out for the public if I can help it.'

They walked the remainder of the way to the terminal. There was a ferry due to leave in fifteen minutes. They bought tickets – he wanted to get hers but she wouldn't allow it – and went on board.

Considering how calm the weather had seemed during the journey down to the south coast, the sea was unexpectedly choppy and Marchbank was glad to feel solid ground beneath his feet again. As they emerged from the terminal at their destination, Ryde, a figure waved and Evelyn waved back. It was her father.

'Daddy.' Evelyn kissed him fondly on the cheek. 'This is Tony Marchbank.'

'Marchbank.'

'Dr Hope. How are you sir?'

They shook hands.

'You're on time then,' he commented to his daughter as he ushered them towards the car park.

Dr Marius Hope was barely taller than Evelyn. He had ruddy cheeks and a weathered and suntanned face, more befitting a sailor or a farmer than a retired GP. He looked fit and was dressed in sturdy, country clothes. They stopped beside a Jaguar. So this is where her taste for fast cars was born, Marchbank thought to himself.

'Come on. Jump in,' he instructed. 'Your mother won't be pleased if we're late for lunch.'

Ryde was not a pretty town, Marchbank decided, but once they had passed through it the remainder of the island looked largely unspoilt. It took them half an hour to reach the Hopes' home; past Newport and the Norman stone of Carisbrooke Castle to a small village near the southern tip of the island. The house was a single whitewashed storey standing in half an acre of garden that was vibrant with the colours of summer.

When Marchbank met Mrs Hope he recognised immediately the font of Evelyn's handsomeness and style. Her mother was one of those women who grew more radiant the older she got.

'Dr Marchbank. Evelyn has told me about you.' Rather than shaking his hand she grabbed hold of it with both of hers as a child might. It was a carelessly welcoming gesture.

'Go with Evelyn,' she told him as they stood in the hallway, having completed their introductions. 'Marius will find you a glass of sherry. I have things to do in the kitchen.' From the rear of the house came the conspiracy of smells that signalled a meal in preparation.

Roast leg of lamb, crisp on the outside while the flesh remained pink and succulent inside, roast potatoes, mint sauce; Marchbank tried to remember when last he had sat down to a traditional Sunday lunch. Many years ago now, he realized. It might even have been his own mother who prepared it – dead now since seven winters.

The Hopes treated him as if he was an old friend of their daughter and it wasn't long before he felt like one of theirs too. He couldn't avoid the impression that Evelyn had briefed them thoroughly about him.

No mention was made of Roughburn or the purpose of his visit until they had finished their meal.

'Why don't we go for a walk, Marchbank?' Dr Hope suggested, rising. Marchbank did likewise. It was warm outside and he left his jacket behind.

'I've been following the unravelling of your research in

Roughburn with some interest, as I expect you can imagine,' Evelyn's father told him as they started to amble along a road that led away from the village and towards the sea. 'What put you on to it?'

Marchbank was still being circumspect about Hamble's involvement. He explained about the study however and the fact that Roughburn had been one of the controls. How he had managed to piece together the evidence that convinced him about the radioactivity.

'It's a remarkable coincidence. You sound as if you have been very thorough. Mightn't it have been better to publish your findings in a journal though?' There was the faintest hint of criticism in his voice.

'I tried. They weren't interested. But Evelyn said you had some information that might be of relevance,' Marchbank prompted, trying to move Dr Hope to tell his own story.

The older man seemed in no hurry to get to the point. 'Roughburn was only my second practice you know, after I qualified. If you'd told me I'd spend the rest of my professional life there I'd have laughed in your face. But it's an easy part of the world to live once you get settled. No pretence. The people speak the truth and that's what they want to hear. Realise that and you're home and dry. I suppose we might have moved on after a few years, but by then it would have been too much of an upheaval.'

'The cancer deaths?' Marchbank suggested, trying not to sound too impatient.

'Yes, of course. It's an odd thing. You see my own suspicions were aroused many years ago. It was for a completely different reason, but I wonder now if there could be some connection. It would have been around the time you have pinpointed.

'The business I am talking about started with all the doctors in the town receiving a letter from some special unit in London. Apparently Roughburn had been chosen as one of a group of areas across the country that were to be monitored over a period of several years. Part of a national research programme to gauge the health of the British public.

'What they asked of us was that we report details of all illnesses among our patients. We were supposed to compile three-monthly synopses and send them off to an address in St

James. Jermyn Street, I think it was. Names, symptoms, diagnoses, everything. There were a few of my colleagues who weren't very happy about that I can assure you. They take confidentiality very seriously in that part of the world. It's a conservative community. But eventually we were all persuaded that none of the personal information would ever be divulged and so we complied.

'This went on for years; at least four or five if my memory serves me. I must say that at the beginning I wondered what was happening to all the reports we'd sent off. I never saw any results from the programme. But you get so into the habit of doing something that eventually it becomes second nature. That's how it was with the three-monthly reports. After a while I never even thought about what I was doing.

'Until one day, that is. During 1957. We sent the reports off as usual from our practice and a few days later they came back marked "Not Known at This Address". We sent them back again, of course. Had to be a mistake. But it wasn't. The same thing happened with all the other practices – those I spoke to anyway. Whoever had been collecting the information suddenly upped sticks and disappeared.'

'And you never heard any more?'

'We tried to find out what was going on. I remember writing to the Health Ministry several times. Even contacted our MP. Drew a complete blank. If anybody knew anything about the address in Jermyn Street and what had been going on there they kept it to themselves. As far as we were able to find out there had never been a national research programme. Our reports had disappeared into one of those black holes.'

'How extraordinary. And you never discovered what was behind it?'

'I've puzzled over that for years. Never got anywhere. But now; with what you've found out. I wonder if there's a connection? Is it possible, do you think?'

Marchbank wondered. It was certainly a curious coincidence.

'I'm not sure. The timing's right.'

'You will let me know if you find anything?'

'Of course,' Marchbank assured him, smiling wryly. 'That is if you don't read it in the newspapers first.'

As they turned around and headed back towards the house Marchbank tried to pick over the GP's memory of Roughburn. But although the doctor could remember the children dying, he could offer no further insight. Nobody had considered at the time that the deaths might be linked. Marchbank was disappointed. He had expected more.

But when they got back to the house Dr Hope had a final surprise for him.

'My former practice is still thriving in spite of my absence. I rang up the senior partner last week, after I knew you were coming. I had a sneaking suspicion that my old file on this business might still be there. I was right. Here.' He proffered a buff envelope. 'It's a copy of the original letter we were sent when the reports' business started. I thought it might be of some use to you.'

Marchbank took the envelope with thanks and stuffed it into his pocket. He would study it later.

The afternoon was nearly over. Soon it was time to leave. Evelyn's mother gave them tea and they set off for the ferry. The crossing back to Portsmouth wasn't nearly as uncomfortable as the one coming out; or maybe Marchbank knew what to expect this time.

It had been a long day. Both were feeling tired. Little passed between them on the journey back to London. Evelyn concentrated on her driving while Marchbank, reclining comfortably, made a feeble attempt to fit Dr Hope's revelation with what he already knew. But before he had made any progress he fell asleep. They were in the outskirts of London again when he awoke.

As they approached Shepherd's Bush, Evelyn insisted she take him directly to his door. In return he persuaded her to come in for a drink.

'I hope you'll excuse the mess. I've reverted to my bachelor ways since my wife left.'

'Don't worry. I'm sure my flat is much worse.'

'What would you like?'

Evelyn settled for coffee and Marchbank poured himself a large gin and tonic while he waited for the water to boil.

'I enjoyed meeting your parents,' he told her when they were seated. 'You're lucky.'

'I suppose I am. Life's always been good to me. Too good, I sometimes think.' She sounded wistful.

'What do you mean?'

'Oh, I've always had the best of everything. And whatever I've wanted has been mine without any effort. But I suppose I shouldn't complain.'

'Then why do you?'

'It's just that sometimes ... oh, never mind. I don't want to end the day on a maudlin note. I've enjoyed it too.' She drained her cup. 'Thanks once again for your company. I really should be going. I've an early start in the morning.'

Now that she was about to leave, Marchbank found he didn't want her to go. He followed her to the door.

'Can I repay you? How about dinner one evening?'

'Yes. I'd like that.'

'Soon?'

'Please.' She kissed him, like a bird, a tiny peck on the cheek and was gone.

When her car had disappeared he laughed to himself. She liked him. The realization made him feel happy.

Marchbank shut the door and went back to his drink. The buff envelope, the one Dr Hope had given him before they left that afternoon, was lying on the table. He opened it.

It was much as the GP had described, a letter from something describing itself as the British National Health Survey, or rather a photocopy of it. He read the document through.

Dear Doctor.

In order to provide a yardstick for judging the state of the British national health the government has decided to institute a countrywide survey. This survey will be based on selected towns and rural areas throughout the country, chosen to furnish a complete and balanced sample of the population.

Roughburn has been chosen as one the participating sites and as your practice falls within the designated catchment area I would be grateful of your co-operation in this matter. It is important that the protocol of the study is strictly adhered to if the survey is to make a fruitful contribution towards understanding the health needs of the British population.

I will require from you a regular report providing full and detailed descriptions of all the ailments and illnesses among your patients, either treated by you or referred by you for treatment. This report should be prepared at three monthly intervals and dispatched to the address shown above.

In order to facilitate analysis of the information I am sending you Forms A-RBN 02. Please use these to compile your reports. Your stock of these will be replenished as the need arises. THESE FORMS ARE STRICTLY NUMBERED AND MUST NOT BE USED OUT OF SEQUENCE.

The study is officially launched on 1 January 1952. Your first report should be compiled on 1 April 1952, covering all incidence between 1 January and 31 March. Please lodge it immediately. Successive reports will be expected on 1 July 1952, 1 October 1952, 1 January 1953 and regularly thereafter.

Thank you in anticipation of your co-operation.

The letter was dated 12 October 1951 and it was signed by Dr Marion Crawford. The name struck a chord with Marchbank but he couldn't instantly recall why. Then it came to him: one of the stories Lambeth had found in the Roughburn paper had contained a comment by a scientist from London. His name was also Crawford. They might very well be the same man.

Marchbank awoke feeling groggy, a nagging, insistent sound buzzing inside his head. He opened his eyes and then realized that the sound was the telephone ringing downstairs. Reluctantly, he pulled himself out of bed and struggled clumsily into his dressing-gown then tumbled down the stairs expecting the ringing to stop any moment.

It was still going when he picked up the phone. 'Tony Marchbank. Hello.'

There was no answer. Damn, he thought to himself, replacing the receiver. Whoever it was must have rung off just as I got here. He looked at a clock. The time was ten minutes past three. Who the hell would ring at this hour?

He went upstairs again and climbed back into bed but he had

barely shut his eyes when the phone started again. This time he left his dressing gown where it was, ran down the stairs taking two steps at a time and grabbed the receiver. 'Hello,' he gasped.

But again there was no reply.

'Hello,' he said again, 'who is it? Evelyn? Margaret?'

More silence.

Eventually he replaced the receiver a second time, then sat by the phone waiting for it to ring again. After ten minutes, when nothing had happened, he went back to bed. His sleep was not disturbed again that night but in the morning when he recalled the incident he was convinced that someone had been trying to get hold of him. Ringing the wrong number once could have been a mistake. Twice indicated clear intention.

As she had promised, Love called Marchbank that Monday morning. But Marchbank found he couldn't tell her about the virus.

'The data isn't ready,' he lied. 'It's taking longer than I expected.'

'How long?'

'A few more days, at least.'

'In a couple of days the story will be as dead as a dodo. Is there a problem of some kind?'

Marchbank was defensive. 'No, there's no problem.'

'Are you sure?'

'Listen!' He was irritated now. 'It isn't simply a matter of turning a handle and numbers come spewing out. If this isn't done properly it won't be worth doing at all.'

'Can I do anything to help?' she asked, disarmingly.

'No.'

'I'll call you in a couple of days then.'

'No! Wait until I call you.'

He was about to put the phone down when he remembered the letter Dr Hope had given him.

'Actually there is something you can do. I've discovered that Roughburn was part of a national health audit carried out during the 1950s. The doctors from the town had to register a report with an address in London every three months. The man running the audit was someone called Dr Marion Crawford.'

'So what?'

'The audit must have had exactly the same information we've collected about the children who died there. Why was nobody alerted at the time? And something else: when there was a problem during lambing in Roughburn in the spring of 1953 a London scientist was sent up. His name was Crawford too. I think they might be the same man. I'd like to talk to him if he could be found. Do you think you'd be able to track him down?'

'What's that London address?'

'Have you got a fax?'

'Yes.' She gave him the number.

'I'll send it to you.'

After he had put the telephone back, Marchbank clenched the bridge of his nose between his thumb and forefinger and closed his eyes. It was only ten o'clock in the morning and he already felt tired. Must be the broken night's sleep, he decided.

As he scribbled out the fax he wondered why he hadn't told Love the truth. He would have to tell her eventually because there was no way he could come up with the figures she wanted. Maybe Lambeth was right and he was becoming paranoid.

Fourteen

Elliot Cromby arrived at Cambridge to start his postgraduate studies with all the right credentials. He had just won a first class degree at Nottingham University and received glowing commendations from his tutors. Any research group should have been glad to count him as one of its members. The lucky one was the team where Marchbank was also taking the first steps towards a scientific career.

The group they had both joined, led by Howard Johns and one of three under Conrad DeWyntz's professorship, specialized in epidemiology. The department was unique and attracted far more graduates than it could possibly accommodate. Resources were limited and only a few of those who applied were accepted. So, in spite of their excellent qualifications, both Marchbank and Cromby were fortunate to gain entry.

Cromby soon started to live up to his star rating. He appeared to have a nose for the subject. By the end of his first year he had already completed an important meningitis study – work which demonstrated the existence of previously unknown environmental links and promised a new understanding of the disease. There had been several recent outbreaks in England which formed the basis for Cromby's analysis. His PhD thesis and future career seemed assured.

Cromby prepared his meningitis work for publication and submitted it to the *New Journal of Epidemiology*. Marchbank's name appeared on the paper too for he had played a minor role in the analysis of the data. When the journal's editor returned the manuscript, together with comments made by the anonymous referees he had asked to judge the work, Cromby was on holiday. Dr Johns asked Marchbank to cross-check one or two minor points that had been raised.

Marchbank was already beginning to feel himself in the shadow of his more illustrious colleague and he took to the task begrudgingly. The two students were not close. Nevertheless he did as he was asked.

One of the referees had queried the way in which the data in the paper had been analysed. He wanted to see a more detailed breakdown of the samples used, showing the number of cases in each postcode district and also the total population for each. To find this information, Marchbank had to go into the database on Cromby's personal computer. He soon found the file he wanted and printed it out so that he could compile the data in tabular form.

When he came to look at the printout, Marchbank discovered, tagged on to the end of the statistics, a list of names and addresses together with some other textual information. He wondered what it was. To his surprise he found that the list contained the personal details of the meningitis cases, confidential information that should not have found its way on to an unsecured computer. Puzzled, he took a closer look and was even more surprised to find that the names of most of the cases appeared twice in the list, under two different addresses.

Now his curiosity was aroused and with growing disquiet he reexamined the data upon which the study was based. It was fraudulent. Cromby had used real cases but he had moved many of them to different addresses; addresses occupied by families with the same surname so the sleight of hand would be impossible to spot. It was obvious to Marchbank that he had decided upon the result he wanted to establish first and then arranged the data to deliver it. In truth, the environmental links were a product of Cromby's imagination.

Marchbank was horrified. He didn't know what to do. Should he take his discovery to the head of the team, Dr Johns? To do so would lay him open to Cromby's accusations of jealousy and spite. Instead he elected to wait until his contemporary returned and confront him directly.

There are some things one prefers not to know. It was a painful week's waiting. When Cromby eventually reappeared and Marchbank told him what he had found the other man was furious, accusing him of spying and eventually of fabricating the whole thing to discredit him. He refused to withdraw the paper, so Marchbank was forced to tell Johns anyway. A few days later Cromby left the research group.

The experience had left a permanent mark on Marchbank. If it hadn't been for a twist of fate the paper would have been published and the medical community set in completely the wrong direction, and all for the sake of one unscrupulous man's ambition. Why had Cromby done it? His success was already guaranteed anyway.

The same twist of fate had also dealt Marchbank a lifelong enemy. He could still recall the man's last words to him.

'I shan't forget the favour I owe you Tony. Our paths will cross again one day.'

Those words were ringing in his ears as he stared at a copy of Wednesday's newspaper, the same paper that had published the damning attack on his work at the end of the previous week. Cromby's picture was staring back at him from the front page.

He knew what he was going to find even before he started reading but, caught in a spell like a rabbit mesmerized in a car's headlights, he couldn't tear himself away from the story.

Roughburn Scientist Linked to Academic Fraud

Marchbank paper withdrawn after discovery of data rigging.

The article recalled the case of the meningitis paper in great detail, explaining how the data had been manipulated to produce the statistically significant results. The facts it reproduced were accurate in all but one of those details. Instead of Marchbank discovering the fraud attempted by Cromby, their roles had been reversed. Now Marchbank was the one who had rigged the data and Cromby the person who had discovered it.

Somebody was trying to destroy his academic career. Of that he was in no doubt. And whoever was responsible was succeeding.

Cromby must have supplied a great deal of the information

that went into the article. It would be comforting to believe that he was responsible for the campaign too. At least then he would know what he was up against. But that couldn't possibly be the answer. Cromby had nothing to do with Roughburn. And it was Roughburn and whatever had taken place there forty years ago that was at the back of everything that was happening to him.

Besides, as Marchbank knew, the other man had settled in the USA several years ago. No, Cromby was just another tool; willing certainly, but not the instigator. The mind behind the campaign belonged to somebody else. The horrifying thing about this story was that it would be virtually impossible to disprove. The only other person who knew the full background of the fraud was Howard Johns. And he had died three years ago after a heart attack in his laboratory.

Cromby should be pleased with his contribution. It nudged Marchbank further into the chasm yawning at his feet. But who would have known to seek him out?

Who else had known about the incident? Marchbank searched his memory. Margaret; he must have told her. DeWyntz, of course. And a handful of other people in Johns' research group who had been aware of the paper. They might not have been told the full story but with the paper being withdrawn and then Cromby leaving Cambridge, it was not difficult to put two and two together. Which of them had informed the newspaper?

Somebody was tightening a noose about his neck, slipping the knot a little closer each day. He had no idea who it was. But a germ of an idea was beginning to form. Somebody close to him was involved. Somebody he knew. Was there anybody in the world he could trust?

It was an edgy Marchbank who waited for Love in a pub on Marylebone High Street at lunch time that same day. He had called and proposed the meeting, ostensibly to discuss the Cromby story. Now he sat nursing half a pint of bitter and nervously counting the cheese dishes on the walls around him – the publican collected them it seemed. He had given up rehearsing how he was going to tell the journalist about the computer virus. Every excuse he thought of to explain why he had lied to her sounded lame.

Predictably, she was angry.

'Friday? Why the hell didn't you tell me when I called you on Monday?'

'I don't know.'

'Let me get this straight. You're telling me that you haven't got any figures to support the claims you made about Roughburn, the ones in my story.'

'Your story?' he quibbled irritably.

'Your story then.'

'No. Not any more.'

'That's great.' She gave him a hostile look. 'It's unfortunate that this should happen on the same day an article appears accusing you of professional misconduct. If I had a suspicious mind I might think you destroyed the data yourself in order to cover something up.'

'Don't be ridiculous,' he countered crossly. 'It happened on Friday, not today.'

'So you say.'

'That at least I can prove.'

'OK, OK. I believe you, though God knows why! Dr Marchbank, you are in a hole. It's time you realized that and stopped digging yourself in deeper.'

'I know.'

'Well, if this is your story, tell me what happens next?'

He didn't reply.

'Then tell me about Cromby,' she suggested.

'There isn't much to tell.' Marchbank swilled the beer around in his glass. 'He graduated from a redbrick university. Top qualifications. We worked together for about a year. He was the sort of person you would describe as brilliant, I suppose. He had no need to cheat – I don't know why he did. Perhaps it was the pressure of suddenly finding himself among people who were just as clever as he was instead of being number one all on his own.'

'People like you?'

'I don't know if I was in his league.' Marchbank sipped his beer. 'He never showed any signs of worry or pressure while I knew him. At the time I came to the conclusion that he had an uncontrollable appetite for success. He was in a dreadful hurry – there were never enough hours in the day for him.'

'What happened to him afterwards?'

'He moved to the States after leaving Cambridge. I heard he got himself another job there.'

'In research?'

'No. He wouldn't dare so long as there were people around who knew what he had done. He went into biotechnology first, then moved into computers. Started his own company. It's very successful, I've heard.'

'So he would know all about viruses.'

'Yes, I expect so.' He caught her implication. 'But then so would any number of other people. I know Cromby and this doesn't bear his signature. I'm certain of that.'

'Who is behind it then?'

'I've no idea.' He stared into his beer.

Love looked at him. 'Why do I get the idea that there's something you haven't told me?'

'What do you mean?'

'How can you be so sure your Mr Cromby isn't responsible?'

'Because....'

Because what? Perhaps it was time he told her about Hamble. Unfortunately that meant admitting to another lie. Storm clouds gathered once again in her face but by the time he had finished the anger was replaced by concern. Not that it came out sounding like concern.

'Why in God's name couldn't you have told me about this in the first place?' she demanded. 'You'll get yourself killed too if you carry on the way you are.'

'I suppose I imagined the pressure would be off me as soon as Roughburn became public knowledge.'

'Well, it looks as if you were wrong. What do you propose doing now?'

He shrugged.

Love changed the subject. 'I've had no luck with your Dr Crawford. I've tried all the government research labs I can find. Nobody has heard of him. And the address in Jermyn Street? It's gone. A nasty 1970s office block there now. I'm going to need more information to have any chance of tracing him.'

'There isn't any.'

'Then we seem to have reached a dead end.' Love drained her glass. 'I have to get back to the *News*. If you think of anything let me know. Otherwise, perhaps you'd better sue.'

He watched despondently as she weaved her way through the lunch-time crowd to the door, then made his own way to the bar and bought himself another drink; this time it was a full pint.

Back at the *News*, Love went straight into McIntyre's office.

'Our bloody Dr Marchbank only told me half his story. And he's lost all the evidence to support his claims about Roughburn,' she said slamming the door.

'He's your doctor. I don't want any part of him. What's the other half?'

She repeated what Marchbank had told her about Hamble.

'And the evidence?'

'Destroyed by a computer virus, or so he says.'

'Don't you believe him?'

Love shrugged. 'He said it was done deliberately.'

'What about today's story?'

'According to Marchbank it's a hatchet job. He wasn't the guilty party. It was the other man, Cromby. He had to leave Cambridge as a result. At least we can check if that's true.'

'It doesn't look good. Curse Maurice and his sodding tip. Whoever is doing a job on your doctor is being disturbingly clever. Either that or we've picked the wrong side. What do you think? Is he a fraud? Do you believe his story?'

Love thought. 'I suppose I do believe him, yes. He's prickly, and naive, but I think he's honest.'

'In that case we'd better try and find out who's putting the screws on him, and why.'

Lambeth retained her faith in Marchbank too, in spite of his increasing coldness towards her. But then she knew all about Roughburn.

When he told her his version of the Cromby story she accepted it without question. However she was still unwilling to believe that the Michelangelo virus had been planted on their computers deliberately. Perhaps she didn't want to accept that they really were the target of a shadowy adversary.

'You're taking all this too seriously Tony. Don't let it get to you. The whole thing will blow over soon.'

But the more she insisted, the more adamant he became. And the more suspicious. In the end he caught himself wondering if she was somehow implicated.

It wasn't just the Roughburn results that had been destroyed by the computer virus. The results of all Marchbank and Lambeth's other work had been eradicated too. The main additional casualty was the industrial accident study. They had already amassed a considerable amount of data when the virus struck. That too would have to be collected again.

It was a daunting prospect. Faced with it, Marchbank found he was getting more and more depressed. He felt himself in the grip of something he didn't understand. Something he was powerless to act against.

And then there was Earnshaw, the person upon whom his suspicions had also fallen. Ever since his outburst after Love's original story appeared in the *News*, the director had been curiously silent.

Marchbank no longer believed Earnshaw had anything to do with the attacks on him. He had thought so after the tax man's visit but recent events convinced him otherwise. He didn't believe the director would have sanctioned the ruthless manipulation of the Roughburn figures. Any professional criticism of Marchbank was bound to reflect on the unit, at least in the director's eyes, and he had become fiercely proud of his fiefdom. Added to that, Earnshaw knew nothing of the Cromby affair.

Nevertheless Marchbank was surprised there had been no further reaction. Even Wednesday's vitriol appeared to have left Earnshaw unmoved. The peace didn't last for long.

On Thursday the director's silence was broken. It was mid morning when Earnshaw loomed at the office door dressed in a sombre, close fitting suit that, nevertheless, managed to contain most of his bulk so only the barest ripple of flesh spilled over the edges. Marchbank wondered whose funeral it was. He should have guessed it would be his own.

'Sit down please Tony,' the director instructed when they were inside Earnshaw's office.

Marchbank did as he was asked.

'I was extremely upset to read this disturbing attack on you in the Press yesterday morning. Most unwelcome for you, and for the unit. I hope there is no truth in it.'

'So do I.'

'This is not a matter to joke about.'

'No truth, none at all, I assure you.'

'I'm relieved to hear that because serious questions have been raised. Questions that I'm afraid must be answered. There will have to be an inquiry. These are grave allegations and it wouldn't be fair to you to let them pass unchallenged. I will conduct it myself, of course. I'll be absolutely scrupulous. Of that you need have no fear.'

Marchbank nodded, resignedly. 'What about my work?'

'There's no reason why you shouldn't continue for the moment. Your funding doesn't come up for review for another six months yet.'

His whole future at the unit was under threat then. He felt worse than ever.

In the early hours of Friday morning the telephone woke Marchbank. Half asleep he struggled downstairs and picked up the receiver, only to find no one on the other end. The clock said ten past three, exactly the time it had rung on Monday morning. Coincidence? He thought not. But it didn't ring a second time that night. However it did the next night and when he picked it up he screamed into the receiver in fury. After that he took to unplugging his telephone before he went to bed. His house was no longer a haven. Its emptiness was becoming a threat.

Life in Putney was not progressing quite as well as it once had either. Cracks were now beginning to appear in the formerly smooth façade.

'God, Chris. Your clothes are so predictable,' Margaret Marchbank exclaimed on a particularly hot afternoon during the weekend following the publication of the Cromby story. 'You always manage to look as though you're clothed by a soft furnishing department.'

'But you said you liked the way I dressed,' she protested, hurt.

'I'm getting fed up with it. Crushed velvet is for covering windows, not people.'

'Don't be so horrible.' She felt a tear welling in the corner of her eye and turned away. The crushed velvet in question, a skirt of Lambeth's, was lying across the arm of the settee.

Margaret checked herself. 'Sorry. It must be the heat. I wish we had a fan in here.'

The apology sounded hollow.

They were sitting in the living room of the flat in Putney. Margaret had on a bikini top and shorts. Lambeth had only that moment slipped out of her skirt and was in her underwear. The windows were open wide over the river but there was no wind and the flat seemed to be a trap for the heat.

Ice cubes clinked as Lambeth drank from an enormous mug of lemonade she picked up from the table beside her. During the past two weeks Margaret had become increasingly irritable and cruel, she had noticed. It wasn't just the weather, or her cycle. She was brooding. Something was wrong.

It was over three months since Margaret had left Tony, nearly four in fact. In that time she and her husband had met on three or four occasions at the most. Yet it appeared to Lambeth that the pair of them were still riding the same sea of fate. Tony Marchbank was sinking into a pit of despair and, for no reason that Lambeth could discern, his estranged wife was behaving like a dyspeptic porcupine. And here was she, Chris Lambeth, being tossed this way and that in a boat that was not her own to sail, by a storm she could not escape.

'How's Tony getting on with his new girl friend?' Margaret asked, stealing into her thoughts.

'What, the woman he went off with last weekend? I've no idea. Are you jealous?' she added acidly.

'Don't be stupid. The sooner he finds himself a nice girl and settles down, the sooner he'll agree to a divorce. I just wish he'd get on with it.'

Now that the subject of Marchbank had been raised, Lambeth took advantage of it to voice her own concern. 'I'm worried about him, Marg. He gets telephone calls in the middle of the night – when he answers there is no one on the other end.'

'He should tell the phone company.'

'And a couple of weeks ago the tax man was round asking about some teaching money he hadn't declared. What, with the newspapers too, he's becoming paranoid. I don't like it. He's beginning to think we're all in a conspiracy against him.'

'Well I hope he keeps out of my way. The last thing I want is him finding out about us.'

'How can he? He hasn't even got the address. Anyway, you were the one who wanted to tell him, not so long ago.'

'That was before I left him. Now I've changed my mind.'

'What are you frightened of?'

'I just don't want him to know. That's all.'

No, Lambeth thought to herself, I don't want him to find out either. He's not capable of adding things up and getting the correct answer in his present state. But I'd pay good money to know what's prompted your change of heart.

Margaret levered herself from her chair and went across to the fridge to refill her glass with lemonade. 'More?'

Lambeth shook her head. She was still thinking about Marg's behaviour. Margaret hadn't been able to see her at all during the previous week, or so she had claimed. Too busy at work. That was an excuse she had used endlessly with Tony before she left him.

Stop it, Lambeth told herself. You'll end up paranoid too.

The Civil Service might appear to be a homogeneous monolith beating with a single heart but in reality it is more like a sponge; an elaborate heterogeneous structure constructed from individual organisms. It is a building of innumerable rooms each with its own clock. And those clocks do not always strike on the same beat.

One occasionally erratic chime belonged to a man whose job it was to advise the government on matters of safety pertaining to the invasion of the human body by chemical agents. Perfidious dioxins emanating from waste disposal plants, the safe dose of radiation that could be absorbed by a worker in a nuclear power station, asbestos and all its ramifications: these were matters that fell within his terms of reference.

It was this man's job to keep abreast of every new development that might possibly influence the place where the line between life and death was drawn in each case, the threshold below which the presence of these agents was deemed to be safe. And in this capacity his attention was drawn to the furore that developed in the Press concerning Roughburn. However it was not solely on account of the claims and counterclaims and their possible significance within his field that his curiosity was aroused. Although he did not know the name of the town he recognized the case. He had come across it before. Where? That was the question that exercised him.

The paths that his research coursed were labyrinthine. Where in that maze was the coincidence that had stimulated his imagination? He strove long before he finally identified in his mind the corpus that he was certain matched the northern town of the newspapers.

It should not have taken him so long. He had reviewed the material within the last month, two at the outside. But memory is not linear; it does not conform to the laws of time. Once recalled, however, he knew exactly where to find the papers and went directly to them in order to confirm his suspicions.

The papers were not there. Nor was there a marker to indicate that the enquiries of another had led to them. Had he been mistaken? Perhaps his memory was fallible and they were kept somewhere else. He consulted the index system that was the map to the collection. The papers he sought were mentioned nowhere. It was as if they did not exist.

Slowly it dawned on him that as surely as night follows day, the material he was looking for had been destroyed. It had become an embarrassment.

The servant of the government was not an arrogant man, nor was he fired by a desire to see that the executive acted for the people, not on its own behalf. But he was a man of principle. The principle he adhered to was that history, in all its manifestations, was sacrosanct. Once a thing had been done it belonged to no one individual; it was common property. The general good might demand that knowledge of it remained secret, that he accepted; but to attempt to rewrite history, to erase an event, that was the vilest of crimes.

Nor was this the first time he had become aware that such a thing had happened. Unlike their predecessors, this current generation of men of power considered it their right to interfere with the truth as they saw fit.

A man can stand by and see his principle violated once. He may remain mute in the face of a second violation. Then he must either abandon his principle or defend it. The civil servant decided to act. Yet he felt impotent. The material was gone. What could he do? His prodigious memory provided him with the solution.

He was able to recall sufficient of the vanished papers to pursue their tendrils through the collection, backwards, forwards and sideways in time, until he found something that the cleaners had missed. It was not much; the link was tenuous but it was better than nothing. Surreptitiously he removed the document and made a copy, taking care to blank all identifying marks that would indicate its origin. Then he replaced the original.

The papers were burning a hole in his briefcase that evening when he left his place of work. He had never felt so nervous. But nobody took the slightest notice. He went by so often the men on the door didn't even see him any more. He put the case into the pannier on the side of his motorbike before climbing astride the machine. And as he rode home his nervousness was replaced by a feeling of exhilaration.

Fifteen

The human mind is mysterious and unpredictable. Marchbank's was no more peculiar than most. Did it control him, or he it? He could no longer be certain. He began to feel as though he was losing control of his own thoughts.

Ideas would swirl, uncalled, through his consciousness, then disappear again when he tried to trap them with logic. He would find himself entertaining hypotheses that he couldn't possibly accept and at the same time could not banish. Conspiracies of international proportions were ranged against him.

At home alone he would conjure up a hired killer stalking the streets of Shepherd's Bush, waiting for the perfect moment to bring his life to its bitter end. Eyes watched him from behind the net curtains and locked doors of Gower Street as he walked to the laboratory in the morning or home again in the evening. And closed doors in the building where he worked almost inevitably hid listeners and watchers. He burst in on them once, only to find himself face to face with a bewildered secretary touching up her make-up. It was an unmarked ladies toilet. Marchbank beat an embarrassed retreat. After that he learned to tolerate their unseen presence.

Although Marchbank began, seriously, to consider the possibility that he was becoming unhinged, in reality he was experiencing the natural reaction of a person subject to unreasonable levels of psychological pressure. He was under attack and his brain was reacting in his defence, analysing the situation as best it could and presenting him with scenarios that might provide insight into the events engulfing him. And if it didn't have sufficient information to make sensible appraisals it did the best it could with guesswork.

After several days of torment, he was eventually able to rid himself of what seemed the more improbable phantoms that stalked his mind. There was no faceless international conspiracy ranged against him. Whoever was responsible had a human face and was within his grasp – if only he knew where to look. With growing confidence he tried to narrow the net.

A more analytical approach was needed and he attempted to bring one to bear on the source of his torment. His mind generated possibilities. And as he worried away from every angle one idea began to surface with increasing frequency. Roughburn might be the reason behind this attempt to discredit him, but it had to involve a person close to him. Somebody who knew he hadn't declared money earned from teaching; somebody who knew about Cromby and knew that he would be only too pleased to lend his aid to Marchbank's discomfiture. Someone who knew that Dr Johns was dead. Someone with access to the letter that he and Lambeth had been unable to get published. In short, someone he knew and knew well.

Eventually his unconscious analytical engine, fed with the limited amount of evidence available, jumped to a conclusion. This was a professional matter; it revolved around his work. Therefore it seemed likely that it was one of his professional colleagues who was involved. Who was it? Someone consumed with professional jealousy. That hardly seemed likely.

He looked at the people around him and considered each in turn. Earnshaw? Much as he would like to blame the director he already had too many strong reasons for dismissing him. Colin Derwent? He knew about computers and viruses so he had some of the right qualifications. What could his motive be? Marchbank could think of none.

When he had eliminated everybody he was left with one name. Chris Lambeth.

How could it be Chris? She hadn't known about Cromby. Nor would she have been able to tell Her Majesty's Inspector of Taxes he was in dereliction of his duty. But she had access to the letter. And she was quite capable of planting the virus – she knew the computers better that he – and nobody had greater opportunity. She also had a plausible motive. His job. After all if he found himself forced to leave, who better to take over than his assistant? Slowly the germ began to develop.

He started to watch her surreptitiously, to study her behaviour, and it didn't take him long to notice that she was constantly on edge. More than once over the course of two or three days she was sharp with him or flared angrily as a result of some inconsequential mistake or accident. Her usual ebullience and sense of humour had evaporated.

When he asked if there was something bothering her she told him to mind his own business – then apologized – but offered no explanation. It was unlike Lambeth. What was worrying her? Perhaps the strain of playing a double game was showing itself. The germ took root.

This is madness, Marchbank told himself. It can't be Chris. I would have noticed something before. But you weren't looking before, the analytical engine told him; now you are and you've found something suspicious.

If she really were involved then she must have co-conspirators with whom she was in contact. He decided to test the hypothesis that they existed. He started to follow her from the office. The germ was now pushing forth strongly on its own, out of his conscious control.

The first day he planned to follow Lambeth was a Thursday. But he had overlooked the fact that she often cycled to and from home and the problems this would cause. As soon as she had changed and left the building he went after her. Instantly he realized his difficulty. It was impossible to keep up with her unless he also had a bicycle. In half a minute she had threaded her way through the traffic and was gone. He went back and rethought the plan.

The next day, Friday, she came to work on public transport. Marchbank used the opportunity when it was offered and set out to follow her again that evening. This time it was simple. Lambeth had no reason to suspect he was behind her; why should she? She walked to Goodge Street underground station and took a train north to West Finchley. Marchbank simply buried himself in the crowd and kept her in sight. He had a season ticket so trains and buses posed no difficulty.

At the other end of her journey the crowds thinned out and Marchbank let her move farther ahead of him. Now he began to worry she would turn and see him but she never once glanced back. After a walk of ten minutes she let herself in through a door on the side of a large semidetached house.

So this was her home. Now Marchbank was faced with a quandary. Should he wait until she reappeared – she might stay in for the rest of the evening – or go home and come back in his car, risking the chance that she had gone out before he returned? Give her an hour, he decided. It proved a wise decision. In less than half an hour she reappeared, her clothes changed and a capacious bag over one shoulder.

Again the task of following her proved simple. Lambeth returned to the underground station and, with Marchbank in tow, crossed London. Where were they going? Adrenalin coursed through his arteries and his excitement mounted.

The answer proved to be Putney. By nine o'clock Marchbank was stationed outside a block of flats near the Thames. Though he knew his former wife lived in this part of the world he didn't make the connection. After another hour he was feeling tired and very hungry and Lambeth was not coming out again. He went home.

There was no point in returning the next day. The trail would be cold, he realized, and he could waste two days outside the Putney flats for nothing. He spent an impatient weekend.

By Monday he had solved the bicycle problem. He would drive to the unit in his car. If Lambeth cycled to work then she would cycle straight home afterwards, he reasoned. He would know if she had come by bike and could drive to her home and wait. It worked perfectly but he immediately refined the scheme further, parking his car in Finchley near her home and then using the tube to get to work. That way the vehicle was ready for him whether she cycled or travelled by train. Over the next four days she stayed at home twice after work, went to her women's group once and to Putney once more.

Putney, that was the key. He had to find out who she met there.

There was a problem. When Lambeth went to Putney he had no choice but to follow in the train. His car stayed behind in Finchley. So, on the next Friday, he took a chance that she would go there and didn't follow. Instead he drove directly to the block of flats. It was a hot, close evening, an evening ripe and sticky with expectation. He parked the car where he could see the entrance and waited.

The time passed nervously and he thought he had made a mistake. She wasn't coming. Then, at a quarter to nine, and still light, she arrived and let herself in.

Let herself in? He hadn't noticed before that she had a key of her own. He filed the new piece of information away and then settled down to watch. Another sticky hour passed before two figures appeared in the doorway of the flats and started up the road. They were going to walk along the pavement directly opposite the car. By now it was dark and if he kept perfectly still they probably wouldn't see him watching. He took the chance.

The two walkers approached slowly. As they got closer he was able to pick out Lambeth. But the recognition of her companion struck him like a bolt of lightning. Margaret! He recoiled, physically.

In a split second of searing illumination, all the missing pieces tumbled into place. Lambeth may not have known about Cromby or his tax declarations but his former wife did. Between them they had all the information required by his tormentor – and the motives. At last it made sense.

The office had been hot and uncomfortable all week and Lambeth was glad to get away that Friday evening. It wasn't just the weather. Marchbank himself was an oppressive presence. She bid him good night and left without bothering to wait for his answer.

Marchbank had become very quiet and introspective over the preceding few days. She couldn't make her mind up whether this was a good sign or a bad one. It could be his way of coming to terms with his problems or equally it might be him retreating from them. Lambeth hadn't tried to find out. She had her own problem to contend with, Margaret Marchbank.

Throughout the spell of hot weather that lasted from the middle of June until the first week of July, Margaret remained irritable and irrational in her behaviour. She too was withdrawn for a lot of the time – when she wasn't being acerbic. And whenever Lambeth probed to try and discover why, Margaret always claimed her work was to blame.

They generally only met at weekends now. Margaret declined to see Lambeth during the week, again citing work.

There was one notable exception, a Tuesday, when Margaret rang her unexpectedly at the laboratory. This in itself was unheard of. She normally avoided ringing there on the grounds that she might get Tony on the line. On that day she broke her own rule. What was more she wanted Lambeth to meet her at the flat in Putney that same night. Could she come?

Lambeth agreed, and duly turned up at the flat feeling extremely anxious. Her fears turned out to be totally unfounded. For once Margaret was delightful. She had bought Chris an enormous bunch of flowers and cooked her a wonderful meal. Yet Lambeth couldn't help the feeling that some conscience salving was going on.

By Friday the old, irascible Margaret had reasserted itself. Oddly, Lambeth discovered she preferred this to the one she had met the previous Tuesday. She suspected it was a more honest version. She had no illusions. Their relationship was grinding inexorably to its conclusion.

That Friday night the weather was close and humid. A storm was brewing. To escape the flat they went for a drink at a nearby pub but both were too tired to engage in any serious bickering and, back home again, soon fell soundly asleep in spite of the weather.

Next morning, Saturday, the hot spell finally broke with a torrential downpour and with immaculate timing Margaret dropped her own bombshell. She had to go into the office. There was an important meeting to discuss strategy for the launch of a new product on the coming Monday. She wouldn't be back until late in the evening – she couldn't say what time. Chris was welcome to stay if she wanted. The implication was that she wouldn't want to.

'Why didn't you tell me this before I came over?' Lambeth asked crossly.

'I didn't know until yesterday evening. It was a last minute decision. I know I should have said something last night but I thought you'd be upset.'

'Too right.'

'What will you do?' she asked a little too eagerly.

'I'll see you tonight.'

For Lambeth it was a very long day. Having nothing better to do, she went into London by herself and window shopped.

The summer sales had started. The streets were crowded and it was wet everywhere after the rain. She tried on a couple of dresses but neither looked right. Anyway, her heart wasn't in it. All the time she was being drawn to the flat in Putney.

By six o'clock she was already back there waiting. She switched the television on at least five times, only to turn it off again almost immediately each time. She couldn't settle to watch anything. Time dragged. Seconds seemed like minutes, minutes like hours. What was Margaret up to? At nine she packed her things and almost went home, then changed her mind. It was ten when she heard the sound of a key in the lock.

Lambeth knew Margaret had been with a man as soon as she came through the door. She could smell him. It was like the scent left by a wild animal and it was obscenely sexual. Instantly she felt sick. Yet her mind, which had been racing all evening like her heart, quieted and became perfectly calm.

'How was it?' she asked coldly.

'The meeting? It was deadly. Thank God it's over.' Margaret smiled tentatively.

'Not the meeting, the coupling.'

Margaret looked startled. 'What do you mean?'

'Come off it Marg. You know perfectly well what I mean. I can tell by the way you're walking that you spent most of your so-called meeting on your back. What was it like being pumped full of semen again?'

There was a tiny instant of time, of perfect quiet, before Margaret reacted. Then her eyes blazed.

'You bitch! Get out of my flat! Now! I don't want to see you ever again!' The way she held her body intimated violence barely contained. This was another Margaret, a primitive, dangerous creature.

Lambeth found her bag was beside the settee, already packed though she couldn't remember filling it. With deliberate movements she picked it up and then walked out of the door which her former lover was holding open, never looking at Margaret directly but always keeping her in sight from the corner of her eye. Only when she was through the door did she turn and look into her eyes. She said nothing. There was nothing more to say. She remained staring until the door slammed in her face.

She walked down the stairs slowly, like an automaton. By the time she reached the bottom she was shaking uncontrollably. But it wasn't until she was outside in the street that her own emotions finally broke through.

On Sunday the sunshine returned but the wind had changed direction so the weather was fresher than it had been during the preceding three weeks. Lambeth spent the day trying to sort out the physical and mental remains of her relationship with Margaret.

The tears of the previous night had washed away most of her pain. She had been living in anticipation for several weeks anyway so the final break was in part a relief. But a dull ache still lingered and would for many days yet.

Memories were piled up. Good times. Bad times. Times that had been promised but never realized. No holiday. They hadn't made it to Tenerife after all. Perhaps she should go on her own. The future looked empty. But at least there was her work. She could throw herself into it, just as Tony had done. Now they had both been tossed aside by the same woman; they were both her victims, both sucked dry and jettisoned.

On Monday morning Lambeth cycled to work. As had been usual recently, Marchbank was there already when she arrived. She left her bike outside the office and changed into one of the velvet skirts that had vexed Margaret so during the twilight of their affair. Dressed, she made her mug of coffee and went through to their laboratory.

'Hi, Tony.'

Marchbank muttered something from the other end of the room.

'What?' she asked walking towards him.

He was seated in his private office, just beyond the door that divided the room into two. His face was lined with tension. Lambeth realized immediately that something was seriously wrong.

As she approached him, Marchbank stood up and came to the doorway, looking as if he had come to a decision. 'Shut the door, will you, Chris?'

She gave him a puzzled look before turning round to close it but he offered her no further explanation.

'Sit down please.'

Again she looked puzzled. 'What's up?'

Whatever it was had him worried. He took a deep breath, then a second before starting to speak.

'I know what's been going on. I know about you and Margaret.' He spoke quietly but now that he had started the words tumbled out. 'Why did you do it Chris? I thought I could rely on you, of all people.' There was pain in his voice.

Lambeth stared at him with a look of horror. 'What?' The question was involuntary.

'It's no good pretending. You've both been involved in the campaign against me from the beginning haven't you? It's clear to me now. Why are you putting me through this? What have I ever done to you?'

This time her confusion was real. 'What are you talking about Tony?'

Marchbank began to get angry. 'Don't play the fool with me Chris. I followed you to Putney. I've seen the two of you together so it's no use denying it. You planted the virus on the computers, didn't you? You and Margaret told the paper about Cromby. And it was you tipped off the tax man too.'

Lambeth was barely listening. 'You followed me?' she asked incredulously. 'Good God Tony, you really have flipped.'

But now he was a runaway train, rolling with increasing momentum towards the inevitable crash at the end of the line.

'Don't try and change the subject. That won't work. Why did you do it? I have a right to know.'

Then she laughed in his face. She had understood.

'You really think that me and Marg are responsible for the things that are happening, don't you? Well I've got news for you Dr Marchbank. We've been involved, all right, but not in the way you think. We haven't had time to worry about you. We've been far too busy worrying about ourselves.'

Marchbank's mouth had dropped open. 'What do you mean?'

'I mean Marg and I have been having an affair. We've been screwing one another to buggery. Your wife left you for another woman – me!'

His face flushed red. He felt hot and dizzy. This made no sense. He had got everything worked out. Now his theory had been thrown back into his face. He sat down heavily in a chair.

'You and Margaret?' he stammered.

'Surprised eh?' she mocked.

He didn't answer her. Instead he began to breathe in and out rapidly, too rapidly, caught in a spasm he couldn't control. He looked ill. Lambeth realized something was wrong.

'Tony!' she shouted, grabbing his shoulders and shaking him in panic but she couldn't stop him.

Eventually he did calm down. When she was sure he was breathing normally once more she brought him a cup of tea.

'Do you want a doctor?'

He drank from the mug. 'No. I'll be OK in a minute.' His voice was almost a whisper.

'You should go home. You're in no state to work.'

But he appeared not to hear.

Both Marchbank and Lambeth had reason to feel remorse for what had happened. Lambeth had carried on an affair with Margaret Marchbank behind her husband's back. In return Marchbank had suspected Lambeth of conspiring against him. Worse, he had followed her about London, invading her privacy to satisfy his fevered suspicions.

But Marchbank felt no remorse. He was incapable of it. In the immediate aftermath of their confrontation his mind effectively stopped functioning. He couldn't cope with the conflicts facing him, so he shut them away in a compartment of his subconscious and switched off.

To Lambeth, Marchbank had become a fatalist, impassively awaiting the next turn of the screw. Instead, it was she who bore the immediate burden of guilt, and with it a further burden, Marchbank himself. She felt responsible for pushing him too far and blamed herself for his state. In her own mind, he had become her responsibility.

Gradually though, in the days following her revelation, Marchbank's mind appeared to reawaken and some semblance of normality returned to his persona. But it was a peculiar normality. He never alluded to Lambeth's affair with his wife and while outwardly he appeared to be functioning normally, to Lambeth, at least, there was a gap in his personality. A part of him had vanished. It was as if he had become two-dimensional. She worried and tried several times to persuade him to visit a doctor but he refused. Eventually, despair, she decided to contact DeWyntz.

'It's about Tony.'

'Tony? What's wrong?' DeWyntz sounded terrified.

She explained what had happened and he seemed to calm down. Finally he promised to do what he could. Later the same day he called Marchbank and persuaded him that it was time to pay a visit to Cambridge.

When he finally set eyes on his protégé, DeWyntz was shocked at the change that had come over him. Marchbank was gaunt. His cheeks were hollow and the skin on his forehead was pulled so taut it had lost all colour. He was thin and his clothes no longer fitted. His eyes were lacklustre. He looked to his mentor like a man doomed.

'Tony, m'boy. How are you?' he asked, trying to hide his concern.

'Oh, I don't know Conrad.' Marchbank's voice was flat.

'Sit down while I make us both a cup of coffee.'

This was a break with tradition – the coffee didn't normally come until later – but Marchbank barely noticed. When he drank it, however, the flicker of a spark appeared as if the thick and gritty brew was stirring a memory, buried deep inside his mind, of their last meeting.

'Margaret has left me you know Conrad.'

'I'm sorry.'

'Probably the best thing.' He looked distracted.

'I think Earnshaw believes Cromby,' he started again, his train of thought erratic. 'He asked if the Roughburn figures were fabricated too.'

'Phh. He wants it to be true. Then he has an excuse to rid himself of an embarrassment.'

The conversation rambled on in this uneven fashion with Marchbank jumping from one subject to another and DeWyntz following the switches as best he could until Marchbank exhausted the kaleidoscope swirling around in his brain.

'What's happening to me Conrad?' The words burst out of him, a sudden, desperate plea.

There was a look of sorrow and of remorse in the old man's eye but Marchbank couldn't see it. All he could see was the wasteland that was his own bleak future.

'Oh, Tony. Why did you have to rake the embers of this Roughburn business back to life? Why couldn't you leave it to smoulder and die? Now it will consume you too unless can find iron for your will and a fire in your belly.'

They looked at one another. DeWyntz was as helpless as Marchbank. He was in the autumn of his life. Now, the cold threat of winter had arrived early to haunt him.

Sixteen

The package was sitting in the middle of Love's desk when she arrived at the *News* one Tuesday morning at the start of July – a heavy manilla envelope and about half an inch thick. She had no idea what it was so as soon as she had taken off her jacket, even before sitting down, she tore it open and pulled out the contents. In her hand she had a loose wad of photocopied sheets, fifty in all at a guess. It looked to her like some sort of report. She read the title on the top sheet.

An Evaluation of Our Current Understanding of the Threshold Theory in Relation to Radioactivity

What?

Love started to read the first page of the report but was soon lost in a maze of scientific gibberish. She looked at the second and third pages. They all appeared to be couched in the same incomprehensible technical jargon. Why had it been sent to her?

Then something on the title page caught her eye – a name. The report was the work of two authors, G. Winfield and M. Crawford and it was the second that had jumped off the page. Crawford! Could it be the same Dr Marion Crawford she had been trying to trace in connection with the Marchbank story?

Love retrieved the envelope from the bin beside her desk and examined it. There was no postmark. In fact, apart from her name scrawled across the front in longhand there was nothing at all. No clues as to its origin.

She picked up her phone and called down to the reception.

The woman on the desk had no recollection of the package being delivered but the concierge who guarded the door remembered clearly.

'A man on a motorbike brought it, first thing. He was in one hell of a hurry. Never even took his helmet off. Shoved it into my hand and was off without so much as a ...'

'Thanks Ben.'

She put the receiver back into its cradle and picked up the report again. Its contents meant nothing to her. When had it been written? And where? There was only one thing to do. She called Marchbank.

In his world of shifting substance Marchbank now followed routine blindly. He was in a dreamlike state for much of the time and routine was the only way he was able to get from home to office, from one day to the next. But at least it indicated that his instinct for self-preservation was still intact.

It was the week after Marchbank's visit to Cambridge and he was sitting inside his private office, the inner part of the room he shared with Lambeth. The door was firmly closed. He was daydreaming. Images and ideas haunted him. Fire? A fire in Roughburn. A fire in his belly? DeWyntz's words were chasing round and his head.

What fire? The ideas had become confused. He was in the hospital again. He could feel the heat of the flames.

It was as if there was a gauze separating him from reality. He couldn't grasp anything clearly. He felt as if he was slipping gently into an incorporeal world.

Abruptly, his thoughts set off in another direction, towards his wife. Margaret Marchbank. Not long ago they had shared a bed. Now his memory of her felt as if it belonged to someone else. She was a stranger to him – and in such a short space of time. How was it possible? Perhaps he had never known her in the first place.

Margaret and Chris. If Lambeth had been a man Marchbank would have been able to understand and react. Then his belly would have been a raging furnace. But two women? It ought to be simple enough but he couldn't make sense of it. Screwing? What did they do in bed, for God's sake?

His thoughts drifted on elsewhere. He had no sense of purpose.

The telephone rang in the office outside, breaking through his reverie. He heard Lambeth pick it up and echo the number of her extension – two-four-six – then listened to the conversation through the door but didn't hear it. She replaced the receiver. There was a knock and his door opened.

'Tony, hi. Want a cup of coffee?'

He shook his head.

'I've just had Lisa Love, from the *News*, on the phone. She's bringing over a report somebody sent her. Something to do with the Threshold Theory. Could be by our mysterious Dr Crawford. Better have a look. Might be important.'

'If you think so.'

She looked at him despairingly and left him on his own again.

Love arrived within the hour. When she saw Marchbank she gasped. The change in him since their last meeting was frightening. She caught Lambeth's eye and raised her eyebrows questioningly.

Marchbank was oblivious to her reaction.

'What have you brought?' he asked, interrupting their silent conversation.

'Here.' She passed him the report, now in a pink folder. 'It was delivered anonymously this morning.'

The desks in the outer office were cluttered as usual. Marchbank sat on one of the chairs and then clumsily cleared a space for the report, knocking a map on to the floor as he did so. Lambeth hurried to pick it up. He opened the pink folder and took in the title page of the report, then turned over and began to read. The others might just as well have not been there.

Lambeth and Love had little choice but to watch. They both sat down too and waited, at first patiently, then with increasing impatience. Time crept along on tiny feet as he worked his way through the full fifty pages. When he finally reached the end they were fidgeting like patients in a doctor's surgery.

'Well?' Lambeth asked.

'It's about the Threshold Theory.'

'Jesus, Tony, I could have told you that. What does it say about the theory?'

'Here, read it yourself.'

Marchbank dropped the report into her lap and she had to grab the folder quickly to prevent the pages spilling across the floor. Before she had time to issue a curse he disappeared into his office again and shut the door.

'What's happened to him?' Love asked in a whisper after the door had closed.

'It's a long story.'

'Is he all right?'

'No, he's not all right. I think he's probably off his trolley,' she added crossly.

Lambeth made no further effort to explain so Love returned to the report. 'What is this theory?'

'The Threshold Theory? It's a clumsy way of predicting the effect of radioactivity on people. The idea is that there is a level of radiation which is harmless. Provided the dose doesn't exceed that threshold level it causes no damage.'

'What has that got to do with Roughburn?'

'I'll have to read this lot myself before I can tell you that.'

And then she buried her head in the report, leaving Love once again the impatient observer.

But in a moment Lambeth looked up again, taking pity on the journalist. 'There's a kitchen along the corridor. Why not make us both a mug of coffee?'

'Do you know what radioactivity is?' Lambeth asked a little while later, putting the report aside.

'Atoms, rays: something like that?'

'Not quite. Perhaps I'd better explain.

'There are three principal types of radioactivity. The first is gamma radiation. A gamma ray is more or less the same as a light ray or an infra-red ray except that it carries a lot more energy. Gamma rays have more energy even than X-rays and they have a much shorter wavelength. If you like you can think of them as being smaller than X-rays and light. Like X-rays they can pass straight through a human body, unless they happen to bump into an atom on the way. The fact that they're so small means it's by no means certain they will hit one. You need several inches of lead to absorb them completely. But when they do strike an atom all their energy is absorbed by the target.'

She looked at Love who nodded her head knowingly.

'That's one type of radioactivity. Then there are alpha particles. If it means anything, an alpha particle is the nucleus of a helium atom, two protons and two neutrons. That's not really important. What is important is that it is a fragment of an atomic nucleus and it's big, too big to pass through matter without colliding into the atoms that compose it. You can stop an alpha particle with a sheet of paper. That doesn't mean it cannot do any damage however. It can.

'Finally there are beta particles. Beta particles are electrons. They are much smaller than alpha particles and correspondingly more penetrating but not as powerful, or as small, as gamma rays.'

'I'm not sure I'm much wiser,' Love said when she had finished. 'Why are they called radioactivity?'

'It's historical. They are all produced during nuclear reactions of elements like uranium or plutonium.'

'They sound so different.'

'They are. But what all three have in common is energy. It's the energy they carry that ultimately does the damage to living tissue. An alpha particle hitting a cell is like an express train hitting a palace. A beta particle is much smaller and consequently more selective in what it destroys, a howitzer shell rather than a train. The gamma ray is more selective still, a high velocity rifle. These are very crude analogies.'

'Where does the theory fit in?'

'Try and imagine, if you can, what happens to a living organism close to an atom bomb when it's detonated. It becomes saturated with radioactivity and a large number of its cells are destroyed, sufficient to kill it for that reason alone in most cases. When the organism is farther away the dose it receives is somewhat lower and it may initially survive but its cells probably won't be able to replicate any more, or they may become rogues and replicate improperly. Eventually it too will die.

'However, the most interesting case is when the dose is much lower still.'

'You scientists have a macabre curiosity,' Love suggested jokingly.

'I don't think we have time to discuss scientific ethics,' Lambeth told her curtly. 'May I go on?'

'Sorry.'

'You and I can afford to lose a few of our cells without coming to any serious harm. Cells in our bodies are dying all the time anyway and being replaced. On the face of it, therefore, a low dose of radiation shouldn't do any lasting damage. Unfortunately the situation isn't quite that simple because radioactivity is insidious. Instead of simply destroying a cell it may damage it in such a way that it mutates and then ...'

'You have cancer?' Love interrupted.

'Exactly. Which brings us to the Threshold Theory.

'According to the Threshold Theory there is a minimum radiation dose, below which this organism suffers no serious or lasting damage. But what is that minimum level? It's an important question to answer because the threshold level will determine what is a safe dose for people who work in nuclear power stations and other installations where they are constantly exposed to radioactivity.

'And that's what the report is about?'

'No. The report is about trying to establish a theoretical basis for the theory. And it's way out of date.' At exactly that moment Marchbank's door opened again.

When Marchbank had disappeared, leaving Lambeth scrambling to stop the pages of the report cascading across the floor, he hadn't been aware that he was behaving oddly or rudely. His consciousness peered out at the world from the dreamlike state he inhabited as if through a telescope. He was aware of the existence of other people but they were remote, not part of the world he occupied.

Having finished reading the report, he wanted to think. Where better to do it than in his own office? Inside his muddled mind something had begun to stir.

It struck Marchbank immediately, as Lambeth had subsequently noted, that the report was out of date. The ideas it put forward were extremely old fashioned. In fact they were of about the same vintage as the incident at Roughburn. What did it mean? He thrashed around inside his mental prison. His instinct told him there was something to be found. But it was still some time before he realized that age itself was the connection.

So what? His mind was in the habit of going its own way now and he had difficulty forcing it to follow a single line of thought. Crawford – Roughburn – the Threshold Theory. Did they all belong to the same puzzle? If so, they led back once again to the elusive Dr Marion Crawford. It was then he remembered the list of references at the back of the report.

'About thirty years out of date,' Marchbank capped Lambeth's comment, as he appeared through the doorway. 'Will you pass me the report please.' There was a look of childish pleasure on his face.

Lambeth gave it to him and he immediately turned to the back.

'I thought so,' he exclaimed excitedly. 'Look!'

The last two pages of the report consisted entirely of references, in alphabetical order by author's name. Marchbank was pointing to the Cs. The other two looked over his shoulder. There were eleven articles by Crawford cited. Nearly all dated from the late 1940s – the latest was from early 1950 – and several of them were internal reports from an atomic research laboratory in Berkshire.

'I think we've got you now, Dr Crawford,' he said. For the first time in over a month he was smiling.

But if a Dr Crawford had worked at the laboratory, he didn't any more. 'Try the other author,' Marchbank whispered noisily to Love who had been delegated the job of making the enquiry. That name too drew a blank.

'Look, Tony. We are talking about thirty years ago. He could be anywhere now,' Lambeth pointed out.

'But at least we know there is a real Dr Crawford somewhere.'

'A lot of help that is.'

As it turned out, it was a considerable amount of help.

It was Love's idea to consult the records of births, deaths and marriages. She wasn't surprised to find that Crawford was a common name. But Marion Crawford was less so and Dr Marion Crawfords were positively rare. Theirs was dead. Fortunately for them he left a widow.

How do you trace a woman when all you have to go on is her name? The answer, they found, was with great difficulty. In the end the only way Love could think of was to use the telephone directory. There was a complete set at the *News*.

Searching through every directory in the country for the name L. C. Crawford and then ringing each number was both an extremely tedious and time-consuming task, even with Marchbank's help such as it was. He had latched on to her, a constant companion whether she liked it or not. And at the back of her mind was always the thought that the woman might have remarried, or emigrated or disappeared for any one of a hundred other reasons.

Ironically Dr Crawford's widow hadn't strayed any distance in the thirty years since her husband died. They traced her to a small village in Berkshire, not far from the laboratory where he had worked. Marchbank and Love went to see her together. Marchbank drove.

Lilian Crawford's was a small, neat house, one end of a terrace of four, with a carefully tended garden. The woman matched the house, small and neat. They found her in the garden making cosmetic adjustments to her rose bushes.

'You're the lady who rang?' she asked when they appeared at the gate.

'Lisa Love.' Love held out her hand over the top bar. 'This is Dr Tony Marchbank.'

'How do you do? Please excuse me not shaking hands. Mine are filthy from the garden,' she apologised.

She opened the gate and let them through.

'It's not been a good year,' she told them, fussing about the roses still. 'Not enough rain.'

To Marchbank the blooms looked perfect: they could have been painted by hand. There was a shallow basket full of dead and discoloured flower heads on the lawn beside the rose border. Mrs Crawford picked it up.

'I expect you'd both like a cup of tea.' She took them into the house, disposing of the contents of her basket in the dustbin on the way.

'Now,' she asked over tea and homemade cake, 'you mentioned something about my late husband.'

'I'd like to know what sort of work he did,' Marchbank told her bluntly.

'And why is that, young man?' she asked, piercing him with

her grey eyes.

'Does the name Roughburn mean anything to you? It's been in the news recently because it was discovered – I discovered – that a lot of children died there from cancer forty years ago.'

'I thought your name sounded familiar. So you're that Marchbank.' She peered at him closely as if to make sure she wouldn't forget his face. 'But what has this got to do with Marion?'

'I came across his name twice in connection with Roughburn. The first time was a letter sent to all the doctors in the town, in 1951. It was signed by a Dr Marion Crawford. Did he ever work in Jermyn Street by the way?'

'No, never. He hated London. Why?'

'The letter was addressed from there.'

'You said his name came up twice.'

'In 1953 they had a terrible lambing season around Roughburn. Hundreds died. A scientist was sent up to the town to find out why. His name was Dr Crawford too.'

Crawford's widow was unimpressed.

'I think I'd better tell you something about Marion, Dr Marchbank, he worked for the ministry. All his work was top secret. He wasn't allowed to tell anybody about it, not even me.'

'But he must have mentioned what he did; dropped hints from time to time.'

'It would be disloyal to his memory for me to repeat his confidences to you.'

'Mrs Crawford. I don't want you to be disloyal to him but I do want to find out why those children died. Please help me.'

She looked from Marchbank to Love and back again.

'Marion was a clever man. He was working at the Cavendish laboratory when war broke out. I don't think I would be giving away any secrets if I told you he got drawn into the atom bomb programme. After the war the work continued and he stayed too. He thought it was important for the sake of the country. I don't know precisely what he did. He would never have told me that. But during 1951 and 1952 he travelled to the north of England several times. Usually to Windscale. Although he never mentioned it, he could have visited this town Roughburn too I suppose.'

She paused, looking distant. She's back there, with him, Love thought.

'My husband enjoyed his work, Dr Marchbank. Much as you enjoy yours, I imagine. It totally absorbed him. And he was dedicated. But towards the end of his life something changed. During the two or three years before his death he became increasingly unhappy.'

'Do you know why?' Marchbank enquired.

'He never told me why before he died.'

'What happened to him?'

Mrs Crawford looked at him again and for an instant uncertainty appeared in her face. Then it was gone.

'You don't know? My husband committed suicide. One night in the summer of 1957 he shut himself in the garage and switched on the engine of the Morris. I found him there next morning.'

'I'm sorry.'

'So am I. But it's a long time ago now. I've forgiven him. Would you like some more tea?'

Marchbank declined, but Love accepted her offer.

'Mrs Crawford,' Marchbank continued, 'somebody sent Lisa, anonymously, a report written many years ago by your husband. It was about something called the Threshold Theory. I'm sure you know nothing about the report but there was another author. Someone called Winfield. Do you know who that was?'

'George? Yes, I knew George. He practically lived in our house at one time. He was the apple of Marion's eye. We never had children and I believe Marion thought of George as a son. I tried to like him too.

'I haven't seen George since Marion died. His suicide turned me into an outcast. I was shunned by all his old colleagues afterwards.' She spoke sadly but without bitterness.

'Do you know where I can find him now?'

'That shouldn't be difficult. George gave up his career as a scientist and went into politics.'

Love's mouth dropped open. 'Not *the* George Winfield?' she asked.

'The Secretary of State? Yes, it's the same George Winfield.'

Marchbank could only stare.

* * *

The unexpected appearance of the Threshold Theory report marked the nadir of Marchbank's decline. From that time forward his grasp on reality began to improve. But it was the visit to Mrs Crawford which provided the stimulus to finally clear his mind. At last he had something firm to hold on to; a way back from the brink of the abyss.

In the car on the journey back to London pieces of the puzzle began to jostle around again, looking for ways to fit together.

'Crawford committed suicide in 1957. It was in that year the Jermyn Street operation closed down.'

'Why do you suppose he killed himself?' Love asked.

Neither of them knew.

'Does Winfield fit into all this?' Marchbank asked.

Again they drew a blank.

'What's the link between Crawford and the deaths?'

'It must have something to do with the Threshold Theory.'

But neither Marchbank nor Love could have guessed how terrifyingly simple the truth was.

Marchbank didn't expect to hear from Crawford's widow again but the day after their visit he received a telephone call from her. She wanted to see him. Alone. He drove out to the house that afternoon.

'Thank you for coming all this way again,' she said, greeting him at the door.

'What can I do for you Mrs Crawford?'

They were seated in her living room. Crawford's widow was staring at him, weighing him up, he thought.

'Do you believe in your work, Dr Marchbank? Is it important to you?'

'Yes I think so.'

'And do you think scientists have to accept a moral responsibility for what they do?'

'For their research? Yes, I do.'

'Then you can imagine what it would be like for you to realize that something you had been doing was morally indefensible.'

He looked at her closely before answering. 'I think so, yes.'

'That is what happened to my husband.' She paused. 'Dr

Marchbank. In the few months before he died Marion had a haunted look about him. When you were sitting there yesterday afternoon I saw the same look on your face. That is why I asked you here again. You see, I misled you yesterday. I do know why Marion killed himself, though I didn't find out until after he was dead. He left me a letter. I've never told anybody about it. I was too frightened of the consequences. The ministry has looked after me since he died. Paid for my house. Everything. But now, well. Here, see for yourself. I think this will answer all your questions.'

She handed him an envelope. Inside he found several sheets of neat hand-written text. Marchbank began to read.

Seventeen

Dearest Lilian.

I am sorry. Sorry to leave you alone. Sorry because you will have to sort out the mess after I've gone. But I cannot go on living. God knows I've tried. I've been struggling to live with myself for these past three years but it gets no easier. Now, for me, the struggle is over.

I hope you will be able to forgive me for abandoning you but I'm no good to you as I am. I'm no good to anybody any more.

You want to know why? You, of all people deserve to know why. I ought to have sat down and told you but somehow it is easier to put it on to paper than to say it out loud. Why is that?

I must write it down anyway. It will not be recorded anywhere otherwise. What you do with this when I am gone is up to you. Am I passing on the responsibility for what I have done? I don't think so, but I don't seem to be sure of anything any more.

I'll tell you the story from the beginning. It's easier that way.

It was George's idea in the first place you know. He's a very bright young man. Bright but ruthless. I think he knew right at the start what I came to realize only when it was too late. The morality he subscribes to is a different one than mine. I understand that now. I suppose I am guilty of naivete. How can innocence lead one so far astray?

The point of departure is clear. Our military people want to know if we can survive a war fought with atomic weapons. A simple question, you may say, but its answer is not so easy to uncover. Oh, we can put forward theories. We can perform our experiments with rats. But men of a military bent are not really interested in rats. What they want to know is whether their soldiers can survive. They want to know if they can win. And if they can win, whether there will be any prize left worth claiming.

189

It is our job to tell them.

We'd done all our experiments with rats and monkeys and pigs so we thought we knew pretty well what the radiation threshold was for survival. What the limits were. But to be absolutely certain we needed to carry out one more experiment. With human subjects. That's where George's bright idea came in. A harmless double check, he called it. The bottom line of the proof.

What George proposed was that we expose a group of civilians to a level of radiation below the threshold. It would do them no harm and at the same time give our strategists the unequivocal answer they needed – the confidence they could win their war. To my eternal damnation I agreed with his proposal.

At the time it seemed a perfectly reasonable and justifiable proposition. The risk would be minimal and we needed the information. It was for the good of the country.

What iniquities we justify in the name of our country. There can be no justification for using innocent civilians as our laboratory animals, exposing them to ionizing radiation with – or as in this case – without their knowledge. No justification whatsoever. We do not have the right. I did not have the right. But for me and for them it is too late. However I digress from the story.

The strategists settled on a town in the Borders called Roughburn, a conveniently out of the way little place of no interest to anybody except the people who happen to live there. It took me a long time to put the necessary monitoring in position but by the middle of 1952 we were ready.

August 15. That was the date we chose. The met boys had predicted a fine night over the whole country and a light wind from the west. Ideal conditions. I went up to the aerodrome at Abingdon to help load the planes. Two of the latest Vampire T10 night fighters had been modified especially for the job. How is it that machines of war look so magnificent?

I won't go into the details of the load they carried beneath their wings that night. Suffice it to say that it was a cocktail of radionucleides carefully calculated to approximate as accurately as possible the fallout from an atomic explosion. The cores of our research reactors provided most of the material.

The two Vampires took off at ten o'clock into a star-bright sky. It was an exciting moment. We watched them from the air traffic control tower. *Two streaks of silver in the moonlight with two brave young men sitting in their cockpits. They had no idea what they were carrying but we protected them as best we could. I wonder if they will survive to old age?*

I had calculated the height and dispersal pattern very carefully and they followed my plan to the letter. I know that to be true because of the monitoring we carried out on the ground immediately afterwards. Roughburn had never seen so many engineers searching for problems with its water supply in one day before. The radiation levels on the ground were precisely what we had predicted. There were no hot spots that we were able to detect. Everything had gone perfectly. Now it was simply a matter of watching and waiting.

I had arranged for the doctors in Roughburn to send reports every three months to a collection point in London. We didn't expect to find anything of course. That was the whole point of the experiment, after all. And we did find nothing – at first.

The first sign that something was wrong came in the spring of the next year, 1953, during the lambing. Still births increased alarmingly that season. There were grotesque deformities too. If I were a God fearing man I could believe them the spawn of the Devil. But I know better. It was man who created them.

The Ministry of Agriculture sent a team up to have a look and I tagged along with them. We blamed it on lichen. I think I even believed our explanation for a time. There were a number of unusual specimens in the area. But sheep don't eat lichen. Now I am convinced that the lichens, like the sheep, were affected by the radiation we doused them with.

Everything happens faster in sheep. It was three years before there was any weight of evidence from the human population. But when it became clear it was devastating. It was the children who were suffering. They were dying.

I refused to believe the evidence before me. I didn't want to believe it. George concurred. It had to be something else causing the deaths. Nothing to do with our experiment. But why else are they dropping like flies? What else could cause cancer on such a scale? Because that is what they are dying from, cancer.

Over thirty children from the town have died of cancer since we carried out our experiment. More will die, I am sure. That is what I have on my conscience. It is my responsibility and I cannot live with it. If there was something I could do – but there is nothing. I cannot seek absolution because what has taken place in Roughburn will never be made public. As far as the world is concerned it never happened.

I don't feel bitter towards George. It was his idea, but ultimately my authority to say yes or no. He hid nothing from me. But how could I have been so blind? George can live with this. He believes that if the experiment is to blame, it is an acceptable price to pay. As for the military men. I don't think they believe what we tell them anyway. They think we must have botched the figures somewhere along the line. They still want to win their war, you see, and they are not keen on anything that will prevent them.

That leaves me. But I cannot go on. Perhaps I am being a coward. I don't know. Forgive me Lilian. I would like to think that one day we may be together again, but if there is a heaven and a hell then I will surely end my time in the latter and I wouldn't wish that on you.

Goodbye.

Marion.

When Marchbank had finished the letter he sat, in silence, for several minutes, holding the last page limply in his hand. To read Crawford's graphic testimony was shocking. It was horrifying. And it touched him personally. What would he have done? Would he, could he, have performed the experiment Crawford had designed? It was too easy to say that he could never have agreed to it. Not now perhaps. But then? He pitied Crawford.

Lilian Crawford sat and watched him. Eventually she broke the spell.

'Would you like a cup of tea?'

'Please.'

He carefully folded the letter and replaced it in the envelope while she was gone. How many times had she read it, he wondered.

'Was my husband a coward, do you think, Dr Marchbank?' she asked him when she had returned with two cups of tea on a tray.

'I don't know, Mrs Crawford.'

'What would you have done in his position?'

'I don't know if I could find the will to kill myself. Perhaps that is cowardly. He wanted to atone and there was no other way open to him. I think he showed bravery in making his choice, not cowardice.'

'I like to think so too. I was fond of him. He was a good man, I believe.'

'What of George Winfield? Is he a good man?'

'Who am I to condemn him?'

'But you don't like him.'

'No, that's true. I found him ambitious. You may think that a strange reason not to like a person but ambition pervaded every aspect of his character. It fuelled everything he did. I felt he was using my husband, using his friendship to further his own ends. Marion couldn't see that, not until it was too late anyway.'

'What was he ambitious for?'

'What do men seek? Power I suppose. Fame, perhaps.'

'He has got his wish then. Do you think he is ruthless?'

'Yes, I'm sure he would be ruthless if he had to be.'

'Mrs Crawford. I have to ask you a personal question. Why have you shown me this letter?'

'Marion wrote that he didn't know whether he was shifting his responsibility on to my shoulders. He was. I had nothing to do with the children dying, you understand, but knowing about the events that led to their deaths is a responsibility too. I have kept it to myself for all these years out of fear but also because I didn't believe there was anything I could do anyway. Things are different now. Besides, I need to share this with somebody before I die. That somebody has turned out to be you. Now you know and you must bear the responsibility with me. I hope that doesn't sound too selfish.'

'If I am to discharge the responsibility in the way I see fit, I will have to make the contents of your husband's letter public.'

'I know. I have thought about that. It is what he would have wished, I think. I will just have to learn to live with the consequences.'

Marchbank called Love as soon as he got back to London and

arranged to meet her that evening in the cheese-dish pub. Her surprise was obvious when he told her that he had been to visit Crawford's widow again, this time at the old woman's request.

'What did she want?'

'To show me this.' He handed her a photocopy of the letter.

'What is it?'

'Read it.'

She did as he suggested.

Love was visibly shaken. Her face was almost white by the time she had finished. Her response, however, was more practical than Marchbank's had been.

'Is it true?'

'I've no reason to think otherwise.'

'But nobody could be so callous. Surely?' She sounded as if she didn't want to believe it possible.

'Callous? No, I don't believe he was callous. You're judging him by our standards today.'

'Time doesn't reverse good and evil,' she retorted.

'Maybe not, but even so the situation looked different thirty years ago. Things were black and white then, not our infinite shades of grey. Besides, the atom was a brave new act on the world stage and men like Crawford and the others were its stars. To be an atomic scientist. Once that was every boy's dream. These men were the elite. They thought they could do anything.'

'Even murder?'

'Oh, come on.' He found himself automatically jumping to Crawford's defence. 'You can't call this murder.'

'What would you call it?'

'Something else. Not murder.'

'Are you trying to justify it?'

'No. It's just that I can see it from his point of view.'

Love looked at him coldly.

'Look. Don't get me wrong,' he told her. 'I don't condone what Crawford did. But I can understand it, from a scientific point of view.'

'Do you scientists protect one another's backs at all costs?'

'It's not a matter of ...' Marchbank was about to go on the defensive again when he realized what he was doing. 'You're right. There is no excuse. But let's settle for manslaughter?

Crawford was wrong, he was naive, but he wasn't evil. I think he was an honourable man. That's why he killed himself.'

'Sure.' Love still looked wary. 'You're certain it happened then? This isn't the distorted view of a depressed man about to commit suicide?'

'It makes perfect sense, from their point of view. Don't you believe it?'

'Yes, if you do. I'm thinking as a journalist. One man's testimony – a man who's dead – it's not much to base an exposé on. Who's going to speak for the defence when the critics start pulling it to pieces?'

'This is the closest we're going to get to the events in Roughburn. There isn't going to be hard evidence. Any that existed has either been destroyed or is buried under layers of official secrecy.'

'What about Winfield?' she asked. 'If what Crawford says is true he must know.'

'He won't talk to us.'

'It's worth a try.'

'You'd be wasting your time.'

But she was determined to have a go.

'Have you got a safe at the *News*?' he asked before they parted.

'The editor has one.'

'Put this in it will you?' He handed her the original letter Crawford's widow had given him. 'I don't want that to go missing.'

As Marchbank had predicted, Winfield refused to see Love.

'His PPS claims he's too busy to take any interviews this week,' she told Marchbank on the phone, next day. 'If I submit my questions in writing he'll do his best to see Winfield responds to them. In other words, forget it.'

'Perhaps he'll see me.'

Marchbank made the suggestion without thinking.

'What? You're the one who said it was a waste of time.'

'I'm curious to meet the man.'

'Suit yourself.'

'Have you got the number?'

* * *

Why had the politician agreed to the meeting? Marchbank was in the antechamber to Winfield's office, waiting nervously and trying to sort out in his mind what he was going to say. It was all very well for Love to talk about getting the man to admit that Roughburn had been used as a laboratory. Now he was almost face to face with Winfield he had no idea how to go about it. On top of that was a niggling doubt. Winfield must know who he was, surely, if there was any truth in Crawford's testimony. In which case why had he allowed the meeting to go ahead? Unless he had plans to dispose of Marchbank, once and for all. But he wouldn't do it here, not in Whitehall, surely?

'Good morning Dr Marchbank. Won't you sit down please?' Winfield greeted Marchbank effusively when his secretary ushered him into the room.

'Thank you Clive.' He dismissed the secretary and they were alone.

Winfield was older than Marchbank had expected though he had seen him on television often. Maybe the image of Crawford's ambitious assistant still lingered in his memory. The politician had a good head of hair, greying slightly at the temples and a strong, lined face. He wore a charcoal suit and black brogues and exuded a relaxed authority that comes only with practice, and access to considerable power.

'Now, what is it I can do for you? Something about ...' – he looked at a sheet of paper on his desk – 'research for a book on the British atomic weapon's programme, I think you told my secretary? I should have thought that had been thoroughly raked over already but perhaps you have a new angle?' There was a suspicion of a smile on his lips.

He's playing with me, Marchbank thought. This is a game. He couldn't help feeling very insecure and took a deep breath to steady his nerves.

'I should apologize. That was a small deception on my part. There is no book. Actually I'm trying to find out what happened forty years ago in a town called Roughburn.'

The admission had no effect on Winfield's demeanour whatsoever.

'Yes? I believe I read something about the matter in the

newspapers. A cancer cluster, I think you claimed. From what I can remember the whole business backfired rather and you ended up in the firing line yourself. Why have you come to me?' The smile played across his lips again.

'You were working on the atomic programme at the time.'

Winfield dismissed the suggestion with a wave of his hand. 'I don't see what relevance that has. Besides, so were a hundred others. Have you spoken to anybody else?'

'Not yet no.'

'Well I don't see how I can help.' He sat back in his chair challenging Marchbank to prove him wrong.

Here goes, he thought, feeling stickiness spreading under his armpits. He steeled himself.

'According to a Dr Crawford you were intimately involved in the experiment at Roughburn.'

Winfield sat up in his chair and his face suddenly hardened. Then he relaxed again. 'Marion Crawford? Don't talk rubbish. He's been dead for over twenty years.'

'So I believe. He left a detailed account of the reasons why he decided to kill himself. Your name was mentioned more than once.'

'I don't believe you!'

They weren't playing a game any longer.

'I can assure you it's true. I have read the letter he left. I see no reason to doubt what he said.'

'And what did he say?' Winfield demanded sharply.

'That the residents of Roughburn were used as guinea pigs in an experiment to prove that humans could survive exposure to a radiation dose below a certain level unharmed. An experiment that should never have taken place and that has led to wholesale death among the hapless residents of the town, particularly the children.'

Winfield jumped up from his seat. 'I think you had better leave, Dr Marchbank.'

Marchbank remained in his chair. 'You don't deny that you were involved in the experiment or that it was criminal, tantamount to murder?' Love would be proud of him.

Marchbank expected Winfield to call his secretary and that he would be ejected bodily from the office. But he had calculated without the other man's arrogance. Winfield knew he had been right all those years ago. He meant to make sure Marchbank knew it too.

'You don't know what you're talking about. How can you? The whole perspective was different then.'

'Different?'

'We're talking about a time before you were born. How can you expect to understand? We had just emerged from what was probably the ugliest conflict the world has seen. We were victorious, but victory hadn't been assured until the last round was fired. Hitler nearly got the bomb before us. Be thankful that never happened.

'Yet, no sooner had we disposed of him than a new and even deadlier enemy reared its head, an enemy that did have atomic weapons. And it was prepared to use them. Make no mistake, the fate of the world was balanced on a knife edge. We needed to keep ahead and we needed our strategy in place, fast. If we were going to fight we had to know we could win. That meant knowing we could survive an atomic attack if needs be. Roughburn was necessary. It was the price that had to be paid.'

'You weren't the one who had to pay it.'

'Don't be a fool man. There was no room for niceties. I suppose you would have preferred the scientists to carry out the experiment on themselves. A fine mess we would have been in if they had been killed.'

'I can't accept your argument. The premise upon which you justify the experiment is false. You say I can't understand because I didn't live through the events. Will you explain to me how anybody could propose fighting and winning an atomic war after seeing what happened in Japan? It's preposterous.'

'It isn't preposterous. It's perfectly feasible. Roughburn proved that.'

Marchbank looked at him in astonishment.

Seeing his reaction, Winfield pushed home his advantage. 'You imagine the experiment was a failure. I can assure you it was not. We overestimated the threshold, but not by much. Most of the people in the town survived and are still healthy. I'm afraid Marion failed to appreciate just how successful we had been. We established without any doubt that an atomic war was survivable.'

It took Marchbank a moment to recover himself. Winfield

was right. He hadn't for one moment considered that the Roughburn results were considered valuable.

'But the Threshold Theory? It's a complete fantasy. Surely you must accept that?'

'Our government still appears perfectly happy to allow the principle to guide it in setting maximum levels of exposure for workers in nuclear facilities. I take that to be an endorsement of the theory.'

'Are you telling me you endorse the theory too? You know of course that there is no physical basis for it? The only threshold that can have any meaning is zero. In principle one single gamma ray can disrupt the molecular structure of a DNA molecule and turn a normal cell into a rogue.'

'Where's your proof?'

'It's accumulating slowly. Only last month a paper was published with evidence for inherited abnormalities in cells that were offspring of a parent struck by a single alpha particle. One particle is sufficient. It is only a matter of time before research finds the causal links to prove that beyond doubt.'

Winfield appeared to be tiring of the discussion. 'Perhaps, Dr Marchbank, perhaps. We shall see. I still stand by everything we did. The safety of our country demanded it.'

'And the people of Roughburn? The ones who have lost their children? The others who must have lost husbands, wives, mothers and fathers by now? What expression of gratitude can they expect for the service they have given to their country?'

Winfield must have called his secretary without Marchbank realizing for at that moment the office door opened.

'An interesting discussion, Dr Marchbank. Now if you will excuse me.' And without a further word he was gone, leaving Marchbank to be guided out by his secretary who stood at the open door.

Winfield didn't go far. As soon as Marchbank had left he returned to his office again and took a telephone from one of his desk drawers.

'Hello Guy. It's George. Marchbank has just left. You might be interested to know that Marion Crawford did leave an epistle after all.'

'Did he indeed?'

'Yes, Marchbank has got hold of it, somehow.'

'Then it might be advisable to relieve him of the responsibility.'

'I think that would be a very sensible course of action.'

Eighteen

When Marchbank got back to his office he was elated. Winfield had confirmed everything in Crawford's letter. It was more than he could have dared hope.

Lambeth was out that day collecting data for the industrial accident survey they were both supposed to be working on, data to replace that destroyed by the virus. It was as well that she kept up their work. He had devoted scarcely any time to the project since the virus had struck.

Nevertheless it was a pity she was away. If she had been there he might have been moved to dance between the desks with her. Such a spontaneous act might have been just the lubricant needed to reestablish their relationship. There was still a great deal of untilled ground lying between the two of them. While Marchbank had been withdrawn and depressed there had been no option but to leave it lying fallow. But now, if it weren't turned over soon, wild and untameable growths would gain too strong a hold.

Marchbank was about to call Love and tell her how he had fared with Winfield when Earnshaw's secretary knocked at the door and told him the director craved his presence; Earnshawspeak for get in here on the double.

'What can I do for you Oliver?' he asked, seating himself and forgetting for the moment that he was still under suspicion in the director's eyes.

'It has come to my attention that you have a document that can shed some light on this Roughburn business.'

Marchbank's eyes narrowed. 'What?'

'A letter, I believe, that contains information pertinent to my inquiry. I think you had better let me have it, don't you?'

'Who told you that?'

'My sources are confidential. Now. May I see it?'

Then Marchbank laughed. 'Thank you Oliver. You've just done me a valuable service. Of course you shall see it. I'll only be a moment.'

He disappeared out of the door leaving a perplexed looking Earnshaw staring after him from behind his desk. Moments later he was back with one of the photocopies of Crawford's letter he had made earlier in the week.

'Here. Read it. I think you'll find it illuminating.'

Earnshaw did as he was asked. But his response was not quite what Marchbank had expected.

'A fine piece of flummery, I'm sure. You can hardly expect me to take this seriously.'

'Why not?'

'How am I to know you didn't cook it up yourself?'

'That would be absurd, and you know it.'

'This is only a photocopy. It really isn't good enough. It could be a collage for all I know. If you want me to give this serious consideration I think you had better let me see the original.'

'I think not Oliver. That is in a safe place and I intend it to remain there. Nice try though.'

He left the director going pink in the face and looking distinctly apoplectic.

Back in his office, Marchbank didn't feel quite so happy. Who's fooling who, he asked himself? He wasn't sure he knew the answer.

'I want Winfield!'

'Fine sentiments. How do you propose to get him?'

'With this.' Marchbank was waving another copy of Crawford's letter. 'And with what he admitted to me himself this morning.'

'It won't work,' Love told him. 'It won't stand up. It isn't enough.'

'Tell me why not.'

'It's simple. Winfield has taken you up the garden path and back again. Nothing he said this morning is of the slightest use as evidence. He might just as well have said nothing. And he knows it.'

'But he confirmed everything in the letter.'

'Prove it.'

'I....'

'Did you record the conversation?'

'No.'

'Take any notes?'

He shook his head.

'Then there's no way you can. It's your word against his, a secretary of state. Worse, he'll probably claim his PPS was listening in to the conversation and will back him up. It's what journalists call an off-the-record briefing. Repeat one word he told you and he'll sue for libel before you can draw breath again. He has to. Otherwise it's tantamount to admitting the story is true.'

Marchbank was crestfallen.

'There's something else. Read Crawford's letter again carefully. I have. It doesn't actually mention Winfield once.'

'Yes it ...'

'No. It mentions someone called George. How do we know that the George is George Winfield?'

'Crawford's widow told us.'

'Do you suppose she'd testify against him?'

'I think she might, yes.'

'I'm not so sure. But I hope he doesn't see a copy of the letter, just in case.'

Marchbank's face fell a notch further.

'It's too late. What a bloody idiot I am. And I thought I was being so clever.'

'Why? What have you done?'

He explained about Earnshaw and the photocopy of the letter.

'He'll know then. It looks as if you've given away the whole shooting match to friend Winfield.'

Marchbank refused to accept defeat. 'This is ridiculous. You and I know what happened in Roughburn. We know Crawford's account is true. Winfield has confirmed it. Why can't you print the story? Surely that's exactly what newspapers like yours are supposed to do?'

'Forget any ideas you may have about our duty to the truth. One whiff of libel and we run for cover. Newspapers are run by accountants these days, not journalists.'

'It happened, damn it, and the people of Roughburn, if no-one else, have a right to know. Why can't we call Winfield's bluff? I don't believe the government will want a case like this dragged through the courts.'

'Maybe you are right. Unfortunately it isn't me you have to convince.'

'Then take me to the person I need to persuade.'

'OK. I'll see what I can do.'

A meeting was convened late that afternoon. At it were Marchbank, Love, Fran McIntyre the features editor of the *News*, Gerald Walpole the editor, and the paper's legal adviser.

Before they went into the editor's office, Love issued Marchbank with a quiet warning. 'Don't be surprised if sparks start flying. Fran can't stand Walpole and he's terrified of her. They usually get on famously.'

Now they were seated together, Marchbank could appreciate the editor's apprehension. McIntyre was a *force majeure*, a tall brash woman with a smouldering mouth and a fiery temper to match. Love her or hate her, he soon realized you couldn't ignore her.

The editor, Walpole, was a small, dapper man. Marchbank wouldn't have been surprised to find him selling brushes, door-to-door. It was a spectacle in itself to see the interplay between him and McIntyre, the one holding the seat of power and the other radiating it, but not one he had time to enjoy. They were there to discuss a serious issue, whether to run a story about the Roughburn experiment as outlined in Crawford's letter; a story that would nail Winfield once and for all.

'Why do you think we should stick our necks out on this, Dr Marchbank?' Walpole demanded.

'There are mothers, fathers, brothers, sisters, who have lost relatives, sacrificed for the sake of a bankrupt military strategy. Don't they have a right to know why?'

'Are you sure they will want to? They might be happier left in ignorance.'

McIntyre muttered something unintelligible but clearly disparaging. Walpole pretended not to hear.

'I think the truth should be told, however painful it may prove, if only to prevent the same thing ever happening again.

Besides, the relatives are probably entitled to considerable compensation from the Government.'

Walpole grunted. 'It seems to me, from what you have told us, that the credibility of your claim rests entirely on the evidence of this Crawford. It is a sound journalistic principle, Dr Marchbank, to ensure that information of this sort is corroborated by one, preferably two other sources. How are we to do that in this case?'

'Don't be so pompous Gerald,' McIntyre interrupted. 'George Winfield has confirmed it. Dr Marchbank already told you that.'

'Off the record, Fran, I believe. I don't consider that adequate.'

'Come off it. Winfield is a pillar of the government. This is a dream story. Better than Profumo. Winfield is in a corner. He won't be able to hold the lid on, once the pot starts boiling.' She defied Walpole to contradict her.

The paper's legal adviser came to his rescue. 'You would be straying over extremely treacherous ground Fran,' he warned. 'Winfield could take us to the cleaners on this one as it stands today.'

'What it all comes down to, I think,' Walpole summarized, 'is whether we have faith in Dr Marchbank's interpretation of the available information. We only have his word for Winfield's confirmation.'

'May I make a suggestion,' Marchbank interjected.

'Please do.'

'Run the story under my name. I'll take the blame if he sues.'

'With all due respect, you are not a journalist,' McIntyre immediately objected.

'A moment Fran, please,' Walpole stopped her. 'Would that serve any purpose?' he asked the lawyer.

'If we give him the platform to air his views we are equally culpable.'

'How much is this going to cost us?' Walpole asked.

'How long is a piece of string? It probably depends how quickly we apologize after he issues his writ.'

But for all his perceived faults, Walpole was at heart a journalist. He could resist a good story no more than McIntyre.

'I think we should run it,' he announced as if it was the view he had supported all the time. 'But I want every word checked five times.'

Even before they had time to sit down and start writing the article, one of their main planks was removed. Lilian Crawford disappeared.

When she didn't answer the phone, Marchbank drove out to her house. It was shut up.

'She got taken bad,' a neighbour told him. 'The ambulance was here yesterday.

'Which hospital?' he demanded.

But his informant had no idea where she had been taken.

Neither had anybody else. None of the local hospitals had a record of her admission. It was as if she had ceased to exist.

'Coincidence?' he asked Love. 'Or Winfield?'

Marchbank blamed himself. It was his stupidity that had revealed Lilian Crawford's role. But what could he do? She could be anywhere. She might even be dead.

Without her, the letter from Marion Crawford lost most of its credibility. There was no way now that they could mention Winfield by name. Walpole came close to pulling the story but he eventually relented and let it run. He had no cause to regret his decision. It sank effortlessly.

As far as Marchbank could see it created no ripples whatsoever. True, the paper that had previously been his harshest critic resumed its role with another piece condemning the experiment theory as unconfirmed speculation and lamenting the unnecessary pain it was causing the families in Roughburn. But that was it. The rest of the media gave it a wide berth. There was no public outcry, no parliamentary questions, no pressure on the government.

'We should have named him,' Marchbank complained to Love a couple of days later. 'At least that would have stirred things up. We've no ammunition left now.'

'Don't be a fool,' she told him. 'It was impossible, and you know it.'

He had no way of knowing that he was wrong. Out of sight the conflagration was still building slowly. It might yet make a funeral pyre.

* * *

Flight Lieutenant Rod Bartram, (retired), was a sick man. He had cancer of the thyroid. Most of the gland in his neck had been surgically removed over two years earlier and he had to take drugs constantly to control his body weight. Now he had developed secondary tumours. The truth was that his body was riddled with the disease. The doctors had given him six weeks to live. That was optimistic.

Bartram read the newspapers each day from cover to cover. It was one of the few things he was capable of accomplishing without pain. Yet mostly he read for the sake of something to do, to fill in the spaces he might otherwise spend dwelling on his fate. The information he took in rarely registered. So it was with the story in the *News* under Marchbank's byline.

He had already decided the story couldn't be true by the time he had finished the first paragraph. His instincts and background rebelled against the idea that such a thing could happen. Habit alone carried him on down the page.

It was when he read about the Vampire T10 night fighter that Bartram's senses were alerted. The Vampire was an aircraft he knew well – he had flown it himself. Then he came to the part about two planes being specially modified for the Roughburn operation. Odd. He looked back up the page to check something.

August 15. His brother's birthday. But he had missed most of the party his brother held in 1952 to celebrate the start of his twenty-first year because he was on duty – flying a special mission in a Vampire night fighter.

The name Roughburn meant nothing to him. He had flown to a grid reference. But he was in no doubt. There had been no other flights that night, and no other missions with the two modified planes.

So what? He had followed his orders for that mission in exactly the same way as he had a hundred times before and since. It was nothing to do with him if he had been flying with a load of radioactive dust. He'd had no idea then and he could do nothing about it now. Bartram felt tired. He closed his eyes and let the newspaper slip to the floor.

The story stirred memories and they wouldn't let Bartram be.

He remembered the silver body of the leading night fighter as it shone dully in the moonlight on the perimeter track. He saw the plane take up position on the runway. He watched the glow from its engine and felt the tremor as it rolled forward, slowly at first then faster and faster until it powered into the night sky.

His turn came. RT crackled in Bartram's ears, clearance for take-off from the air traffic control tower. He pressed the face mask to his mouth and acknowledged, then let it dangle free again. They were supposed to use oxygen for the whole flight but Bartram had ignored the order. His hay fever left him feeling suffocated inside the mask, though he refused to go to the MO for fear of being grounded.

The pilot couldn't see the point of the order anyway. They hadn't been at a high enough altitude. On top of that he was irritated at having to fly the mission tonight instead of being at home, celebrating, with his brother who had just turned twenty-one.

Now the aeroplanes were flying in formation, Bartram slightly below and behind the wing leader, following a flight path that took them west from the Oxfordshire aerodrome before turning to the north. Forty minutes flying time brought them to their target. The moon winked from the canopy of the first plane as it banked to begin its run over the dropping zone.

The two pilots had practised the pattern twenty times if they had practised it once. Bartram was to fly an identical path, but two hundred feet higher than his leader. So what was he doing beneath him?

Bartram hadn't been concentrating. He was at his brother's party, the party he was missing. His senses were numbed by the incessant pounding of the Goblin engine beneath him. He had almost reached the release point before he realized. Hell! He had shrugged, mentally. What difference would it make? Those damned boffins would have them spraying crops next. He swung down the lever that activated the pods beneath his wings.

Bartram emerged from his reverie. The idea sneaked up on him. He didn't know where it had come from. It was just there, in his mind.

What if he was a victim too?

No. It was impossible. He would have been told if he was in any danger wouldn't he? But the more he fought it, the stronger the notion became. Somebody should find out. He had a right to know.

It was another twenty-four hours before he eventually decided to ring the *News*.

The single additional piece of evidence, Bartram's testimony, was enough to tip the balance. Suddenly everybody was interested in Roughburn. Marchbank was once again fêted by the Press but this time it was as a celebrity. Fortunately, his relationship with the *News* served to protect him from the excessive attention of the paper's rival publications. They assumed he must be under contract and although no such document actually existed he didn't disabuse them of the idea.

But, for all the support he had gained from the *News*, it was the clamour raised by the tabloid press that really took the pressure off him. As soon as Bartram's account was published, they immediately decided the story was true and began, once again, to develop their own angles. In particular they took up the case of the people in Roughburn who had suffered.

It was outrageous. They wanted blood. And with tabloid hacks going through the dustbins it could not be long before they got it.

Yet Winfield, the man who in Marchbank's eyes was the real villain, remained unscathed. Without Lilian Crawford there was nothing to link him to Roughburn. Marchbank and Love redoubled their efforts to find her.

It was fruitless. She could not be found. Then luck broke their way, if it could be described as luck.

Bartram was dying. He asked to see Love. Passing through one of the wards on the way to see him, she found herself staring at Mrs Crawford's face. The woman had been in the same hospital as Bartram all the time!

Love called Marchbank and he got there as quickly as possible. But what he found made him wish they had never tracked her down. In place of a bright, compassionate woman, growing old gracefully, he found a dull, lifeless vegetable. She clearly didn't recognize him and could barely hold a conversation.

'What's happened to her?' he whispered to a nurse.

'Stroke,' the girl told him.

He didn't believe it. It was too much of a coincidence. There were tears in his eyes as he left the hospital with Love, and a bitterness and hatred in his heart that was directed towards one man. George Winfield.

Marchbank was in the laboratory one evening a few days later, trying to generate some enthusiasm for his work. The industrial accident study was progressing slowly; he didn't expect it to achieve anything anyway so he wasn't bothered by that. He had one or two other ideas of his own that he ought to follow. But he was finding it difficult picking up the threads again.

Lambeth had gone home. He had the lab to himself. He moved around restlessly and found himself sitting at her desk. In the middle of it was a large, old fashioned blotting-pad which she used for doodling and to jot down odd notes. Across one corner was a telephone number. It was a number he knew. He had seen it before. A chill gripped him when he recalled where.

Somewhere in his office was the telephone bill he had pocketed on his final visit to Hamble's house. He found the envelope containing the bill, knowing, without looking, that he would be right. The number on the pad was the same as the number on the bill. The number someone had called from Steven's house the night he died. The call someone had made after he was dead.

Marchbank couldn't believe it. Lambeth was involved after all. He felt sick. It was all over now; he wanted it to be over. No more revelations. No more tragedy. His head began to throb and he squeezed his knuckles into his temples.

Eventually he went home but he might just as well have stayed in the laboratory. He didn't sleep. Next morning he was there, waiting, when Lambeth arrived.

When she saw him, sitting at her desk, Lambeth felt terrified. She had seen the look on his face before; that Monday morning after he had found out about her and Marg. What now?

But this time he didn't say anything. He just pointed to the corner of her blotter. She followed his finger.

'Whose is this number?' His voice sounded wooden and hollow.

She stared, not recognizing it. Then she remembered.

'It's Conrad's. I got it from Directory Enquiries when I was worried about you. The day he persuaded you to go and see him?'

'That's not Conrad's college number.'

'Not his college, his home.'

Marchbank seemed to sag as he absorbed the information.

'What is it? What is that number?' she demanded.

'That's the number that was called from Steven's house on the night he was killed. Somebody used his phone after he was dead. Used it to call Conrad.'

It wouldn't end. The tendrils of the bloody affair went deeper and deeper.

'Why Conrad?' Lambeth looked shocked. But it began to make some sort of sense to Marchbank.

'He would have known what to look for in the papers Steven had in his house.'

'Look for what?'

'Anything about Roughburn.'

'They took them all away.'

'Probably decided they couldn't be certain.'

'What will you do?'

'I don't know.'

But he did know, even as he spoke. He would have to go and see DeWyntz. He would have to find out the real reason why. The reason why he had betrayed their friendship, the friendship Marchbank had thought so special.

Marchbank couldn't bring himself to telephone so he arrived unannounced. Standing on the threshold he almost left without knocking. But it had to be done. He steeled himself.

The door opened.

'Conrad!' He didn't know what more to say.

'Come in m'boy. I've been expecting you.'

There was no light in the old man's eyes any more.

'I don't understand.' Marchbank found it hard to look straight at DeWyntz. 'Tell me why.'

DeWyntz spoke with a rasp. His old, guttural vowels had

crept back.

'I owed a debt. It had to be repaid. This country of yours is not my natural home. But it took me to its bosom. Made me welcome after the war. It saved my life. In return I did what I could. All I had to offer was my expertise so that is what I gave.

'Roughburn? They asked for my help. How could I refuse?'

'You were involved from the start?'

But of course it made sense.

'What about Steven?'

'Believe me, m'boy, I didn't know. By the time I found out it was too late. I tried to warn you but you wouldn't listen.'

Did Marchbank believe him? It really didn't matter. Hamble was dead. There had been a conspiracy. But to make it public would destroy DeWyntz. There could be no winners, only losers.

Marchbank stood up. He had heard enough.

'Won't you stay for coffee?'

But there would be no more coffee. He closed the door quietly behind him as he left.

After DeWyntz, the bitterness drained slowly from Marchbank. Even when fate finally caught up with Winfield it gave him no satisfaction.

It was Love who told him. She called him one day, several weeks after they had found Lilian Crawford.

'Winfield has resigned his job. He has cancer. He's dying.'

'Perhaps nature has its own form of justice.'

Or was it just another statistic; probability not fate catching up with the politician?

Another phone call, however, gave Marchbank pause for reflection.

'Marchbank? Dr Hope here. How are you?'

'Fine. Thank you.'

'I see you finally got to the bottom of the Roughburn business.'

Marchbank remembered a promise he had made to tell the doctor if he discovered anything, a promise he had failed to honour.

'I should have called you. Please accept my apologies. It's been rather a difficult time.'

'Forget it. I'm sure you've been too busy to worry about me. I was shocked when I read what had really happened. Good Lord, man, Evelyn might have been one of the victims. It doesn't bear thinking about.'

Evelyn! He had forgotten she even existed.

'How is she?'

'Very well. But I think she has been hoping to hear from you.' There was a trace of disappointment in Dr Hope's voice.

'Yes. I must call her.'

'Do.'

The doctor rang off.

He had made another promise too, he remembered now. It seemed so long ago, in a previous life. He recalled their trip to the Isle of Wight together. He had wanted to see her again then.

But now? He had no enthusiasm for the idea, he realized with a shock. He didn't even want to think about it. Why was that? He had thought he was getting back to normal but there were still empty spaces, places where life had been lived before. Now they were barren.

Life in the office was almost back to normal. Earnshaw had kept a low profile since the truth about Roughburn had come out, which was just as well as far as Marchbank was concerned. His putative inquiry into Marchbank, launched after the Cromby affair was publicized, appeared to have been buried without ceremony. Even so Marchbank wasn't happy. That the director was a fool, he had always known. Now he knew he was a disingenuous fool. He could no longer ignore the man.

Lambeth, meanwhile, continued with the work on the industrial accident study and Marchbank did, slowly, pick up the threads of it again. But they kept one another at arm's length. Work was their only common subject of conversation. One afternoon it got too much for Lambeth.

'Good God, Tony. What do you want me to do? Slit my throat?' she shouted at him.

He looked at her with alarm. 'What's the matter?'

'I'm sick and tired of you making me feeling guilty about Marg. And I'm pig-sick of you. Loosen up or that's it. I've had enough.'

'It's not my fault that you feel guilty.'

'Like hell it isn't. You come in here, day after day, looking as if the world is about to end. And you didn't even like her.'

'What do you mean I didn't like her? I married her.'

'That doesn't prove anything. Most married couples hate one another's guts. You never brought her flowers. You never took her out. You never made her feel loved.'

'And you did, I suppose?'

'As it happens, I did.'

'So that makes it all right, does it, for you to steal her from me?'

'Don't be pathetic. She was looking for a way out. I just happened to be handy.'

'You know how to be a bitch when you want, don't you?'

'That's it. Go on. Insult me. Perhaps you'd like to bloody my nose too.' She offered her chin to him mockingly.

'Don't be childish.'

'Childish, me? You should take a look at yourself in the mirror sometime.' She stormed out, leaving him feeling slightly stupid.

When he thought about it, he realized Lambeth was right. He hadn't liked Margaret very much, not at the end. And at the beginning? Why had he married her then? Perhaps Chris had done him a favour after all.

The next day he brought a large bunch of freesias for Lambeth. She looked sheepish when he handed them to her.

'I shouldn't have got so mad yesterday.'

'You were right though.'

'Can we be friends again?'

'On one condition.'

'What's that?'

'There's something I want to ask you. What did you two do when you were in bed together?'

Lambeth turned bright pink.

Nineteen

Roughburn in the heat of summer was a new experience for Marchbank. Autumn, winter, spring; the sun had shone before but it had never been warm. The cold-edged wind, his familiar companion during the previous visits, was absent, and absent too was the bleakness he identified with the town.

He was on foot, his car safely ensconced in the municipal car park. The graveyards that had drawn him to Roughburn on the first occasion beckoned him again and he answered their call. When Marchbank had first visited Roughburn he had been seeking the answer to a riddle. He had begun to unravel it in these graveyards, among the stones commemorating the children who had died of cancer. Why was he here now? To say goodbye? Or to lay to rest their ghosts?

He stopped at the gate of one graveyard and leaned over the top bar. There was no point in going further. He had done what he could for the memory of the children lying beyond. He and they should leave one another in peace now.

He turned his back on the silent stones and ambled down towards the town centre, enjoying the warm afternoon sun. As he walked he tried to remember the town as he had seen it for the first time. Had it changed as a result of the things he had discovered, the publicity he had aroused? Was there greater pain here than when he had first laid eyes on the place? Or perhaps a greater peace? The slow, ruddy stones of the buildings were no different. But if there was a difference it would be in the minds of the people not in their architecture.

Near the town centre, the sight of a new building arrested him. When he looked closely he realized it wasn't new. It was nearly a year old, the town's recently built health centre. For some reason he had never walked this way before, never seen it. There was the stone commemorating the day it had been opened by the Right Honourable George Winfield: the same day he had made his own first visit.

Had Roughburn been on Winfield's conscience all those years after all? The possibility had not occurred to Marchbank before. His only meeting with the man had convinced him that Winfield felt no remorse whatsoever. But if not why the health centre? It couldn't be chance.

It was time to lay his bitterness aside.

The people of the Lake District were enjoying the hot summer sun too and the crowds of visitors that it brought. Good for business, though bad for anyone seeking solitude. Marchbank was lucky to be able to secure a room in the hotel. He arrived early, cutting short his perambulation around Roughburn in the hope of a pleasant amble round Ullswater. But in place of ghosts he found himself tripping over real people. Only too real. It was impossible to escape them.

Marchbank felt apprehensive. He retreated to his room, regretting his decision to come. It had been a mistake. What he was seeking couldn't be found here. Later, however, he plucked up the courage to change and step downstairs for dinner.

The lounge was as he remembered it, but more crowded. All the guests had turned out to eat at the same time and there didn't seem to be any seats remaining. From the doorway he looked to his right, at the rear of a sofa placed to one side of the fireplace and at a familiar head of hair, a blonde bob. Evelyn Hope! But even as his heart somersaulted he felt the bottom fall out of his stomach. She was seated next to somebody, a man, and the two of them had their heads bowed, deep in conversation.

He was on the point of turning to go when the man stood up. It was the hotelier taking her order for dinner. He caught the look in Marchbank's eyes and was about to speak but something stopped him.

Marchbank felt hot. Beads of perspiration were forming on his upper lip. She would rebuff him. He didn't want to see her. But his feet took him where his heart couldn't.

She didn't notice him at first. Then there was an instant of bewilderment followed by a look of pure delight.

'Tony! What are you doing here?'

'I ... Your father said you would be here. I wanted to surprise you.'

'You have. Now sit down quickly, before you fall.'

It was going to be all right after all.